"Will remind readers what chattering teeth sound like."
—*Kirkus Reviews*

"Voracious readers of horror will delightfully consume the contents of Bates's World's Scariest Places books."
—*Publishers Weekly*

"Creatively creepy and sure to scare." —*The Japan Times*

"Jeremy Bates writes like a deviant angel I'm glad doesn't live on my shoulder."
—Christian Galacar, author of GILCHRIST

"Thriller fans and readers of Stephen King, Joe Lansdale, and other masters of the art will find much to love."
—*Midwest Book Review*

"An ice-cold thriller full of mystery, suspense, fear."
—David Moody, author of HATER and AUTUMN

"A page-turner in the true sense of the word."
—*HorrorAddicts*

"Will make your skin crawl." —Scream Magazine

"Told with an authoritative voice full of heart and insight."
—Richard Thomas, Bram Stoker nominated author

"Grabs and doesn't let go until the end." —*Writer's Digest*

BY JEREMY BATES

Suicide Forest ♦ *The Catacombs* ♦ *Helltown* ♦
Island of the Dolls ♦ *Mountain of the Dead*
♦ *Hotel Chelsea* ♦ *Mosquito Man* ♦
The Sleep Experiment ♦ *The Man from Taured*
♦ *White Lies* ♦ *The Taste of Fear* ♦
Black Canyon ♦ *Run* ♦ *Rewind*
♦ *Neighbors* ♦ *Six Bullets* ♦ *Box of Bones* ♦
The Mailman ♦ *Re-Roll* ♦ *New America: Utopia Calling*
♦ *Dark Hearts* ♦ *Bad People*

The Man From Taured

World's Scariest Legends 3

Jeremy Bates

ISBN-13: 978-1988091440
ISBN-10: 1988091446

The Man From Taured

PART I

Narita International Airport

CHAPTER 1

According to the clock on the screen affixed to the aircraft seat in front of me, it was 12:05 p.m. Lunchtime. My least favorite meal of the day. In fact, it was a meal I usually skipped, preferring to make up the calories with a gluttonous breakfast that would power me through the day until it was time for a reasonably sized dinner. If I had been seated in economy class, I would have told the flight attendant I wanted neither the fast food teriyaki burger nor the soggy tonkatsu she was likely peddling. However, I was in the front of the aircraft in first class, and the fare on this side of the curtain was pleasantly palatable. Despite considering myself a connoisseur of fine food, I hadn't been in the mood for the Japanese offering of soft-shelled turtle and simmered eel. Instead, I'd ordered the Wagyu beef sirloin from the Western menu. It had been meltingly tender and up there as one of the best steak meals I'd had on a flight. I skipped the dessert of mint profiteroles (I've never had much of a sweet tooth) but paired the beef with a light Californian pinot noir.

Now I was enjoying a second glass of the wine with the chair in my Sky Suite reclined to a comfortable position and my feet propped up on the padded ottoman. I raised the glass to my lips—just as a shock of turbulence rocked the plane. The glass jumped in my hand. I cursed in surprise and scanned my starchy white dress shirt for crimson stains. Finding none, I cursed again, this time in frustration at the turbulence. I returned my seat to the upright position and finished what remained of the wine in one long swallow.

"Everything okay over there?" asked the passenger in the Sky Suite next to mine.

I glanced over the privacy screen and saw an attractive woman, about forty, with a blonde pixie cut and twinkling hazel eyes. She was dressed smartly in a houndstooth blouse and clingy leather slacks.

"Reflexes like a cat," I replied in my French-accented English, which cared little for the subtleties between stressed and unstressed syllables.

"Turbulence is why I don't drink red wine on planes," she said.

"How do you know I was drinking red wine?" I asked her.

"I heard you order it from our lovely attendant." She raised a small tumbler filled with a clear liquid above the privacy screen. "Vodka, on the other hand...well, you can actually use this stuff to get stains *out*."

"Vodka it is on the return trip," I said agreeably, despite the fact the only spirits I drank were of the brown variety.

"I'm Hallie Smith," she said.

"Gaston," I replied. "Gaston Green."

"Like from Clue?"

"Excuse me?"

"The murder mystery board game. You know, how the characters were all named after colors? Miss Scarlet. Mrs. White. Professor Plum. Oh, who was the yellow one?"

"Colonel Mustard," I offered.

"Yes! So—how long are you in Tokyo for, Mr. Green?"

"Ten days," I replied, not sure I liked her addressing me by my surname after the association she had made.

"Plenty of time to enjoy the city. It's one of the finest in the world."

"I am afraid this trip is for business, not pleasure."

"Yes, me too. I've been based in Manila for the last five, six—oh God, maybe it's even been seven years already! I work at the British embassy there."

"Do you enjoy living in the Philippines?" I asked. Most male expatriates I knew appreciated the abundance of young, friendly women, many of whom had no qualms dating foreign men old enough to be their fathers. Female expats, on the other hand, were more of a mixed bag. They enjoyed the Filipino people and the happy-go-lucky culture but often found it difficult to look past the endemic poverty and polluted cities.

"Love it...until I hate it," Hallie Smith said, confirming what I'd suspected. "But then I love it all over again."

We soared through another pocket of turbulence, which caused the aircraft to skate left and right, as if it were a terrestrial vehicle that had hit a patch of ice. A moment later the Fasten Seatbelt sign pinged on and a female voice requested everyone to buckle up.

I obliged. Then I slipped my laptop from my carry-on bag and opened it. While the machine booted up, I realized—and regretted—I hadn't asked Hallie Smith for her phone number. I'd noticed she wasn't wearing a diamond when she'd raised her drink—*reflexes like a cat, eyes like a hawk*—and she seemed to be pleasantly sophisticated and outgoing. In other words, a woman with whom I might enjoy sharing a drink.

Once my laptop was ready, I was greeted by the desktop wallpaper of my slobbering, grinning bulldog. He was back in my house in the Makati subdivision of Forbes Park, Manila, being looked after (and no doubt spoiled) by Grace, my live-in maid. I didn't need Grace, but help in the country was cheap, and my company insisted on supplying me with not only a live-in maid but also a driver and a gardener. It was overkill, of course. I was a neat and tidy person by nature, so much so I had caught Grace ironing the drapes, simply for want of something to do. Raphael, my driver, was on call 24/7, and considering I spent most days working from home, he could often be found snoozing on the front seat of the Volvo SUV parked in my driveway (windows and doors hanging open due to Manila's relentless heat). Mark, my gardener, came by each day to spend several hours trimming different sections of the front and back lawns with a pair of clippers, despite a brand-new lawnmower I'd purchased for him.

With a click of the laptop's trackpad, I opened the Excel document I'd been working on and began reviewing my most recent expense accounts.

When I tell someone I'm a whisky ambassador, I often get bemused looks. Yet that was indeed my job title. Ambassador to East Asia for Glenfiddich. Most brands of Scotch whisky have such ambassadors, whose mission was to educate the public of the premium brands they represented. Or, as I liked to put it, spread world peace through whisky, one dram at a time.

I'd lost count on how many occasions I'd been asked enviably how I'd landed such a gig. The answer, I'd tell them, was passion. I'd had an unrelenting passion for Scotch whisky since I was old enough to legally drink it, which was around the time of my first job managing a Four Seasons restaurant and lobby bar. Later, I started my own company that hosted private events and whisky tastings. It grew, and fast...as did my appreciation for single malt whisky. Over the years I'd gone out of my way to befriend master distillers, blenders, stillmen, mashmen, and warehousemen, all in the name of learning everything there was to know about the drink I so adored.

Truth be told, however, I did not seek out the position of brand ambassador; it found me.

Ten years ago I received an unsolicited call from a headhunter looking to fill a role at William Grant & Sons Distillers

Ltd. I brushed him off. My company was turning over a decent profit, and the position he pitched sounded too much like a sales gig.

A week later I received a second unsolicited call, this time from the top of the totem pole: W. Grant & Sons' head of sales and marketing. Her name was Liz Gordon, and she insisted on flying me to London to meet for lunch. She was a witchy-looking woman with ebony hair, pale skin, and lips painted the color of smoldering coals. For most of the meal we talked about everything under the sun but whisky. It was only when we had finished our main course that she leaned forward and said, "Most people know *shit* about whisky, Gaston. Bartenders, clients, consumers, they know nothing. It's an uneducated category. We need to educate them. And to do that, we need an educator."

I took a sip of the light beer I was nursing. "And you want me to be that educator?" I asked.

She leaned forward farther—her gold necklace resting in the snug valley of her cleavage—and smiled in what I swear would have been a seductive manner had she been anybody else except my potential future boss. "You have the expertise, Gaston, but more important than that, you have the *look*. That's why I wanted to see you in person. Pictures online can be deceiving. But, yes, there is no question about it, you have the look."

"And what look is that?" I asked, intrigued.

Her smile grew. "The industry is no longer pipes and armchairs. It's young. It's dynamic. It's full of energy."

"You have not answered my question," I said.

"*Sexy*, Gaston. You're *sexy*. But we can make you even sexier. Glenfiddich is the bestselling brand of single malt Scotch in the world. Our market share is twice that of the next two single malts combined. As the face of our company, we'll make you into the James Bond of the whisky world. How does that sound to you?"

Pretty darn good, I had to admit. "I was told I would have to relocate to the Philippines?"

"Glenfiddich has eighteen ambassadors worldwide. We'd like you to be the ambassador for our East Asia operations, and our East Asia headquarters is located in Manila, yes. There will be a lot of travel involved, make no mistake. But I don't think we have to worry about your stamina, do we?" Now the coquettishness that had been in her smile touched her eyes.

"No, you do not," I said.

"I'm glad to hear that. Coffee?"

"No, thank you."

Liz Gordon stood. "That's it then. We'd really love to have you on board, Gaston. Take a few days to think over the offer before getting back to me, will you?" She tucked her small black handbag under her arm and left the club.

I didn't need a few days to consider the offer. I'd always had a passion for traveling. Throughout my twenties I'd visited every country in Europe and spent three months looping through half the countries in Africa, so jet-setting around East Asia suited my nomadic nature and sense for adventure just fine. Getting to talk about, and drink, whisky sealed the deal.

I called Liz Gordon to accept the position that evening. After a furious week of preparation, I relocated to a mini mansion in downtown Manila, where I hit the streets running with instructions and organized a last-minute whisky dinner in Singapore for that Friday. The dinner was a hit, the reviews were positive, and Liz Gordon called me to offer her congratulations.

What followed was a decade-long blur of lavish parties and product launches, expensive hotels, fine dining and VIP booths, and schmoozing and boozing with the crème de la crème of society from Shanghai and Macau to Bangkok and Seoul.

The job wasn't all fun and games, mind you. I worked ninety-hour weeks, including weekends, and spent more time in airport lounges and hotels than at home, whatever down time I had was swamped with administrative work and training staff at restaurants and bars, dinner-hour events, after-hour visits to key accounts, and conference calls with the marketing team.

Yet would I prefer to be doing anything else with my life? No, *monsieur* or *mademoiselle*, I would not.

Now I massaged my temples, realizing the two glasses of wine had made my thinking sluggish. I worked on my expense accounts for another ten minutes before I began struggling to keep my eyes open. I closed the laptop and glanced over the privacy partition at Hallie Smith. She was sleeping, her lips parted slightly, her chest rising and falling in slow, steady intervals. She really was quite attractive, and I reminded myself to get her number before we debarked.

I reclined my chair so it was 180-degrees flat, folded my hands together on my belly, and closed my eyes. The 787 Dreamliner's twin Rolls-Royce engines purred quietly as they thrust the aircraft along at its cruising altitude. Every now and then turbulence jiggled the cabin, though I traveled enough that this didn't bother me, and soon I was asleep.

I do believe one can never outrun their past, especially one involving any sort of traumatic event. In my case, I may be in my Volvo on a traffic-clogged Manila street, or watching the news in my lounge room, or, like now, reclined in a seat on an airplane, and all of a sudden, out of the blue, I'll find myself thinking about the ski trip I'd taken when I was twenty-two years old.

It had been November, 2001. I'd finished university earlier that year and had recently returned from a three-month backpacking sojourn through Europe. Four of my friends—Dominique Noiriel, Gérard Baker, Laurence Abélès, and Miley "Smiley" Laffont—had organized a ski weekend in the Pyrenees Mountains. Gérard pulled out at the last minute and I took his spot. Dom drove us to a small village situated at the base of a sprawling ski area known as Cinq Valées. We ended up spending all of our first day holed up in the wooden alpine house we'd rented because the snow was wet and heavy and not suitable for skiing. The following morning conditions improved, though many of the more challenging runs were off-limits due to killer winds at the upper elevations. The four of us spent the morning on the easy hills. By noon we had grown bored and we took the lifts as high as we could and went off-piste searching for deep powder.

After about an hour of hiking without discovering any skiable routes, Dom and Laurence decided to turn back. Smiley and I were determined to carry on and told them we'd meet them back at the house for Happy Hour. After another half hour of difficult hiking we discovered a backcountry area covered in pristine powder. With great delight, we strapped on our skis and hit the slope.

I remember skiing the fall line, cutting a series of fluid S's through the snow, when Smiley overtook me. I did my best to catch up and was retaking the lead when I accidentally collided into her. I flew off my skis and cartwheeled at breakneck speed down the hill. Even as I was tumbling head over heels, I heard an inexplicably loud *WHOOSH*, as if dynamite had gone off in the distance. When my momentum slowed, and I came to a rest, I looked up the steep slope—a split second before a moving wall of snow crashed over me.

The next thing I knew I was suspended in an empty blackness, focusing on a bead of light. I continued to focus on the light until it brightened and the darkness around it lightened. I thought it might have been a ray of sunlight pushing through a barricade of black clouds. But as the light stretched and faded and stretched again, I realized it was not the interplay of sunlight and clouds but rather my mind struggling to regain consciousness.

I opened my eyes.

And could see nothing but a stinging whiteness.

My first thought was that I might be blind, and my second thought was that I might be dead, before concluding with relief that I was neither and simply staring at snow a centimeter or two from my face.

At this point I wasn't yet thinking clearly enough to understand what had happened or why I was cold as a winter gravestone. But it didn't take long before I recalled the wall of rushing snow and realized I'd been swept up in an avalanche.

Terror came then, saturating me, possessing me, ferocious and unapologetic. My heart rate spiked. I began breathing dangerously fast. I could shift my left arm the slightest bit from the elbow down, and I could wiggle my fingers and toes, but I couldn't move any other part of my body. It was as though I were encased in cement. This paralysis boosted my terror to a new level.

I screamed for help at the top of my lungs, knowing I was exhausting my finite supply of oxygen but unable to simply lie there and wait to suffocate to death. I continued to scream with everything I had. Yet due to the crushing weight of snow atop me, and my flattened lungs, it became excruciatingly painful to keep this up for long.

My throat burned. It felt as though I were breathing through a heavy cloth. My eyelids grew heavy, but I forced myself to keep them open, knowing that if they closed they would likely never open again.

I'd been skiing ever since I was a child. I'd taken numerous lessons over the years. I'd learned a lot about avalanches, and what to do in the event you became an unfortunate victim of one. One piece of advice was to spit so you know up from down. I spat now. The saliva struck the snow just below my mouth, which meant I was facing down. I'd also learned that you should urinate so the rescue dogs can find you. But I doubted doing so would help. In the words of one of my instructors: if you're looking for someone who's been covered by an avalanche for more than eleven minutes, then you're looking for a corpse.

How long had I been buried? I wondered. Five minutes? Ten? Did I only have one minute left to live? This seemed impossible. So utterly unfair and impossible. I wasn't supposed to die. I was going to start looking for my first real job soon. I was going to start my own business one day. I'd already told my brothers I would hike the Appalachian Trail with them the following summer. I've never even owned a car! Dozens of other abstract thoughts came and went in a mad flurry as my unrealized future, not my past, flashed before my eyes, and then as a quiet, peaceful darkness folded me into its embrace, my final coherent thought was: *What a shame...*

ΔΔΔ

Even as I felt myself sliding comfortably into sleep on flight JL077, I continued to think about the 2001 ski trip. Although I hadn't known it at the time, Smiley, eight feet above me, had heard my screaming and was frantically working to dig me out with nothing but her gloved hands. After about fifteen minutes she discovered my right arm. When she reached my head and found me lying facedown, she dug the rest of my body out before rolling me over and performing CPR.

As the aircraft rattled through another pocket of turbulence, my semi-waking thoughts transitioned to a dream, and I watched the action unfolding on the mountain, watched as Smiley gave me the kiss of life over and over again until, miraculously, I opened my eyes and sucked a huge mouthful of air into my bruised lungs.

I don't remember much of what happened next—the moments after being resuscitated were a haze—but in this dream I kissed Smiley like I did almost every time I dreamed about her, and she kissed me back—even as I did my best to ignore the foreboding knowledge that it would be me who would kill her in a few hours' time.

ΔΔΔ

More turbulence shook the 787, ejecting me from sleep. I pushed myself upright, my heart in my throat, feeling as though I were strapped into a too-tight corset.

A dream, I told myself with a mix of fading dread and immeasurable relief. I curled the fingers of my right hand, which were still stiff from the frostbite they'd suffered twenty years ago.

I conjured Miley Laffont's face as I remembered it, her amused blue eyes and elfish features framed by locks of flaxen golden hair. And of course her oversized smile, hence her nickname.

As much as it pleased me to think about Smiley, if I did so for too long the pain would come, the guilt and regret and self-loathing that she was gone and I was responsible for that sad fact, and so I reluctantly let go of the image of her.

From the Sky Suite next to mine came a deep, wheezy snore.

I clunked my seat to the upright position. According to the clock on the media screen, it was now 2:35 p.m. I'd been asleep for almost two hours.

Another snore, almost a snort.

Finding it hard to imagine such a boorish sound coming from the petite Hallie Smith, I peeked over the privacy panel—and blinked in surprise.

A man who must have been pushing three hundred pounds sat in her seat.

CHAPTER 2

The stranger's silky silver hair was shorn short. The beginnings of a salt-white beard dusted his meaty jowls. His oily eyelids were closed while a fine trickle of drool leaked from the corner of his lips.

So immense was this man's girth, I couldn't be certain poor Hallie Smith might not be squished like a pancake beneath him. The flippant thought recalled when I was trapped beneath tons of unyielding snow, and I brushed it from my mind.

The plane jounced, causing the luggage in the overhead bins to slip and slide.

The man opened one eye, pirate-like.

We stared at each other for an uncomfortably long moment.

I cleared my throat and faced forward in my seat, frowning.

Where had Hallie Smith gone?

I looked toward the front of the cabin. I didn't see her standing in either of the aisles. Not that this would answer why the big man had taken her seat. You simply didn't annex vacated seats on airplanes.

Had she voluntarily swapped seats with him then?

Because of me?

But...why? I had done nothing inappropriate. I replayed our conversation from beginning to end, searching for a potential faux pas. I could discover none. I had been taciturn and polite. Nothing I had said or done would have been cause for her to—

Maybe it hadn't been Hallie's decision to move then, I thought. Maybe it had been the fat man's...or the person seated *next* to the fat man. The *snoring* fat man.

Pieces of the puzzle began to fall into place. The fat man had been snoring most of the flight. The person next to him had complained to the cabin crew, who had decided to move him to a different seat. And who better to move him next to than a man who was sleeping himself?

Anger built inside me.

So now *I* had to put up with this man's snoring for the next several hours?

I scavenged through my carry-on bag for my noise-cancelling headphones—realizing belatedly I had packed them in my checked suitcase. I tried on the ones the airline had provided. They didn't do the job, and I tossed them back in the storage nook.

The fat man snorted—once, twice...*three times!*—and just when I was becoming hopeful he might have expelled the last of the nasal congestion from his system, he began that deep, bovine breathing once more.

I think not, I decided, glancing at the call button above me. Had I been seated in cattle class, in which the cabin attendant to passenger ratio couldn't be better than 50:1, I would have waited for a stewardess to pass me by. Now I jabbed the button. After all, I wasn't after butler service; I had a legitimate complaint.

While I waited for the flight attendant to arrive, I went over in my head what I was going to say to her. Demand the fat man return to his proper seat? Request a different seat myself? I wasn't going to be rude about it. The flight attendant who'd transplanted the man beside me was just doing her job...only she wasn't, was she? Not really. She'd put him there to make her job *easier*. So she didn't have to deal with the passenger who'd complained about him in the first place.

The flight attendant who appeared at my Sky Suite half a minute later was pretty, peppy, and young—all requirements to be a flight attendant with JAL. "How can I help you?" she asked me.

I hooked a thumb at the big man in the adjacent Sky Suite and said, "He is not supposed to be sitting there." My voice straddled the line between indignation and conspiratorial.

The flight attendant seemed surprised by this statement, which meant she hadn't been the one who'd sanctioned the swap. "Excuse me, sir?" she said.

"At the beginning of the flight," I explained, "a woman was sitting there. Now she is not. Did she change seats?"

"I don't think so. She shouldn't have. Are you...sure?"

The fat man snored, a honking, bubbly sound.

I made an amused face. "I can differentiate between a petite British woman and..." I let her fill in the blank.

"I'm sorry for this inconvenience," she said. "Let me check the passenger manifest. I'll be back shortly."

While I waited for her to return, I plucked the in-flight shopping magazine from the seat pocket in front of me and browsed through the items for sale: pearls, watches, shawls, neckties, cosmetics, fragrances. Ballantine's whisky was on offer, and I made a mental note to ask my colleagues in the marketing department if it would be worth our time getting Glenfiddich into airline magazines.

I was admiring a Polo Ralph Lauren scarf (though at twenty thousand yen it was a little on the pricey side) when the perky flight attendant stopped in the aisle next to my neighbor's Sky Suite. She bent close to him and spoke *sotto voce*.

The man woke with a nasty throat-clear. "Huh?" he grunted.

"I'm sorry to wake you, sir," she said. "Are you Tony Musset?"

"Yeah. Something wrong?"

"No, not at all. Thank you for the confirmation."

The flight attendant came around to my suite. "It appears all the passengers are in their correct seats, sir," she told me.

I was frowning. "But what happened to the woman who was seated there? Where is she now?"

"Do you know her name? I can check—"

"Hallie," I said. "Hallie Smith."

While the flight attendant scanned the printouts in her hands, the big man scowled over the privacy partition at me. "Something wrong?" he said.

"Why did you change seats?" I asked.

"Huh?" he grunted.

I wasn't going to get into an argument over it with him. To the flight attendant, I said, "It does not matter."

She glanced up from the printouts. "Are you sure?"

"Yes, I am sure."

She bowed twice, appearing relieved to have avoided a potentially embarrassing situation, then moved on to resume her duties elsewhere.

The fat man, who was still glaring over the privacy screen at me, settled back into his seat.

I opened the JAL SHOP magazine again. I wasn't able to focus on any of the pages and set it aside. While I'd been sleeping, the Fasten Seatbelt sign had been turned off. I stood and pulled on my tweed jacket. Most airlines had a 1-2-1 layout in business class, to ensure each passenger had direct aisle access. This aircraft had a 2-2-2 configuration, though due to the jagged alignment of the rows, my window seat had its own little walkway to the aisle, allowing me to bypass the fat man without disturbing him.

The cabin's aqua mood lighting was currently set to low. Most windows were dimmed to an opaque navy, creating the illusion of being in a cocoon at the bottom of the sea. The dozen or so passengers seated behind me either wore headphones or were sleeping.

Hallie Smith was not among them.

I started up the aisle toward the front of the cabin, wondering what I'd do when I saw her. Smile? Stop for a chat? I preferred not to socialize in quiet public spaces, such as the aisle of an airplane, but at least I'd find out why she'd moved seats.

Many of the big entertainment screens I passed were playing Hollywood films or Japanese manga. Several passengers were sleeping. A few were working on laptops or tablets.

No blonde British woman anywhere.

I counted two empty seats. Given both lavatories at the front of the cabin were occupied, the Sherlock Holmes inside me deduced she must be in one or the other.

I stopped near the door to the lavatory at the end of my aisle. Deciding it might be embarrassing for Hallie Smith to bump into me just as she got off the toilet, I parted the thick bulkhead curtains and stepped into the galley.

The flight attendant who'd fetched the passenger manifest for me was there.

"Oh," she said, surprised by my appearance. She snapped closed a clam-shaped mirror and slipped it, as well as a tube of cherry-red lipstick, into a pocket in her jacket. "Can I get you something?"

"So this is where you hide so you do not have to deal with passengers like me," I said in jest.

"You are a very good passenger," she said.

"Sorry to involve you in that situation earlier. It really does not matter."

"That's okay. That's my job."

I found I could barely look away from her chestnut eyes.

"*Watashi no namae wa Gaston Green desu,*" I said.

"You can speak Japanese?" she said, impressed. "*Watashi wa Okubo. Hajimemashite!*"

"*Hajimemashite,*" I replied. Then, "You have a lovely name. I do not think I have ever met an Okubo before."

She blushed. "Do you come to Japan often?"

"About once a month. I have not seen you on this flight."

"I've just been transferred from the Tokyo-Brisbane route. Are you sure there isn't something I can get you?"

"How about a drink?"

"*O-nomimono wa nani ni nasaimasu ka?*"

I translated out loud. "What would I honorably like for my honorable drink?"

"Your Japanese is excellent!"

"A whisky, please, neat."

Okubo opened one of the galley's smaller storage containers and produced a bottle of Suntory Hibiki 17, which she held up for my inspection.

"*Mon Dieu!*" I said. "I thought Suntory had discontinued that brand years ago."

"Maybe this is an old bottle? Would you prefer something else?"

"No, no, please." Due to its rarity, the street value of Hibiki 17 was about a grand a bottle.

To my amusement, Okubo poured two fingers into a plastic cup, though I said nothing of her choice of glassware—or plasticware. She handed me the cup. I sniffed the whisky, then took a sip, pleased with the smooth flavor. "Excellent," I said.

Okubo bowed.

"I suppose I should let you get back to work." I raised the whisky. "*Merci, madame.*"

"If there is anything else, please let me know."

I made to leave the galley, though I hesitated at the curtain. I turned back to her. "Have you heard of a sushi restaurant named Matsuoka?"

"In Ginza, yes. Isn't it very expensive?"

"I have an event organized there on Thursday. I would feel rather foolish attending it by myself—would you by chance be in Tokyo then?"

Okubo's already large eyes seemed to double in size. She didn't say anything.

I didn't know how to take this and stammered, "I am, uh, I am sorry, I should not have—"

"No," she said quickly. "I mean, yes. Yes. I'm working this weekend, but I'll be back on Monday and in Tokyo until Friday. So yes, yes, I'm here on Thursday."

"Fantastic! What is your number? I will call you."

She recited the digits but seemed skeptical I would remember them. "I can find a pen—"

"Do not worry, *madame*, I have an excellent memory for

numbers—"

Just then the curtain behind Okubo opened and one of the European-looking cabin attendants entered. She gave me a quick up-and-down, then whispered something in Japanese to Okubo I didn't catch, though it sounded work-related.

Not wanting to get Okubo in trouble for socializing with a passenger, I raised the glass of whisky, said, "*Arigatou*," and left the galley.

ΔΔΔ

The lavatory on my side of the aisle was now vacant

I entered it, sliding the lock closed behind me, which automatically activated the overhead fluorescents. Looking at my reflection in the mirror, I ran a hand through my thick brown hair, then smiled, to make sure I hadn't had any beef from lunch stuck in between my teeth while I'd been speaking with Okubo. Nothing, thankfully. I kept the smile in place for a few moments, because it wasn't every day that I smiled at myself. Presently, the smile didn't reach my golden-brown eyes—it could probably be described as more of a strained grimace—but I had been told by enough women that it was one of my best features. These same women had also told me they liked my eyes. Admittedly, they could be compassionate, intelligent, and lively, sometimes all three at the same time. Yet if you knew what you were looking for, you could detect the pain in them as well.

I noticed the Shiseido amenities arranged neatly near the corner of the sink: moisturizer, lotion, and mouthwash. I used all of them, then urinated while studying the toilet seat's control panel, which featured three buttons displaying pictograms of people getting water shot up their anuses. These buttons were ubiquitous on bidets across Japan, though I'd never been brave enough to push one.

I rinsed my hands and left the lavatory.

I scanned the cabin for Okubo but didn't see her anywhere—and then remembered why I had gotten up in the first place.

Hallie Smith.

The lavatory across from the one I had exited was unoccupied. I counted forty-two business-class seats across seven rows in total—and the two seats that had previously been vacant were now occupied. A Japanese businessman in a snazzy suit sat in one, while another businessman, disheveled and deflated, sat in the other.

The British embassy woman, it seemed, had vanished into thin air.

CHAPTER 3

The 787 Dreamliner made a firm landing at 5:05 p.m. Japan Standard Time, five minutes behind schedule. The touchdown included a few jarring jumps that made me feel like a stone skipping over water before the pilot deployed the aircraft's spoilers, thrust reversers, and brakes, dissipating our speed until we slowed to a crawl.

Once we taxied to our designated terminal and the seatbelt sign pinged off, I collected my carry-on bag and stood. The big man next to me did the same. When our eyes met, his lips curled into a sneer before he diverted his attention to his cell phone. The cabin door opened and passengers around me began shuffling to the exit. I joined the queue, thinking one of the most underrated perks of flying business class was your ability to disembark first and quickly.

Okubo and her European counterpart stood in the galley, thanking everybody for flying with Japan Airlines. As I passed Okubo I mouth the words "I will call you" and was pleased to see her smile.

Yet as I made my way to the immigration area, I found myself not so much thinking about Okubo as Hallie Smith. She'd been on my mind for the latter half of the flight. I'd eventually convinced myself her disappearance was a big mix-up. The fat man was mistakenly given an economy-class seat, while Hallie was given his business-class seat in place. This could also explain why she'd seemed so bubbly. She'd thought she'd scored a massive upgrade. At some point during the flight, however, the fat man realized he should have been seated in business class and raised this concern with a cabin attendant, and he and Hallie were reassigned to their proper seats.

A flimsy explanation certainly, but it was the best I had come up with.

Which was why I was keeping my eyes open for the British embassy woman. If we crossed paths, a brief and lighthearted "What happened to *you*?" would sort out the entire mystery. But I didn't see her among the other deplaned passengers, and by the time I reached the immigration area, I had no patience to wait for her to arrive. Instead, I flashed my travel card to a uniformed attendant, who gestured me down a special fast-track priority lane to a stern-looking immigration officer in a glass-walled booth. I passed him my disembarkation card and passport.

"Why are you in Japan?" he asked, barely raising his eyes as he accepted the travel documents.

"Business," I told him.

"Where are you staying?"

"The Park Hyatt in Shinjuku."

"How long are you staying?"

"Four days."

He scanned my passport and checked the information that had appeared on his computer screen. He scanned my passport again, then flipped through the booklet's pages, which were marred with a cornucopia of stamps from East Asian countries. He frowned at the computer screen.

"Is something wrong?" I asked him.

"A moment," he said, distracted. Then he stood. "Please wait here." He left his booth with my passport.

I glanced over my shoulder at the queue forming behind me. I always rolled my eyes at people who got held up at immigration, berating them for not having all their documents in order.

And now I was that guy.

ΔΔΔ

When the immigration official returned, he said, "Is this your only passport?"

I frowned. "Yes, why?"

"Please come with me."

The man exited the glass-walled booth once again and waited for me to join him. Seeing no other option—if there was one person in the world it wasn't wise to argue with, it was an immigration officer on his home turf—I picked up my carry-on bag and met him at the back of the booth.

"This way," he said, beckoning me.

Reluctantly, I followed.

ΔΔΔ

We didn't go far. To the right of the immigration booths were a series of Special Examination Rooms. The one I entered was white and windowless and redolent of stale coffee. The immigration officer left me alone, closing the door behind him. I waited a moment, then tried the handle. Locked. I noticed a dome video camera in the center of the acoustic-tiled ceiling. Ignoring it, I took a seat in one of two chairs tucked beneath a small table. For a long moment I simply stared at the floor in perplexed thought before I dug my cell phone from my pocket and sent a short text message to my boss, Stephen Seville, who had replaced Liz Gordon as W. Grant & Sons' head of sales and marketing five years ago.

I pressed Send and immediately received an error:

Not sent. Tap to try again.

I tapped and got the same error.

"*Sacré bleu*," I mumbled, and was about to send another message to a different colleague when the door opened and the immigration officer reappeared.

"One big mistake?" I asked cheerfully.

"May I have your phone?"

"You are confiscating my phone?"

"For the moment." He held out a hand.

"Are you going to tell me what the problem is?"

"Your immigration status."

"I do not need a visa to enter Japan."

"Phone, please." He shook his hand impatiently.

"Am I a biosecurity risk? You found an apple inside my luggage? If so, I apologize. I will pay the fine."

The immigration officer's face remained professionally blank. "If I have to ask you for your phone again, I will summon security."

"*Merde*," I swore, handing him my phone.

He indicated my carry-on bag on the floor next to my chair. "That too."

"Why—?" I shook my head, knowing I wasn't going to get an answer. I passed it to him.

"Is there a laptop in here?" he asked.

"Yes," I said.

"Is there a password for it?"

"You are going to search my computer?"

"Do you have something to hide?"

I didn't. "No password," I said. "Enjoy."

He left with my stuff. I glanced up at the dome camera. Was I being watched right then? I settled back into the plastic chair, crossing my legs, trying to get comfortable.

I had an uneasy suspicion I wasn't going to be leaving this small room any time soon.

CHAPTER 4

My intuition was right. I called the Special Examination Room home for the next three hours. When the door finally opened, it wasn't the immigration officer who appeared, but rather two security guards in navy uniforms, peaked caps, and white gloves. One appeared to be in his fifties, the other in his thirties.

I got to my feet. "Who are you men?"

"Your security escort," the older one told me in a voice like a gravel road. "Do you want dinner?"

"Yes, of course." In fact, my stomach was yowling from its emptiness.

"Not free. Twenty thousand yen."

"Two thousand?" I corrected, believing he'd made a mistake.

"Twenty thousand."

"*Twenty?*" I repeated in disbelief. That was close to two hundred dollars.

"Do you want dinner?"

I stared at him. Was I being shaken down? Surely not in Japan. Thailand, yes, or Vietnam, or the Philippines. But not Japan. Still, the man appeared dead serious. I decided I was too hungry and tired to argue with him.

I gave the older security guard—whose quick, fiendish eyes never left my wallet—two ten-thousand-yen bills, which I'd exchanged for pesos in Manila.

"Okay?" I said.

"Follow us," he said, tucking the money away in a pocket.

I knew the layout of Narita Airport well from my past

travels. I expected my security escorts to take me up to the terminal's fourth or fifth floor, where the shops and restaurants were located. Instead, they led me down an escalator to the terminal's second floor, past the baggage claim and customs inspections, to the international arrival lobby, which was now mostly empty.

We stopped before a Lawson convenience store.

"Wait here," the older security guard ordered. He entered the shop.

I turned to the younger security escort. He had a wispy goatee and shifty eyes. "Convenience store food?" I said, unimpressed.

"Quiet!"

I checked my wristwatch. It was 10:34 p.m. "Is Narita open twenty-four hours?"

"Quiet!"

I didn't think the airport was open around the clock. I always booked my own flights, and I couldn't recall ever seeing flights arrive after 11 p.m. or before 6 a.m.

Surely I wasn't going to be held in the Special Examination Room overnight?

The elder security escort returned and handed me a brown paper bag. I peeked inside it.

An onigiri rice ball and some cold soba noodles.

"Do you have some change for me?" I asked him.

He shook his head. "No change," he said.

"I am not an idiot. This cost a few hundred yen. I gave you twenty thousand. Where is the rest of my money?"

He shrugged. "Service fee."

I frowned. "What 'service fee'?"

"For taking you here."

"For taking me down the escalator?" I shook my head. "Where am I supposed to eat this?"

"Here," he said.

"Here?" I looked around. "Right here? Standing?"

He didn't answer. Scowling, I set the bag on the floor. I took out the noodles and slurped them into my mouth with a pair of wooden chopsticks, trying not to splatter any of the dashi dipping sauce on my suit. I exchanged the empty container for the onigiri. An outer piece of plastic covered the triangular rice ball, while an interior piece separated the seaweed from the rice. There was a precise way to unwrap the thing, yet in my haste I tore through the seaweed and broke the rice. Consequently, I had to stuff all the bits into my mouth so I didn't end up dropping them on the floor.

"Best twenty thousand yen I have ever spent," I told the security guards sardonically, brushing my hands clean. I picked up the paper bag. "Where are we going now?"

"Landing Prevention Facility."

I didn't like the sound of that. "What is a landing prevention facility?"

"Follow!"

Sighing, I followed them to a nearby elevator. I dumped my trash in a bin. The older guard inserted a key into a lock and jabbed the Down button. A few moments later the elevator doors opened and we stepped inside the cab. The guard hit another Down button, followed by the Door Close button. We descended to B1, then to B2, before stopping at B3.

The doors slid open. We stepped into a tenebrous concrete tunnel.

"What is this?" I demanded.

"This way," the older guard barked, steering me by the elbow.

I shook my arm free and walked on my own. From somewhere above me I thought I heard the rumbling of a train. Twenty meters onward we came to a metal door that wasn't labeled. The older guard opened it with a key and the younger one shoved me inside.

"Hey!" I protested.

"Wait," the older guard told me. He went to a desk manned by two more security guards, though they were dressed in different uniforms. A conversation ensued. Unfortunately, they were too far away for me to understand what they were saying.

After a minute of this, the old guard returned. He smiled for the first time, revealing nicotine-stained teeth. "You are lucky," he told me.

"Lucky? Why?" I said, immediately distrustful of this statement.

"Tonight the facility is full."

"Why does that make me lucky?" My hope surged. "Are you going to release me?"

"Release, no." He laughed, a grating, arrhythmic sound that could almost be confused for a cough. "We take you to hotel."

ΔΔΔ

The hotel was not the nearby Hilton, where I had stayed several times during previous visits to Tokyo, nor was it the ANA Crowne Plaza nor the Toyoko Inn. It wasn't even the budget capsule hotel located inside Terminal 2.

Rather, it was called the Narita Airport Rest House, a five-minute shuttle ride away. Standing outside the institutional-looking building, the older guard held out his hand. "Thirty thousand yen," he told me.

I scoffed. Not that thirty thousand yen was an outrageous amount to spend on an airport hotel room. In fact, given how much I'd been charged for the meager dinner, it seemed quite reasonable. Rather, I felt like I was an actor in a bad movie. Who were these two security escorts whisking me around the airport and demanding I pay on-the-go for food and accommodation? Whose authority were they working under? Why wouldn't they tell me why I was being held?

Regardless, I wasn't about to deny handing over the money. The airport was nearly deserted and clearly closing up for the night. I lucked out escaping that Landing Prevention Facility in the bowels of the airport, and I had to sleep somewhere. Moreover, once I had my own room, I could make some phone calls, contact my company, or even the Tauredian embassy if I had to.

Whatever the misunderstanding was, it would be sorted out by the time I had to check out of the hotel in the morning.

I took my wallet from my pocket and gave the bastard the last of my money.

CHAPTER 5

The hotel lobby was dated yet clean. A female receptionist was the only person on duty. The older security escort had a few words with her, received an old-fashioned key as opposed to an access card with a magnetic strip, then led me down the first-floor hallway, his cohort trailing closely behind us. We took the elevator to the top floor and went to the room at the end of the carpeted hallway. The guard used the key to open the door, then motioned for me to enter.

I crossed the threshold, then turned around. "I suppose I am not free to leave during the night?"

"He will be outside your door," the older guard said, indicating his younger counterpart. "You cannot go anywhere. Do not try."

I closed the door in his face—taking much pleasure in the action.

As I passed the bathroom, I flicked on the light, glimpsing sand-colored tiles and a yellow-hued sink and bathtub that might have been off-white at some point in the distant past. The room itself was your standard Holiday Inn clone decorated in uninspired, muted tones. I drew back the thin curtain from the window. I had to cup my hands against the glass to see out. There was little to look at except the black expanse of the shuttered airport. No balcony, and the windows didn't open far. Not that I was planning on making my escape down the side of the building Spider-Man style. One, I hated heights. Two, I didn't have my passport, effectively trapping me in the country. And three, I had no reason to flee. I was innocent of whatever I'd been mixed up in.

A flat-screen TV sat on the end of the long desk, next to an electric kettle and some sachets of green tea. Since my laptop and phone had been confiscated, I had no way of accessing the internet. But the telephone would do just fine for now.

Only there wasn't one in sight.

After some searching, I discovered a jack next to the bed... but no telephone anywhere. This gave me pause. Had the older security guard asked the receptionist to send someone up here to remove the phone before we arrived?

I went to the door, knocked lightly to announce myself, then opened it. The young security guard was slumped in a chair across the hallway.

He shot to his feet. "Inside," he said in his poor English, pointing at the room. "Stay inside."

"Phone?" I said, pantomiming holding a receiver to my ear.

He shook his head. "No phone."

"No phone? Where is it?"

"Inside," he said, stepping toward me, making a shooing gesture with the back of his fingers. "Inside, inside."

"I just want to use a phone—"

"No phone!" he barked. "Inside!"

I returned inside the room and closed the door. Although I was disheartened that I wouldn't be unable to get in touch with anybody back home tonight, I didn't dwell on it. The Immigration Bureau couldn't hold me without explanation or charge indefinitely. At some point tomorrow they'd have to allow me to make a phone call.

I took a long, hot shower, which did much to improve my state of mind. I didn't have any pajamas to sleep in, and I wasn't comfortable passing out buck naked with the security guard sitting outside my door, so I checked the closet. Sure enough, draped on a hanger was a white cotton *yukata*, a traditional Japanese garment similar in style to a kimono but lighter and more casual. It doubled as both a bathrobe and loungewear, and it wasn't uncommon to see guests wandering around hotels in them.

I slipped on the *yukata*, went to the queen bed, and crawled beneath the covers, happy to put the contrary day from hell behind me. I closed my eyes and immediately thought of my boy, Damien. He was four years old now and about as rambunctious as you could get without breaking any laws. He had my golden-brown eyes and maybe my nose too. The rest he got from his mother, including his black hair, skin the color of sandstone, and buttery lips. He was definitely going to break some hearts when he got older.

My ex-wife, Blessica Villainz, had full custody of him, while I had visitation rights only. I never had a chance at attaining anything better. The law in the Philippines dictates that a child under seven years of age should not be separated from his mother due to the basic need for his mother's loving care. This rule isn't absolute. But there has to be a compelling reason for the courts to deprive a mother of the custody of her child, such as maltreatment, neglect, unemployment, habitual drunkenness, drug addiction, or plain old insanity. And for all of Bless' faults, she didn't check any of these boxes.

I'd last seen Damien two days before I'd boarded flight JL077. A driver usually picked him up from the international school he attended, though I let Bless know I would be picking him up that day. I took him to Dairy Queen for ice cream and to a toy store, where I told him he could select something under five hundred pesos. This was only ten dollars or so, but it was also about what a McDonald's worker earned for a ten-hour shift in the country. I was trying to instill some money sense into him, because God knows he wasn't getting any from his mother. She bought him whatever he wanted, whenever he wanted it, without batting an eyelid. We argued about such parenting issues all the time, yet Bless wasn't going to change her mindset. She'd grown up a spoiled brat, and she didn't see anything wrong with our son being one either.

I should take Damien to Taured next year, I thought sleepily. *Next summer, or perhaps autumn, when the leaves are turning, and the air is crisp and ripe with the smells of apples, pears, and mandarins. It's time the boy connects with his Tauredian heritage, time he gets a sense of life outside of around-the-clock nannies and drivers and golden spoons...*

Moments later I was asleep, and at some point during the night, I began to dream.

CHAPTER 6

Cold.

So cold.

I felt the coldness deep within my bones and beneath my skin.

"We've got to warm you up," Smiley told me. Her wool-knit hat was pulled down to her blonde eyebrows. Her blue eyes shone fiercely. "You can take my jacket," she added, starting to tug down the zipper.

"No," I said, touching her hand to prevent her from undoing her jacket. "We need to g-go."

"You're shivering."

"I am fine."

"I can't see your skis anywhere. They must be buried. Should we dig?"

I shook my head. "Never f-find them. You go. Down to the res-resort. Get help. I will follow your trail."

"No way, Gaston," she said. "Take my skis. You're the one who needs help. I'll walk."

"I am not leaving you out h-here." An ice-cold shudder scythed through me.

"Please, Gaston! Take my skis!"

"No!" I shoved myself to my feet. "Stay with me then. But we need to g-go."

Nodding, she stood and cantilevered her skis over her shoulder, and we set off down the steep slope together. Snowflakes fell in a silent monochromatic drizzle. Our breath fogged in the frosty air. Despite the steel-gray clouds hiding the sun, the ambient glare off the snow forced us to squint. A slow itch began to spread through the front of my thighs. It was almost a fiery sensation and contrasted sharply with the icy numbness in my chest and arms.

At one point when we stopped to rest, Smiley asked, "Are we sure we're going the right way?"

"We came from that way." I pointed to a sprawling evergreen forest to the east. "As long as we keep going back that way, we should come to a run eventually."

"How long do you think it will take us?"

"An hour? Less?" I checked my wristwatch. It was two-thirty.

This was not welcome news. Winter nights came quickly and early in Taured. We most likely wouldn't reach the nearest trail before it got dark.

As soon as we passed beneath the first boughs of the towering pine trees, the daylight was replaced with somber half-tones and harrying shadows. The snow came to our knees in places, sapping our strength. Soon we began taking turns following in each other's tracks. When we came to a ridge forty-five minutes later, I scampered up it with a burst of renewed energy, expecting to see a groomed run and a chairlift on the other side.

What greeted me was more forest.

For as far as I could see.

Smiley appeared beside me, panting hard. She gasped in despair.

"This is not right," I said. "We should have come to a trail by now."

"We've gone the wrong way," she said flatly. It wasn't an accusatory statement; just a fact.

"But we came west. We have been heading back east."

She looked up at the cloud-covered sky. "Wish we could see where the sun is."

"I am sure we have been going east. We just have to...keep going."

"It's getting dark. We probably only have another thirty

minutes of light."

I didn't know what to say in response to this. Was it possible we were going to be stuck in the forest overnight? We'd freeze to death.

Smiley seemed to be reading my thoughts and added, "We should find some sort of protection from the wind. We'll have each other's body heat. We'll be okay."

"I should not have let you stay with me," I told her. "You would have been safe at the bottom of the mountain by now."

"Or I could be lost on my own. Don't think about it, Gaston. But let's find some shelter."

The lee side of the ridge was steep. My controlled descent quickly morphed into a faster and faster run, then a slide—and about halfway down I lost a glove, though I couldn't stop myself to retrieve it. Smiley tumbled to a stop beside me. She was grinning wickedly.

"I lost a glove," I told her. "Halfway down."

Her grin vanished. We both looked up the ridge.

"I'll go find it," she stated.

"There is no time."

We came across a large rock wall jutting up from the ground. We dug snow from its base, creating a little burrow where we could both take shelter out of the cutting wind. By the time we had cleared enough snow, the stars had come out and it was difficult to see.

Abruptly a distant, persistent noise emanated from the rock, the heavy whumping of a bell clotted with mud...

ΔΔΔ

I opened my eyes, expecting coldness and death, what I'd experienced on the mountain during what would become the longest and most terrifying night of my life. Instead, I was greeted by dull sunlight. For a moment I had no idea where I was. Then I remembered I was in a hotel room. *The Narita Airport Rest House*—and with this name the events of the previous day returned with overwhelming force.

The numbers of the retro clock built into the bedside table read 9:30 a.m. Despite sleeping for nearly ten hours straight, I felt stiff and miserable. As I sat up and pushed the covers aside, I heard the noise that had lured me out of my dream:

WHUD, WHUD, WHUD.

"Yes, yes," I shouted. "I am coming."

I stood and rubbed my eyes. The sash of my yukata had come undone while I slept. I tied it once again, then opened the door. My two favorite security escorts stood in the hallway. The older one looked as though he'd eaten lemons for breakfast, while the younger sported bags the color of jelly under his eyes from a lack of sleep.

"I will have two eggs over easy," I said brightly, "whole wheat toast, two rashers of bacon, crispy, and a glass of orange—"

"Get dressed," the old guard grunted.

"Where are we going?"

"Get dressed," he repeated.

ΔΔΔ

I dressed in my tweed suit that I'd hung in the closet the night before in the hope gravity would straighten out the wrinkles. I brushed my teeth with the toothbrush the hotel provided and combed my hair the best I could with my fingers. When I was suitably presentable, I met my security escorts in the hallway. We walked back to Terminal 1, took an escalator up to the third floor, and passed through the Duty Free and shopping area. In a small room that smelled of fresh paint, a police officer took my fingerprints and mugshot. He made me give a statement about everything that had occurred thus far.

Finally, I was led back to the dreaded Special Examination Room in which my misadventure had begun fourteen or so hours earlier. I entered the little white cube. The door was shut behind me. I took a seat in one of the chairs. With nothing to do but think, it wasn't long before I was once more trying to figure out what had landed me in this ugly predicament. People, I presume, were detained every day in airports for any number of reasons. Intelligence, suspicious behavior, and profiling were the big three that came to mind. I certainly wasn't a spy for a foreign government. I hadn't acted nervous or suspiciously at the immigration counter the day before. And I hardly fit the profile of a terrorist. To the latter point, I wasn't flying into or leaving a troubled geopolitical area. This was Japan, one of the safest countries on the planet.

Eventually all roads led back to Hallie Smith, the British embassy woman. Her disappearing act was simply too out-of-the-ordinary to not be somehow related to my troubles.

Had she slipped contraband into my luggage when I wasn't looking back at Ninoy Aquino International Airport in Manila? Heroin or cocaine? A weapon or explosives? Some other banned item? Was she in cahoots with the fat man? Could they only afford one business-class ticket between themselves, so they'd decided to share it, swapping seats halfway through the flight?

The more I thought about this last possibility, the more frighteningly plausible it became to me. I tried to remember whether I'd seen either of them before the flight at the airport—

The door to the Special Examination Room opened. For a brief moment, I half expected Hallie Smith and the fat man to be marched inside wearing frowns and handcuffs. Instead, a porcine Japanese man in a dark gray suit bustled into the room with a hurried air about him. He bowed slightly before dumping his weight into the chair across the table from me. Puffing for breath, he said, "Good morning!"

He seemed pleasant-natured, which boosted my spirits, and I replied, "Good morning."

"My name is Yasuo Supa," he said, setting a clipboard and micro-recorder on the table before him. "You can call me Supa-san. I'm a Special Inquiry Officer at this airport," he continued in very good English. "I understand you stayed at the Rest House last night?"

I nodded.

"It was satisfactory?"

"Better, I suspect, than the detention facility or whatever it was where they first took me."

Supa-san was nodding. "The Landing Prevention Facility," he said, using a handkerchief to dab perspiration from his forehead. He tucked the hanky away, then used the end of his silk tie to polish the fingerprint-smudged lenses of his dainty eyeglasses.

"Is something like that even legal? It was awfully sketchy."

Supa-san kept nodding. "All major airports have jails of sorts. In Japan, they exist in Narita, Haneda, Chubu, and Kansai."

"Who were the security guards who took me there? They were not immigration officials."

"No, they work for a private security company. By law, airlines are responsible for passengers traveling with invalid travel documentation, so they contract security guards to transfer any such passengers to a detention facility, or to some other appropriate lodging."

"Like the Narita Rest House."

"Exactly."

"I guess that explains the questionable behavior of the security guards."

"Questionable behavior?"

"They demanded I pay twenty thousand yen for some rice and noodles."

Supa-san started shaking his head.

"Not to mention another thirty thousand yen for the hotel room," I continued, galvanizing my indignation. "But according to you, it sounds as though Japan Airlines, being responsible for its passengers, should have paid the bill?"

"They did pay the bill," he said. "Unfortunately for you, some of the security staff extort money from our detainees in exchange for what they call 'good service.'"

"I knew it!" I exclaimed. "Those scumbags. 'Good service.' Right."

"It's shameful," Supa-san agreed. "Shameful for Japan. The

Immigration Bureau needs to implement an official monitoring system to oversee the private security companies."

I recalled the missing telephone in my hotel room. "Is the Narita Rest House funded by the Immigration Bureau too?"

"We own some of the rooms, yes. Usually, they're where we lodge children and minors."

I marveled at the extent to which I'd been pawned. Even so, I was gratified that I was finally starting to get some answers. I said, "Can you tell me why I am being held? You mentioned invalid travel documents. Is something wrong with my passport? Nobody has told me what is going on except that it is an immigration matter."

"We will address that very shortly, just as soon as my colleague—"

The door to the room opened and a squat, angry woman in a navy uniform entered.

Supa-san stood and bowed. The woman bowed in return. They both sat.

"This is Wakako Shimizu," Supa-san said, bowing yet again at no one in particular. "She's an immigration inspector. She will be conducting the interview. Hopefully we will be able to get all the facts and sort this situation out." He turned on the micro-recorder and slid it into the center of the table. "May we begin?"

CHAPTER 7

"What's your name?" Wakako Shimizu asked me brusquely. Her wiry black hair, graying at the roots, formed a triangular helmet. Wrinkles and sunspots marred her face and neck, as well as the backs of her pudgy hands. Drawn-on eyebrows framed eyes the color of coal, and her lips seemed locked in a tight, permanent frown. My immediate impression was of a lady who might spend her free time bullying children on social media.

"Gaston Green," I replied. "Why am I being detained?"

"*I* ask the questions!" she snapped.

I flinched in surprise. Supa-san's polite and unassuming manner had caused me to lower my guard. "You can ask your questions, *madame*," I told her, "but you do not have to be rude about it."

"Do not tell me how to act!"

"Tell me why I am being detained."

"You do not ask the questions!"

"Relax," I said, holding up my hands. "I am going to answer your questions."

"You will answer them now!"

"Hey, *madame*—cool it. I have already told you I will answer your questions. But if this is how you are going to behave, maybe I will not. I am entitled to a phone call, no? Maybe I should call an attorney."

"An attorney?" She snorted. "You are not a Japanese citizen. You haven't been charged with a criminal offence, so you do not have a right to an attorney."

An epiphany struck me. "No, I have not been charged—so I am not being *legally* detained, am I?" I'd watched enough TV and movies to know that often people detained by law enforcement were free to leave at any time during their interrogation, but they simply didn't know enough about their rights to do so. Consequently, perhaps I'd been free to go this entire time, which was why nobody would come straight out and tell me why I was being held. Emboldened, I stood. "I think I would like to leave now."

Both Wakako Shimizu and Supa-san sprang to their feet.

"Please sit back down," Supa-san said.

"You cannot go anywhere!" Wakako Shimizu said.

I remained standing. "If I am not being charged with a crime, you cannot hold me here against my will."

"Of course we can," Wakako Shimizu said. "Narita is a special area."

Supa-san added almost apologetically, "Immigration officials can issue a detention order for an initial period of thirty days when there are reasonable grounds to believe that someone falls under any of the items of Article 24. This can then be extended for an additional thirty days, or until the time deportation becomes possible."

I let the bleak information sink in, then said, "So I am being deported?"

"Stop!" Wakako Shimizu all but screeched. "Stop asking questions! Sit down now!"

I glared at her, but I sat back in my seat.

The two immigration officials sat too.

Wakako Shimizu's stygian eyes didn't waver from mine. Summoning civility with what seemed like great difficulty, she said, "Where did you board your flight to Japan?"

"Manila," I told her, noticing Supa-san scribbling something on his clipboard. Then, so there was no misunderstanding, I added, "The Philippines."

"Do you live there?"

"Yes."

"For how long?"

"Ten years or thereabouts."

"What is your nationality?"

"Tauredian," I said.

Wakako Shimizu—or just Wacky, as I was beginning to think of her as—frowned. Her eyes hardened to chips of black diamonds.

"What?" I asked, looking from her to Supa-san, who seemed preoccupied with his notes.

"I am from Taured," I clarified. "In Europe."

"Where is it in Europe?" Wacky asked.

"Between France and Spain, in the eastern Pyrenees mountains."

"When was the last time you returned to Taured?"

"You have my passport. Check the stamp—?"

"Are you refusing to answer the question? You must say exactly, in detail!"

"Okay, okay, relax." I worked my memory. "2014, I believe. Yes, it was 2014, six years ago. I went back to celebrate my younger brother's thirtieth birthday. I think I stayed for about two weeks."

"Why are you coming to Japan now?"

"For work."

"What is your job?"

I hesitated for only a moment before deciding on my answer. "I am an ambassador," I told her.

"You are an *ambassador*?" Supa-san said, leaning forward so his belly pressed again the round edge of the table. "For your country?"

"For Glenfiddich," I said.

"Where is Glenfiddich?" Wacky demanded.

"In Scotland."

"Ah! So you are from Scotland! You lied to us—"

"I did not," I said, interrupting her. "Glenfiddich is a single malt Scotch whisky owned and produced by William Grant & Sons in Dufftown, Scotland. Maybe you have heard of it?"

"Yes, yes," Supa-san said, nodding. "Yes, I know."

"If you work for a whisky company," Wacky said, scowling, "why did you tell us you are an ambassador?"

"Because I *am* an ambassador, *madame*," I said. "A brand ambassador. A whisky ambassador, if you will. My job is to promote Glenfiddich throughout East Asia."

"Then you are not a *real* ambassador," Wacky said with a heavy dose of asperity. "Do not play games with us, Mr. Green."

I didn't see any purpose getting into a war of semantics with the woman, so I didn't reply.

Wakako Shimizu ran her tongue along the front of her teeth, distending her upper lip, and for a terrible moment I feared she was gathering saliva to spit on me. Thankfully, she only asked, "Have you been to Japan before?"

"Yes, many times," I said.

"When was your last trip?"

"Two months ago."

"In May?"

"Yes, in May."

"What day?"

"The *exact* day?" Seeing her preparing to pounce, I added quickly, "It was near the end of the month. Maybe the twenty-fifth? Or the twenty-sixth?"

"Where did you stay?" she asked.

"The Park Hyatt in Shinjuku. Where I should be right now enjoying the city views." This image hit me hard, as the possibility of getting out of this airport and to the hotel any time soon seemed more distant than ever. Suddenly I just wanted to go home. "*Mes amis*," I said, trying to sound reasonable, "maybe you have me confused for someone else—?"

"Quiet—"

"Do not tell me to be quiet!" I bellowed, slamming my hands on the table hard enough to make it jump. I'd had enough of the woman's truculent attitude. I was not a criminal. I was innocent. And not only that, I was tired, stressed, hungry...and simply fed up with this whole charade. "You have been holding me against my will for more than fourteen hours," I went on. "You are refusing to tell me the reason, other than it concerns some nebulous immigration matter. Well, that is not good enough. I am not answering any more of your questions until someone tells me what is going on!"

Supa-san and Wakako Shimizu exchanged glances. Supa-san nodded slightly. Wacky shrugged.

Taking his handkerchief from a pocket, the Special Inquiry Officer dabbed a fresh sheen of perspiration from his forehead. "You have been very patient with us, Mr. Green," he said, meeting my eyes. "I thank you for that. But I must ask you one more time. Where are you from?"

"My country?" I nearly rolled my eyes. "I told you. I am Tauredian. I am from Taured. Why is that so hard to believe?"

"Because, Mr. Green," he said, pausing almost dramatically, "the country you mention, the country of Taured, does not exist."

CHAPTER 8

I must have sat there for about five seconds simply staring at the immigration officers. Then I issued a stiff laugh. "Taured does not exist? Taured? T-a-u-r-e-d?"

"You seem surprised," Wacky said.

"This is ludicrous! Of course it exists. Is that what all this is about?" I felt a strange mix of relief and fury. The former because the unknown had finally become known. The latter because I'd been through hell all because these boneheads had failed Geography 101.

"We have checked thoroughly," Supa-san said. "There is no country named Taured. Not in Europe. Not anywhere."

"*Mes amis*," I said, finding it impossible not to sound patronizing. "You have my passport. It is from *Taured*."

"Where did you get it?" Wacky asked.

"The Tauradian embassy in Manila! It was issued February 2, 2016."

"Taured does not—"

"Yes, it does!" I exploded. "Get me an atlas. I will show you where it is."

"We don't have an atlas," Supa-san said, "but we can use Google Maps on my phone."

"Type Taured." I spelled it for him once again.

While he typed the country into his phone, I began tapping my right foot. This was incredible. All this drama when all they had to do was a simple online search.

"Taured Sa..." Supa-san said. "Rue Siggy Vue, Luxembourg."

"What are you talking about? It is just Taured. T-a-u-r-e-d."

"That is what I typed. Taured Sa is the only result that appears."

I clamped my jaw. "Can I see your phone, please?"

He passed the device across the table to me. I closed the map app and swiped to his homepage. In the address bar, I typed "TAURED" and tapped Enter. The internet browser opened, displaying numerous results. The descriptions for the webpages were all written in Japanese. I could read hiragana and katagana but not kanji, the characters Japan adopted from China, so little I was seeing made sense.

In the URL bar I typed "WORLD MAP IMAGES" and pressed Enter.

This time a number of colored maps appeared. A couple of taps later and I was looking at a detailed map of Europe. I zoomed in on it—and blinked in confusion. The principality of Taured was incorrectly labeled Andorra. My immediate thought was that the map had been Photoshopped. I was in some conspiracy, and the immigration officers were in on it too. Yet this thought was instantly followed up by a second: *I did the search. I chose the map.*

I tapped the Back button, scrolled down, and randomly clicked a different map.

Taured was Andorra.

Or rather, Andorra was Taured.

"Are you okay, Mr. Green?" Supa-san asked me.

His voice sounded far away. I didn't answer him. I was feeling hot, lost, and muddled.

"Mr. Green...? Mr. Green...?"

I finally looked up. "Is this a joke?" I asked without any real conviction, for I knew it wasn't. Without waiting for a response, I added, "Taured is there. The country is on the map. But it is called...Andorra."

"Yes, Andorra," Wacky said, eyes smoldering. "We know Andorra. Are you from Andorra, Mr. Green?"

"I am from...where Andorra is on the map...but..." I shook my head. "My country is called Taured. I cannot understand this..."

"Is your passport counterfeit, Mr. Green?"

"No—no, it is real. Why would I...? If you think Taured does not exist, why would I...?" I could barely get my thoughts, let alone my words, to make sense. "Why would I ever make a counterfeit passport for a country that does not exist?"

"So you admit Taured does not exist?"

"No! I am saying..."

A sick, empty feeling rushed through me. I looked dully at the two immigration officers. It was like looking at a pair of photographs. They didn't seem real.

"What is happening?" I asked quietly, the question—my voice—sounding alien in my ears.

"We're waiting for you to tell us that," Wacky said.

CHAPTER 9

In one of the first clear childhood memories I could recall, I was kneeling in the sandbox in the backyard of my family home, shaded from the sun beneath the canopy of an old walnut tree, playing with my Tim Mee plastic army men. I moved a prone green rifleman through the sand, sneaking him up behind a blue minesweeper. Before he could strike, a blue bazookaman fired a rocket. I made an exploding sound, vibrating my lips the way you might when blowing air from your mouth underwater. I threw the green rifleman up in the air, mumbling that he was dead now—at the same time as I spotted movement from the corner of my eye. A fox was slinking through my mother's flowerbed not a dozen feet away from me. It pushed past a patch of daisies and came right up to the sandbox, its oversized triangular ears erect, its pointed snout sniffing the ground, following some invisible scent trail. It passed to within a few feet of me, unperturbed by my presence, and continued on its way across the green lawn, disappearing into the forest that bordered the backyard. It had been such a bizarre yet magical encounter that foxes became my favorite animal for years thereafter.

Another early childhood memory was of my fourth or fifth birthday party. I had invited about ten of my classmates over to my house. While we were sitting around the dining room table eating chocolate cake and drinking cola, a girl named Eloise had an allergic reaction to an insect bite and was taken to the hospital. Later that afternoon, when my mother and I paid her a visit, we found her in a room with other kids, sitting on a mechanical bed, her face red and puffy. When I gave her the loot bag I'd brought for her, she kissed me on the cheek—and *she* became my favorite friend for years thereafter.

I had a hundred more equally vivid memories of growing up in Taured, a thousand: trick-or-treating in a Superman costume on a cool October Halloween night; sneaking down the staircase in my pajamas before my parents woke to see how many presents lay beneath the Christmas tree on Christmas morning; the family trips to our lakeside cabin in the summers; swimming in the alpine water and catching frogs along the mucky shores; camping with my brothers and buying homemade pizza from a friendly family in one of the villages we passed. And let us not forget the night I should have died in the mountains.

How could I have all these memories if Taured didn't exist?

Simple: It *did* exist. It had to exist.

Supa-san was saying something to me. I focused on him.

"Do you have other identification on you?"

Nodding belatedly, I took out my wallet and slid the plastic cards free: a Manila driver's license; an Alien Certificate Registration card (a requirement for all foreign nationals living in the Philippines to hold); a debit card; two credit cards (one MasterCard, one VISA); and a green PhilHealth card. "They were all issued to me in the Philippines," I said.

Wakako Shimizu picked up my driver's license. "Gaston Green," she said. "The same name on your passport."

"That is my name."

"May we make copies of these?" Supa-san asked.

"Go ahead."

He collected the six cards and stacked them neatly on his clipboard.

"Do you have an alias, Mr. Green?" Wacky asked me.

"Yes," I said.

An eagerness animated her expression. She leaned forward slightly.

"Mr. Brown," I told her.

"Mr. Brown...?" she repeated.

"If I am in a particularly bad mood," I went on, "I use Mr. Blue. If I am in a sunny mood, I use Mr. Yellow. Angry—Mr. Red."

Wakako Shimizu's face darkened, while Supa-san had enough of a sense of humor to chuckle to himself.

"This is not the place to tell jokes," Wacky quipped.

"I do not have any aliases," I told her with a pleasant smile.

"You don't have an alternative passport—with a different name on it?"

"No, I do not have an alternative passport with a different name on it. The only one I have is the one that was taken from me."

"And that is the passport you used to board flight JL077?"

"Yes," I answered.

"Our problem, Mr. Green," Supa-san said, "is that we can't find a record of anyone with your name or passport number having purchased a ticket for flight JL077."

"I purchased it online from the same website I always use. With my credit card—the MasterCard. Look up my transactions."

"We will do that," he assured me.

"Also, my seat was 6-A. That is connected to my ticket. You can look that up too."

"6-A," he repeated, jotting the information onto his clipboard.

Wakako Shimizu was eyeing me expectantly.

"What?" I asked her. "I do not know what else to tell you. I checked in at the Japan Airlines counter at Ninoy Aquino in Manila with the passport you confiscated. I had a drink in the Sakura Lounge. I went to my gate and boarded the plane. That is it. No aliases. No fake passports—"

Wacky cut me off, demanding, "How is it there is no record of a passenger named Gaston Green on the flight?"

"I do not know! But why would I ever travel on a fake passport, Shimizu-san?" It was the first time I had addressed Wakako Shimizu by her name. Doing so left an unpleasant taste in my mouth. "Actually, no," I added, "why would I travel on a fake passport from a *country that does not exist*?"

"It was a mistake."

"That would be a pretty stupid mistake to make, yes?"

"Mistakes happen, even stupid ones."

"All right," I said. "Let us imagine I commissioned a fake passport, and both the counterfeiter and I were too stupid to realize it was from a bogus country. Let us accept that premise for the moment, *mes amis*. The question remains: Why would I get a fake passport in the first place? Why would I not simply use my 'real' passport?"

"Because you feared it might raise a red flag," she opined. "Passengers often travel on fake passports if they are involved in illicit activity, or have criminal records and are banned by certain countries."

"You think I am a criminal? A murderer, perhaps?" I shook my head. "To be honest, *madame*, if I was a murderer on the run, Japan, with its homogenous population, would not be my first choice of places to blend in."

"I did not say you were a *murderer*, Mr. Green," Wacky said. "But it is a fact that we stop people from Southeast Asian countries—such as the Philippines—every day for attempting to bring drugs into Japan."

"Ah! I see now. You think I am smuggling drugs? The only problem with this hypothesis is that I am not. You can search me, if you want. Search my suitcase too, if you want."

The immigration officers appeared surprised.

"Your *suitcase*?" Supa-san said. "What suitcase?"

"My suitcase. *Merde*, do not tell me it has been sitting down there at the baggage claim all this time? Nobody has collected it for me?"

"There was no unclaimed luggage from Flight JL077, Mr. Green."

"It is bright red. Ben Sherman. You cannot miss it."

"Do you take any prescription medication, Mr. Green?" Wacky asked me.

"No," I replied tightly to the pejorative question.

"Have you taken any illicit or illegal drugs within the last twenty-four hours?"

I was about to offer a glib retort, but I hesitated. *Could* I be tripping out on some unknown drug? Obviously I would know if I were presently high on LSD. But could someone else have slipped me something else? Something that messed subtly with my thinking…something that…what? Made me think I was from a country that didn't exist?

Ridiculous, I thought dismissively.

"If you know of any drugs capable of making one believe he is from a country that does not exist, Shimizu-san, please let me know."

Wacky's lips puckered distastefully. "Do you have any mental illnesses, Mr. Green?" she asked.

"You mean like Alzheimer's? I am forty-two years old."

"There are many forms of dementia—"

"I have never been diagnosed with a brain disease, *madame*," I said. "Nor do I take mind-altering drugs. In fact, I would go so far as to offer that I am in perfect health."

Supa-san spoke to Wakako Shimizu in Japanese at length, then passed her my identity cards.

She stood. "I am going to photocopy these now," she told me.

"I know," I said, using Japanese for the first time. "And you are also going to confirm my seat number on flight JL077 and check the Unclaimed Baggage Center for my suitcase."

Her beady eyes narrowed. "You can speak Japanese?"

"One other thing you might want to do while you are up and about?" I offered. "Check the passenger manifest for a woman named Hallie Smith."

"Hallie Smith? Who is this?"

"She was in the SkySuite next to mine when I boarded the flight in Manila. After lunch was served, I took a nap. When I woke up, a fat man was in her seat. I do not know where she went. I did not see her again."

"This…man…was still in the seat when the plane landed in Japan then?" Supa-san asked.

"Yes. But I do not know his name. He sounded American, if that helps."

Wakako Shimizu exchanged a final glance with Supa-san, then left the room.

"How did you learn Japanese, Mr. Green?" Supa-san asked me.

"Books," I told him. "I enjoy learning different languages. I am a...I think the English word is a *polyglot*."

"How many languages can you speak?"

"French, Spanish, and English fluently. I can get by with most of East Asia's non-tonal dialects, but the tonal ones still give me trouble."

"How many times have you been to Japan?"

"More than one hundred, I would guess."

"For business?"

"Always for business."

"You must have many business associates here then, yes? Is there one we can call to confirm your identity?"

"Yes, of course!" I said, surprised I hadn't thought of this. "I have an event at a restaurant in Ginza on Thursday. It is a whisky dinner. I pair whisky cocktails with the food that is served. I have been in touch with the chef all week. He is a friend."

"Do you know his telephone number?"

"It is your lucky day, *monsieur*, as I have a very good memory for numbers." I picked up his phone from the table and dialed the chef's number. A prerecorded female voice, speaking Japanese, informed me the call had not been successful. Frowning, I hung up and said, "Perhaps I have confused his number. But that does not matter. I can find the restaurant online." I performed a quick internet search for Matsuoka and dialed the telephone number on the contact page of the restaurant's website. When a woman answered, I asked in Japanese to speak to Toru Matsuoka.

"Unfortunately," she replied, "Matsuoka-sama is in Osaka right now."

"Osaka?" I said, surprised. "For how long?"

"Until the end of the month."

"The end of the month! He is supposed to be at Matsuoka this Thursday. He is doing a dinner with me."

"Who am I speaking with, please?"

"Gaston Green."

"Do you have a booking, Mr. Green?"

"A booking? Yes, I suppose. I have booked out the entire restaurant."

"How large is your party exactly?"

"You do not understand. There is no party. No reservation. I am running an event there—"

"I'm sorry, Mr. Green, but I don't speak English well—"

"I am not speaking English! I am speaking Japanese!"

"I'm sorry, I don't understand—"

I jabbed the button to end the call.

Supa-san was watching me with concern.

"At least the restaurant exists," I quipped.

CHAPTER 10

Supa-san excused himself from the Special Examination Room. I used the alone time to try to get my head around the enormity and impossibility of the predicament I found myself in.

Was Taured in fact this so-called Andorra? Was I delusional? Had I had some sort of stroke on the plane? Were my wires crossed?

I almost wished this were the case, but I knew it wasn't, as my confiscated passport was from Taured.

It's got to be a joke, I decided. Some hidden camera reality TV program like *Candid Camera*. But why would such a show target me? And weren't they going too far with it? On *Punk'd* or *Scare Tactics*, the victim was always let in on the prank after a short time. He or she was never held for over fourteen hours.

I recalled that old Michael Douglas movie in which his character's estranged brother buys him a "game" for his birthday that integrates with his everyday life, ultimately blurring the lines between reality and fiction.

Could this airport detention fiasco be a similar kind of game then? But who would go to the trouble of signing me up to something so elaborate and outlandish? Not to mention why would Japan's Bureau of Immigration ever go along with it?

An accompanying line of thinking made the hair on the nape of my neck stand on end:

You're crazy. It's the only explanation. You're crazy and you don't even know it, because that's how it works with crazy people. They don't even know it.

Supa-san returned to the Special Examination Room, sweating and bowing. He sat in his chair and set my identify cards on the table. "You may have these back for now."

"For now?" I retrieved the cards and slid them back into my wallet. "Would you mind if I used your phone again?"

"Who would you like to call this time?"

"My mother. She lives in Taured. She has lived there her entire life."

"Please." He took his phone from his pocket and passed it to me.

"What is Japan's international access code?"

"Zero-one-zero."

I punched this in, then Taured's country code, then my mother's six-digit telephone number (Taured's population wasn't large enough to warrant the use of area codes).

With my mouth suddenly bone-dry, I held the phone to my ear, anticipating the conversation that would ensue when I explained to my mother that I was being held against my will in Japan because the immigration officials claimed Taured did not exist—

Another prerecorded voice told me the call was not successful. I glanced at the screen to make sure I had dialed the right number. I had.

"You said zero-one-zero?" I asked Supa-san.

He nodded.

"You are sure?"

"Very sure, Mr. Green. *You* are sure you dialed the right number?"

"I call my mother once a month," I said, shaking my head. "I do not understand…"

Supa-san leaned back in the chair. "Tell me, Mr. Green," he said, once again polishing his eyeglasses with the end of his tie. "What is Taured like this time of year?"

"Why?" I asked woodenly. "Plan to visit?"

"Is it humid like Japan?"

"The summers are cool and dry."

"And winters?"

"Snowy."

"It is small?"

"No more than five hundred square kilometers."

"The population?"

"Seventy-five thousand."

Supa-san began nodding.

"What?" I asked.

"It's just that your description of Taured could very well have been a description of Andorra."

A queasy feeling rocked my stomach. "Is that so?"

"What is the mother tongue of the people in Taured? I cannot decide if your accent is Spanish or French."

"French," I said.

"What about the flag? What does it look like?"

"It is blue, yellow, and red."

"Very similar to Andorra's, only Andorra's has a coat of arms in the middle."

"What are you getting at, *monsieur*?"

"I just find it interesting. All these similarities between the two countries...but differences too."

"I know what you are thinking," I said. "You think I am making this all up. But I am not. I was born in Taured. I grew up in Taured. I never heard of the name Andorra before you told it to me." I spread my hands. "Am I crazy? Am I sick? Crazy or sick enough to get a phony passport made up to reinforce my delusion? Maybe, but it does not feel like that to me."

"Admittedly, it doesn't to me either, Mr. Green," Supa-san said. "I have never experienced a case such as yours."

"What is going to happen to me?" I asked. "You cannot keep me in this room indefinitely—"

The door opened, and Wakako Shimizu entered.

"Your name was not registered to seat 6-A, Mr. Green," she told me without preamble. "The seat was unassigned. And there was no red Ben Sherman suitcase in the Baggage Claim Office."

I wasn't surprised by these revelations—baffled, angry, desperate—but no longer surprised.

"And Hallie Smith?" I asked.

"No passenger by that name on Flight JL077."

I closed my eyes, feeling as though I were at the bottom rung of a greased ladder with no hope of ever getting to the top.

The immigration officials were speaking to me.

"...but without a valid passport your entry into Japan is denied..."

I looked at Supa-san. "Am I getting deported?"

"That would be the usual procedure," he replied. "But in your case, we can't deport you to a country that doesn't exist."

"You can deport me to the Philippines. That is where I boarded the plane. That is where I live."

"That's what you *say*, Mr. Green," Wacky said. "But without a valid passport—"

"It is valid!" I bellowed. "Taured exists!"

Her hands balled into fists. "*Tell us your real name.*"

"*Gaston! Gaston Green!*"

"*Where is your real passport?*"

"*You took it! You have it—*"

"*Enough!*" Supa-san barked, raising his voice for the first time. He dabbed his forehead with his handkerchief. "I am sorry, Mr. Green," he continued more reasonably. "But we have run out of time to help you resolve this matter." He unclipped a piece of paper from his clipboard and slid it across the table to me. "Please sign here."

The script was Japanese hiragana. I had no patience to decipher the words.

"What does it say?" I asked.

"It's an appeal form," he explained. "It says you have three days to appeal to the Minister of Justice."

"Appeal?" I frowned. "Appeal what?"

"Your detention, Mr. Green," Wakako Shimizu said, smiling with smug satisfaction. "You are under arrest."

CHAPTER 11

A pair of armed security guards handcuffed me in the Special Examination Room before marching me through the airport, which was bustling with morning travelers, many of whom gave me disapproving looks. I kept my chin up and my gaze directly ahead until we emerged outside in a private parking lot. The guards loaded me onto a white coach with tinted windows and two emergency light bars on the roof. They directed me through a cage system that separated the vehicle's front bulkhead and the large holding area. There were seats for perhaps forty detainees in the latter, though I counted only six other men, all of Asian descent. Making as little eye contact as possible with any of them, I took a seat and stared blankly forward.

The driver shifted the coach into gear and weaved through the scramble of airport roads into the grim-gray morning. Through the perforated steel covering the windows, I watched the rice paddies and pastoral towns drift past, barely registering the scenery. Supa-san had told me my destination was the Tokyo Detention House. This, he clarified, was not a hotel such as the Narita Airport Rest House where I had stayed in relative comfort the previous night. It was a correctional facility run by the Ministry of Justice. In not so many words, a prison. And although I had never stepped foot inside a prison before, I had a pretty good idea what life there would be like: physical abuse and mental anguish, solitary confinement and suicides, overcrowding and malnutrition. Riots, hierarchies, gangs, rape. The list of horrors went on and on.

I didn't know how I was going to endure even a day under

such conditions, only that I had no choice in the matter. This understanding was what truly terrified me. My freedom and many of my rights had been forfeited. I was at the mercy of correctional guards and hardened criminals and, God forbid, a sadistic warden.

As the white coach sped along the highway, I repeated to myself that I hadn't done anything wrong and that my incarceration would be resolved within a day or two at most…though this did little to banish the brooding fear in the pit of my being.

PART II

Tokyo Detention House

CHAPTER 12

The hulking form of the X-shaped Tokyo Detention House rose against the depressing sky, dwarfing the nearby apartment buildings and houses. The coach passed through a metal perimeter fence that appeared no different than those around suburban schoolyards. I could see no coiled concertina wire nor intermittent watch towers. These observations might have lifted my spirits somewhat had the prison complex itself not been so forbidding. Twelve stories of austere concrete, it resembled a fortress out of some dystopian future, and I thought:

Some people never come out of prison again. Some people die in prison.

Was I going to be one of those statistics?

The coach passed through an entrance gate with a vertical sign that read:

東京拘置所

I recognized the kanji for TOKYO, and though I didn't have time to work out the rest of the translation, I figured it would be DETENTION HOUSE.

The coach slowed to a stop when we reached the back of the mammoth building. Several guards joined the two in the front bulkhead. Barking vitriolic commands in Japanese, they ushered us off the vehicle and through a pair of glass doors. Inside the reception area, the guards disbanded our motley group of detainees. One shoved my shoulder, directing me down a hallway. He ordered me to stop in front of a cell with Perspex walls.

He opened the door with a key, nudged me inside, and shut the door again with a solid *shuh-clack*. There was no interior handle.

I watched the guard amble off down the hallway the way we had come. I paced in the cramped space. I was a bundle of nervous energy, and I likely could have run a twenty-kilometer marathon right then had I the freedom.

The freedom.

No, I wasn't going to think about that now. No thinking about the future either. Just the present. As long as I focused on that, I could get through this nightmare, one hour at a time.

I continued pacing for the next fifteen minutes, constantly looking through the clear walls for whoever was supposed to fetch me. Eventually all the back and forth was making me go nutty. I sat down on the concrete bench. When another fifteen minutes passed, and still no one came for me, I laid down on my back, my feet near my rear, my knees in the air. There was no way I could sleep right then, yet I closed my eyes. I played over the exhaustive interview with Supa-san and Wakako Shimizu from every angle, but I had no new insight into my predicament.

After Wacky had smugly declared that I was under arrest, I had asked—and been denied—the opportunity to make a phone call. I'd wanted to call Blessica in the Philippines, to get her to contact the Tauredian embassy, so at least somebody with authority would know I had been arrested.

Oh, Gaston, I could imagine Bless saying to me, without a care in the world, had I been able to get in touch with her. *Arrested in Japan, you say? Why am I not surprised?*

We'd met during my first year in the Philippines at an event I was hosting. I'd organized a large fair with tents from several different vendors in Bonifacio Global City, an affluent financial/residential district in Manila. I was doing my rounds, making sure everyone was enjoying themselves, offering my usual whisky-tasting spiels, when I spotted Blessica standing next to a table laden with countless bottles of Glenfiddich and glasses stacked on top of one another pyramid-style. She was with several friends, all of them dressed to the nines in classy dresses, designer handbags, and high heels. There didn't seem to be much of a middle class in the Philippines. The majority of the population was poor, and the rest were rich, and it was those in the latter category who attended my events. They were often a young crowd, the sons and daughters of politicians, business tycoons, self-made entrepreneurs, media and banking magnates. Many worked in glamorous industries such as film and TV, or fashion, while just as many were full-time socialites. They drove new cars, lived in gated neighborhoods, partied incessantly, and in general didn't seem to have a care in the world.

Blessica fit squarely into this second group. Her relatives came from society, her money from a trust. She'd never strayed from her deb-socialite path, and she eventually co-founded an events company representing a portfolio of luxury brands such as Gucci and Cartier. We fell for each other hard and started spending all of our free time together. She seemed to know everyone of importance in Manila and showed me to the trendiest restaurants and clubs on a nearly nightly basis. On my birthday she took me to a bar I had been to countless times before, only on this occasion she led me to a coat check room, an anachronism in a city in which the average temperature could be described as sweltering. We donned fur-lined jackets that didn't belong to us, and a staff member revealed a secret door that led to a freezing cold room composed entirely of ice. It was packed with beautiful people all wearing identical fur-lined jackets and drinking elaborate cocktails.

I proposed to Bless five months after we'd met, and we were married on the island of Boracay the following year. My mother and brothers flew over from Taured, and I think they were blown away by the lavish ceremony (the Porta-Potties, which had been transported from the mainland by helicopters, featured marble sinks and gilded mirrors). In any event, they enjoyed themselves and got along easily with Blessica's family and our friends, and just so my eldest brother Paul would never forget the experience, he got a middle-of-the-night tattoo of a rubber duck across his back (which he swears he doesn't regret).

Bless and I stayed with them on the island for the remainder of the week before returning to Manila and seeing them off at the airport (where Paul continued to deny regretting the tattoo). Bless and I honeymooned in northern Australia. Two months later, in March 2011, she fell pregnant with Damien, who would be born on Christmas Eve, and who, through no fault of his own, would cause everything to unravel between us in the coming years—

An alarming thought unrelated to all the previous ones caused me to snap open my eyes and sit up straight.

I was in an observation unit. Guards were likely watching me on a video monitoring system right then. Making sure I wasn't going to freak out, inflict self-harm, or suffer a thunderclap heart attack from the stress and shock of my incarceration. And they were more than likely forming their first impressions of whether I was innocent or guilty. Because the innocent pace, fidget, and perhaps cry.

The guilty sleep.

"I was not sleeping," I said out loud.

I went to one clear wall and pressed my nose to the Perspex and indeed saw a video camera mounted high on the nearby wall, pointed at me.

I stared at it for a long moment, then began pacing once more.

CHAPTER 13

After about an hour, two prison guards transferred me from the observation unit to a room similar in shape and size to Narita's Special Examination Room, only this one featured concrete slabs for walls. There was a scale and stadiometer in the corner, as well as a blood pressure cuff and pressure gauge on a table, along with a few other miscellaneous medical items.

The guards removed my handcuffs and left. I sat down in one of the hard plastic chairs. A neat man in gray trousers and a white sweater over a plaid button-up entered the room. He wore a white surgical mask over his mouth.

"I am a medical doctor here at the Tokyo Detention House," he said in English from behind the mask. His voice was sonorous and clear. "Do you understand me?"

"Yes," I told him.

"What language do they speak in your country?"

"French."

"I don't know French. English will be okay?"

"Yes," I repeated.

The doctor got down to business, recording my height, weight, and blood pressure in a green file folder. He asked me a constellation of questions related to my health, education, and profession. I wasn't sure why he wanted to know what degree I'd earned in university, or what I did for work, but I suspected it had something to do with my security classification that would determine what part of the prison I would be held in, and what work programs I would be enlisted in.

I nearly told him the questions were unnecessary, as I wasn't going to be in the prison for long, my incarceration was a mistake, until I realized how many times he had likely heard such declarations of innocence.

"Please remove your clothes," he said without looking up from the folder in which he was writing notes.

I shrugged off my jacket and unbuttoned my dress shirt. Soon I stood naked as a newborn, my tweed suit, designer boxer briefs, and socks all folded neatly on the table next to me. The doctor snapped on a pair of blue Nitrile gloves and performed a thorough physical examination, which I endured silently. After he finished, he gave me a pale-green jumpsuit, matching Crocs, a white tee-shit, and a pair of shapeless white underwear. Once I was dressed, he asked for my watch and rings.

"Do I get the all clear?" I asked lightheartedly.

The doctor nodded. "You are in excellent health." He gathered the green file folder.

"What happens now?"

"Someone will be with you shortly."

Be with me shortly? Sounded like I was getting table service at a restaurant.

The doctor left the room. A guard opened the door, holding it ajar until an old man in a green jumpsuit identical to mine entered.

"Who are you?" I demanded.

"Barber," he said, setting a small leather case on the table and taking out clippers and brushes. "Please have a seat."

I relaxed but remained standing. "I do not want my hair cut."

"Are you Jewish?"

"No."

"Muslim or Rastafarian?"

"What? No. *Merde*. Do I *look* Rastafarian?"

"Then you must cut hair. It is rule."

I stared at the inmate-barber for a long moment. He stared back, his eyes resigned, as if he were used to first-timers causing a stink such as this. I sat in the chair.

"Do I get a say in how short you cut it?" I asked.

"No," he said. "No choice."

He slid a very short guard onto his clipper, turned it on, and rode it over my head, moving against the grain of my hair. The clippers whined angrily as clumps of my dark hair fell onto my jumpsuit.

The old man dusted off my scalp with one of the brushes, deloused it with an insecticide, then handed me a small mirror.

"No, thank you," I said, not wanting to see what I looked like.

"You won't see your reflection again very long time."

This statement hit me hard, but I didn't capitulate, stubbornly shaking my head.

The inmate-barber shrugged, tucked away the mirror with the rest of his tools and left, leaving me to wonder who was going to clean up all the hair on the floor.

ΔΔΔ

A beefy man in a blue suit was the next person to pay me a visit. He looked normal enough until he opened his mouth to speak. I'd never seen teeth like this guy had. There must have been twice as many as there were supposed to be crammed into his mouth. They were yellow, leaning every which way, growing out of his gums in all the wrong places, and in several spots, growing in parallel rows. It was almost as if his baby teeth had never fallen out and his permanent teeth had been desperate for new and creative places to sprout.

I had to force myself to look away from the carnival sight. The man's rheumy eyes twinkled amusedly, as if he was used to the reaction his teeth caused in others.

"Sorry?" I said. "What did you say?"

"Please look here." He raised a camera and snapped a photograph of me with my new do. In natural-sounding English, he asked, "Do you know where you are?"

I nodded. "The Tokyo Detention House."

"Do you know why you are here?"

"I know that I am not supposed to be here."

Jaws laughed, tilting his head back and opening his maw wide. To my disgust, I saw he even had a tooth growing out of the *roof* of his mouth.

"If you were not supposed to be here," he said, grinning savagely, "you would not be here."

"There has been a mistake," I said simply.

"If that is the case, 232, then I hope we remedy it quickly so you can get back to where you are supposed to be."

I frowned. "232?"

"That is your prisoner number. You do not have a name while you are incarcerated here."

I didn't say anything. I didn't care what they called me.

"Let me rephrase my question," Jaws said. "Do you know why you have been arrested?"

"Because two immigration officers could not find my country on a map."

"Passport fraud, making false statements, and giving false information," he stated importantly. "Do you accept that you are guilty of these crimes?"

"No," I said.

Jaws leaned back in his chair. "You know, 232, Japan has much in common with many Western countries. But our criminal justice system is uniquely Japanese. So let me offer you a piece of advice. A confession of guilt is looked upon by the courts as a sign of remorse. Consequently, you can be assured a light sentencing." He shrugged the humps that were his shoulders. "If you insist on claiming innocence, and are found guilty, you will be treated much more harshly during the court proceedings and sentencing."

"I would like to speak to an attorney," I stated.

"No, I don't think that is necessary at the moment."

"*Bordel de merde!*" I swore. "Under international law, I have a right to receive legal representation."

"No, 232, you do not," Jaws hissed, his chicanery dropped. "Under the Japanese Code of Criminal Procedure, the police can detain you in this detention center for thirteen days. If you don't admit your guilt, the prosecutor can and will request your detention be extended for an additional ten days. During this time, you have no *right* to an attorney. You have no *right* to anything. You are nothing but a number. *Do you understand what I am saying, 232?*"

I ground my teeth. "You are saying you can hold me for nearly a month without charging me with any crime and without allowing me to speak to an attorney?"

"Yes, 232, that is exactly what I'm saying. Perhaps you are not as stupid as you look."

CHAPTER 14

After Jaws left, two prison guards escorted me to a large holding pen containing ten other male detainees, some of whom I recognized from the white coach. They eyed me warily, their faces ranging in expression from resignation to dismay. I was feeling a lot closer to dismay, but I tried to keep my expression neutral as I took a seat on a concrete bench.

Four Chinese sat together in one corner of the pen, speaking to each other in Mandarin. Three others were Vietnamese. There was also a small black man who resembled a mini Vin Diesel, a taller black man as scrawny as a malnourished mannequin, and an Arab with a long, scraggly beard. None of them looked like hardened criminals.

Mini Vinny saw me studying him and said in English, "Are you American, my friend?"

"I am from Taured," I replied.

"Taured? Where's that?"

"In Europe."

"I have never heard of your country."

"Join the club," I said dryly.

"What have you been sentenced for?"

"I have not been sentenced. I have done nothing wrong."

"You haven't been sentenced?" The small man frowned. "But you have seen the ba?"

"The barber?" I said, deciphering his African accent. "Yes. He told me I must cut my hair."

"No, that is wrong, my friend. Un-sentenced prisoners are not required to shave their heads."

I glanced around the holding pen at the other detainees and realized everyone still had their hair except for me and Mini Vinny, who appeared to be naturally bald.

"Did your clothing feature any foreign-language slogans?" the small man asked me.

"No. I was wearing a suit."

"Perhaps that is why they made you change. A suit in prison is not practical."

Realizing also that I was the only detainee wearing a green jumpsuit, I cursed.

"This is prison, my friend," Mini Vinny said. "You must learn your rights quickly and stand up for them when you can."

"I have been told I do not have any rights," I griped. "I was told I cannot even speak with an attorney."

"Unfortunately, that *is* the case. You are only allowed access to court-appointed counsel after you are indicted."

"*After!*" I bellowed.

"Over the next twenty-three days your interrogators will do or say anything to elicit a confession from you."

"Even if I am guilty of no crime?"

Mini Vinny nodded. "Innocence doesn't matter in this place. Only guilt, or confessed guilt, so that a sentence can be meted out and"—he smiled wryly—"justice can be served."

ΔΔΔ

At what felt like noon, guards brought us a basic lunch of rice (which tasted mostly of chewy barley), a morsel of fish, soup, and tea.

Mini Vin Diesel, sitting next to me, said, "Eat enough of this crap, and even Magdonnas will taste like a feast."

He was right. The food was tasteless, and the thought of a McDonald's hamburger made my mouth water. I hadn't eaten anything since the rice ball and soba noodles the night before.

"Does it get any better?" I asked.

Mini Vinny shrugged. "Once or twice a month bread is

served. That is a treat."

After wolfing down the pitiful meal, I urinated in the lidless, stainless-steel toilet bolted to one wall. Although I also needed to move my bowels, I decided to wait until I was taken to my cell, where I hoped to have more privacy.

I spent much of the long afternoon in the holding pen talking to Mini Vinny, whose name was Ugo Ndukwe. He was from Nigeria and had come to Japan seeking asylum. His application was promptly rejected, and for the last three years he had been incarcerated in the Tokyo Detention House for refusing to be repatriated to his country. Two weeks earlier, while on a hunger strike protesting his unjust and lengthy detention, he was granted provisional release. Then this morning, when he visited the Tokyo Regional Immigration Bureau to renew his release term, an official told him the duration of his provisional release could not be extended—and the next thing he knew he was being transferred back to the prison with no reason for the decision.

"I do not understand," I said, feeling sorry for the man. "Why did they let you out of here, only to arrest you again?"

Ugo Ndukwe smiled sadly. "To set an example that hunger strikes are useless. If you starve yourself, you'll simply be set free, allowed to return to proper health, and then locked up once more."

"How long can they keep you locked up for? You have already been here for three years!"

"Until I give up my 'immigration-mindedness,' as they put it, and 'go home.'"

"Japan must reform its immigration policies! They are archaic in this day and age."

"Good luck getting them to do that," Ugo Ndukwe said with a cynical chuckle. "This country isolated itself for three hundred years from outsiders. Foreigners will always be foreigners and generally unwelcomed. It is the way it is."

ΔΔΔ

Later that afternoon two guards escorted me to my designated cell. They led me up various flights of stairs, across a gloomy courtyard, and down a long wing of cells to the one reserved for me. One of the jailers handed me a booklet, told me to memorize it, then swung the heavy steel door shut.

The cell was three tatami mats in area, or about five square meters. It contained folded bedding on a Western-style bed, a bookshelf, a low table and stool, a washbasin, and a toilet. An opaque window looked out onto a bit of gray sky. All the corners on the furniture, I noted, were rounded, presumably to prevent self-harm. The sink featured a button to control the water, rather than a spigot, to which a ligature could be attached to hang oneself.

The observations made me wonder if anyone had committed suicide in this cell in the past.

Not wanting to dwell on this grim thought, I flipped through the booklet I'd been given and told to memorize. It was written in English and seemed to detail the rules of the prison and the expected behavior of the inmates.

With nothing else to do, I sat down on the toilet and began reading from page one.

CHAPTER 15

The daily regimen for prisoners didn't appear to be too bad, at least not on paper. According to the instruction booklet:

0645 - Wake up, stow bedding, wash face, toilet.
0700 - Roll call and prisoner inspection.
0730 - Breakfast and movement to work location.
0800 - Prison industry begins.
1000 - Fifteen-minute break.
1200 - Lunch.
1400 - Fifteen-minute break.
1640 - Prison industry stops. Prisoners return to rooms.
1700 - Roll call and prisoner inspection followed by reflection time.
1720 - Dinner.
1800 – Unstructured time.
2030 - Preparation for sleep.
2100 – Sleep.

While the regimen didn't seem as unjust as I'd feared, the rules were absolutely draconian, regulating prison life down to the most mundane and inane details. One rule, for example, dictated where and how I must place objects in my cell; another dictated where and on what I could write; another dictated how I must stand or sit; others, how I must sleep and how I must march and speak and so on and so forth. They seemed to never end—and were clearly intended to deprive prisoners of any semblance of personal choice and thus identity.

I slapped the booklet shut and stared at a tear-shaped stain on the wall, sick with dread at what may be in store for me.

ΔΔΔ

A little time later I heard the other inmates returning from their work duties. There was zero conversation, only the metallic *clackity-clack* of cell doors opening and closing. An announcement over the PA system explained that roll call was about to commence, followed by reflection time. I knew from the instruction booklet that I was required to assume a *seiza*-style position during the roll call. I knelt in the middle of the floor with my calves folded beneath my thighs, my butt resting on my heels, my head bowed. I held this yoga-like pose, facing the door, without moving for several long minutes.

From faraway an inmate shouted his prisoner number in Japanese. A second prisoner followed, then a third. They seemed to be starting at one end of the wing and working cell by cell to the other end: *461! 429! 111! 904!*

As my turn rapidly approached, I found my heart beating quickly and my palms sweating. My neighbor called out his number—*711!*—I waited an appropriate beat, then shouted: "*232!*"

A guard's face appeared in the vertical slit window installed in my door. He pounded it with his fist while spitting commands.

It took me a moment to realize he wanted me to lower my eyes.

I did so and heard the door to the cell open. I waited for the man to club me unconscious with a baton for not adhering to the rules. Instead he told me to stand. He patted down my front, back, and sides. He made me open my mouth and stick out my tongue and flick forward my ears to make sure I had nothing concealed there.

Then he ordered me back to the *seiza* position, exited the cell, and continued the head count.

When it was announced over the PA system that reflection time had begun, I wondered what I was supposed to be reflecting on. What were the other inmates reflecting on? How to rehabilitate themselves while in prison? How to reintegrate successfully into society upon their eventual release? How to view their incarcerations objectively? How to set aside their feelings of resentment and hostility? How to stop acting impulsively and illegally to the detriment of themselves and others? Hell, for all I knew some of them were deciphering the meaning of life. All I ended up thinking about was how much my knees and lower back ached.

After twenty minutes of this torture, another announcement instructed all inmates to prepare for dinner.

I sighed and stood, shaking the aches out of my knees. I had no idea what preparations were expected of me—I didn't even have dishes or cutlery to set my small table—so I once again waited in fearful anticipation until a guard peeked through the window into my cell. He seemed to eye me up and down before sliding a tray of food through a slot in the door. I took it to the table and sat on the stool. Rice again, a bowl of noodle soup, and a sliver of beef. I scooped everything back with the pair of chopsticks that came with the meal, dismayed by how quickly and easily I had devolved from fine-food connoisseur to trash rat. I sipped the cup of green tea slowly to make it last as long as possible.

When the guard returned to collect my tray, he shouted through the door. His voice wasn't very clear, and I only caught the word *haburashi*—toothbrush. Figuring he wanted me to brush my teeth, I gathered the toothbrush that had also come with my meal, squeezed some toothpaste onto the bristles, and began to brush my teeth. The guard went ape shit, jabbering at the top of his lungs and smashing the door with his open hand. After a good three seconds of what you might describe as high-voltage panic, I finally understood he wanted to *collect* the toothbrush, most likely so I didn't carve it into a shiv or some other tool overnight. I placed it on my tray next to my chopsticks and slid the tray back through the slot in the door. Glowering, he took it and disappeared from my field of view. I spat the toothpaste from my mouth into the sink and rinsed with water from the tap.

I sank onto the bed, wondering how prisoners who didn't understand any Japanese survived this nightmare.

ΔΔΔ

A few minutes later the door to my cell unlocked remotely. I pushed it open and poked my head into the brightly lit hallway. A few other inmates were stepping from their cells nonchalantly, which confirmed this wasn't some malfunction but our so-called "unstructured time," and we were allowed to wander.

I stepped into the hallway and followed the other inmates. Through the narrow windows in the doors I passed, I could see that all the cells were identical to mine. In several, the occupants had decided to remain put to read or write in private.

I descended the first set of stairs I came to. At the bottom I went left. The cells lining this corridor were much larger than mine, between thirteen to sixteen square meters, designed and furnished to hold several inmates together. They didn't feature Western beds but rather Japanese futons, all of which were currently rolled up. Behind each of these was a large black case, presumably used to store personal belongings. I suspected I hadn't yet received such a case because I didn't have anything except the clothes on my back—and even those weren't mine.

At the end of the wing I arrived at a largish common area. Two dozen or so inmates were seated at tables. Some were watching TV together, others playing Japanese chess or keeping to themselves. I spotted Ugo Ndukwe in a far corner, reading a book. I sat down in the seat next to him.

"What are you reading?" I asked him.

"*Shhh*," he said, his eyes flicking between the uniformed

guards standing watch strategically around the room. "Lower your voice, my friend." He closed his book to show me the cover. It was Stephen King's *Needful Things*. "You are only allowed three books in your cell at any one time," he told me quietly. "I take the fattest ones from the library I can find so they last me until I am allowed to exchange them."

I said equally quietly, "The only book I have is that stupid rule book. Have you read it?"

"Of course I have. I have been detained here for the last three years. I know the rules like the back of my hand."

"They are extreme, no?"

Mini Vin Diesel shrugged. "You are in Japan, my friend. Discipline is instilled in Japanese from a very young age. It is fundamental to their sense of integrity and order and group-thinking. The discipline you find in here is an extension of that mindset."

"Those rules go far beyond discipline. No talking, no looking around, no sitting against the wall in your cell…"

"The purpose of this detention center—and all Japanese prisons—is not merely to punish its prisoners. It is to rehabilitate them, to make them better people, so they will not commit another crime. The rules are very harsh, yes, but they are not cruel. Once you accept them, you will appreciate them, because you will feel safe. In my time here, no other prisoner has once touched me. Yes, the guards yell at you if you break a rule, and in the case of a serious violation, they will give you *shobash*. But they do not carry guns. You don't have to fear being killed here."

"That is a comfort," I said sardonically.

An old man several tables away was watching me with a smile on his face.

I stared at him until he closed his eyes, though the smile remained in place.

"Who is that?" I asked, nodding in the old man's direction.

Ugo Ndukwe looked. "His name is Toshio Takata. As a child, he was pulled out of the rubble of his home when the atomic bomb was dropped on Hiroshima."

"What is he doing in prison?"

"He stole a sandwich, went to the nearest police station, showed the cop the sandwich, and told him he stole it."

"Why would he ever do that?"

"He wanted to get arrested. He was broke and could no longer afford his rent or bills. In prison he knew he would receive a bed to sleep in and three square meals a day."

"A mere *sandwich* got him thrown in here?"

"Japanese courts treat petty theft seriously. That sandwich, however, only delivered him a one-year sentence. So after he was released he took a knife from his kitchen, went to a park, and threatened a woman."

"*Mon Dieu!*" I said, studying the old man, whose eyes remained closed. He was small and slender, his skin dark and leathery. He looked like a frail Buddhist monk—not like a knife-wielding criminal. I mentioned this.

"Oh, he didn't hurt the woman," Mini Vinny assured me. "He simply waved the knife at her, hoping she would call the police. She did. And now he's a repeat offender."

"Are there others like him in here?"

"Many. Japan might be a remarkably law-abiding society, but the basic state pension is very hard to live on, forcing a lot of the elderly to turn to crime to get a free ride in prison."

"What about their children? It is tradition in Japan for them to look after their aging parents."

"It used to be. But many young people in the provinces have moved to the cities, leaving their parents to fend for themselves. And in the larger cities like Osaka and Tokyo, rent is so expensive, and the living spaces are so small, there is no room to accommodate one's mother or father."

I shook my head, still looking at the smiling old man.

"If you ask me though," Mini Vinny said in a conspiratorial way, "I don't think our friend Toshio is in here due to financial hardships, like he claims. I think he's lonely. His parents are dead, his wife is dead, his only child died in an accident, and he has lost contact with his two younger brothers." He shrugged.

"In prison not only does he receive room and board. He also has company."

Ugo Ndukwe and I conversed until a bell rang, signaling the end of unstructured time, and all the prisoners returned to their cells. Inside mine, I changed out of the jumpsuit and hung it neatly on the provided hanger. Wearing only my undergarments, as I'd been given no pajamas, I consulted the rule booklet.

A section titled HOW TO SLEEP read: "During sleeping hours follow these rules: (1) Sleep in your designated place. (2) After lights are out, leave clothing, books, and other recreation material in its designated place. Do not read, talk, or stand up and walk around the room. (3) Do not cover your face with the blanket or futon while sleeping. (4) Do not, on your own accord, use the blanket as a sheet or wrap the blanket or sheet around your waist." The rest of the rules pretty much prohibited any activity other than sleeping so as not to disturb others. The final one was the most ridiculous of all: "You must sleep quietly."

Thank God I wasn't a snorer.

CHAPTER 16

At what I presumed to be nine o'clock in the evening, the light in my cell was dimmed but not turned off, most likely so the guards could make sure I wasn't breaking any of the inane sleep rules.

As quickly as a man on an anesthesia drip, I was out. I wasn't sure how long I slept for, but at some point during the night I woke to find a guard shaking my shoulders.

"What...?" I said, sitting up and wondering through a film of fatigue if perhaps I'd been snoring after all.

"Come," he said.

"Where?" I asked.

"Come!" He yanked me to my feet.

I dressed in my jumpsuit and went ahead of him out of my cell, where a second guard waited. They took me to a room on the prison's first floor not unlike the one in which I had my medical exam.

Inside it Jaws awaited me.

"Sit," the beefy man commanded.

I sat. "What is happening—"

"Shut up, 232!"

I clamped my jaw closed.

"Do you know where you are?" he asked.

"The Tokyo Detention House," I said.

"Do you know why you are here?"

"I—" I was about to tell him once more that a mistake had been made, but he didn't appear to be in the mood for such an answer. "I have been arrested for passport fraud."

"And?"

I tried to remember the other charges he had told me. "Providing false statements and false information?"

"Are you asking me?"

"I am telling you what you told me."

"Are you guilty of these crimes?"

"No," I said simply.

Jaws scowled. "Unfortunately for you then, 232, this is going to be a very long night."

ΔΔΔ

Over the next few hours Jaws, another investigator and a prosecutor took turns interrogating me. They used various degrees of coercion, extortion, leading questions, and brute force (Jaws shook me by the collar of my jumpsuit while screaming in my face on three occasions). None of these tactics were meant to get to the bottom of my passport situation (as Supa-san and Wakako Shimizu had at least endeavored to do), but to elicit an apocryphal confession that I was guilty of my alleged crimes.

I remained resolute in my assertion of innocence, and when I was finally taken back to my cell, the courtyard was bathed in rosy morning light.

Despite being bone-weary, I knew I could not return to sleep. Roll call would be commencing shortly.

ΔΔΔ

When it was my turn to call out my prisoner number I shouted, "232!" I did not raise my eyes this time, but I could sense the guard standing on the other side of my door as surely as a prey animal could catch the scent of a predator upwind.

Then the door opened and the guard came over to me. But instead of ordering me to stand so he could search me, he said, "I know you are guilty. Everybody knows."

I said nothing, though it chilled me to know Jaws was instructing rank-and-file guards to do his dirty work for him. How far was the asshole going to go to elicit a forced confession?

The guard seized the sleeve of my jumpsuit and tugged upward. "Sit straight!"

I grunted but straightened my back as much as I could.

He pushed me down, so my rear pressed into my heels. "Sit straight!"

"I am!" I said.

"Don't talk!" He yanked me sideways. "Sit straight!"

I tried to regain my balance, but as I did so he pushed me the other way, and I fell to my side.

"*Seiza* position!"

"You pushed me!"

"Don't talk!"

He kicked me in the side.

And I knew I was about to snap.

I'd been the recipient of unlawful intimidation and abuse all night, and I was exhausted, furious, and fed up.

The guard kicked me again

"*Stupid bastard!*" I exploded, reverting to French in my fury. "*I shit down your neck, you shit sausage son of a mole!*"

Releasing the string of insults felt good.

The repercussions were not.

ΔΔΔ

I remained locked in my cell for the next hour or so, missing breakfast, before five guards with sanguinary bedside manners escorted me to a different cell in an older wing of the facility. It was damp, moldy, infested with cobwebs, and reeked of urine. It was also gloomy due to a semi-solid plastic panel covering the exterior of the window, filtering the natural light into depressing hues. The tatami mats were rotting in places. All the furnishings had been removed save for a filthy mattress. The guards forced me onto the mattress and told me to sit in the *seiza* position once again.

Deciding I'd rebelled enough for one day, I obliged.

I remained on my knees, my hands on my lap, facing the door, all morning. I was allowed a brief reprieve to eat lunch—about half the allotment of rice and soup I'd received the day before—and then I was back in my favorite pose, Zen-like on the outside, agonizing on the inside.

In truth, I don't know how I managed getting through those twelve hours or so, especially without using the toilet once, but somehow I did (the bugs crawling around on the walls and floor at least provided me some company). When it was announced over the PA system that it was time to prepare for bed, I could barely contain my anticipation.

The current guard outside my door—they had been rotating shifts throughout the day—entered the cell. He read from a piece of paper: "Your rewards have been suspended for three weeks. Your privilege of reading and writing has been suspended for three weeks. Your work duty will be confined to your cell for ten days. You will receive a reduction in food for seven days. If you act against the rules of the prison again, you will be remanded to solitary confinement for two months or less. You are permitted to sleep now."

He left.

ΔΔΔ

I loathed to lie down on the disgusting mattress without a clean sheet separating it from me, but I didn't have one (or a pillow or cover, for that matter). I laid down squeamishly on my back, looking up at the ceiling. I thought I'd be asleep as soon as I closed my eyes. That wasn't the case. In fact, I couldn't sleep at all, even after the lights in the cell were dimmed. I found it hard to believe I'd only arrived in this hellhole yesterday morning. It felt like an eternity already. I couldn't fathom how Ugo Ndukwe had coped with being locked up here for three years. And that crazy bastard Toshio for *wanting* to be locked up here. There had to be a better alternative to poverty or loneliness than *this*.

I needed to reclaim my freedom. ASAP. Spending my coming days isolated in a cell would not only be soul crushing but a colossal waste of my time. I was a busy man. I had a life outside of these concrete walls. I had to smooth over the details for the whisky tasting dinner on Thursday in Ginza. I had to confirm the guest list and fill the spots of those who couldn't make it. I had to collect the cartons of whisky from the distributor. All of this and more should have been started yesterday. What were my contacts going to think when I didn't get in touch with any of them? What would happen to the event? What would happen to *my job*? My boss wasn't going to be happy when he received news that Gaston Green had gone AWOL. Surely he'd understand and forgive when I could explain what happened to me. Yet still…I took great pride in my work, in my professionalism, and this incarceration was unnecessarily pillorying my reputation.

Even as I allowed these thoughts to gain strength and direction, I also couldn't help think I was worrying about my hat blowing off while standing in the path of a tornado. I had not forgotten the reason I was in prison in the first place. My passport was invalid, allegedly because the country to which it belonged did not exist. And after spending a large chunk of my sequestered day pondering this seemingly impossible conundrum, I had been able to draw only one conclusion that didn't involve mental illness.

What had begun as a whimsical and outrageous thought had slowly fattened into a hungry worm, working its way ever deeper into the apple of my mind, solidifying there, for the more I suspended my prejudices and disbeliefs, the thought actually seemed almost *reasonable*, providing a unified explanation for all the turbid questions surrounding Flight JL077, why my name was absent from the passenger manifest, why the record of the ticket I'd purchased was not on the airline's computers, why my check-in suitcase could not be accounted for, why I could not find Taured on a map, why I was unable to place a telephone call to my mother, and why both a petite woman and an obese man had each occupied the seat next to mine at different times during the flight.

And that whimsical and outrageous thought was this: At some point during Flight JL077, I had slipped between the cracks of the cosmos into a dimension that was not my own yet parallel to it in almost every way—with the glaring exception that my motherland, Taured, did not exist.

ΔΔΔ

At some point that night I was woken by two prison guards and once again whisked off through the prison to the interrogation room on the first floor.

"Hello, 232," Jaws said when I entered, smiling broadly to show off his cavern of stalactites. "Do you know where you are...?"

CHAPTER 17

I'd only closed my eyes for perhaps a half hour when the 6:45 a.m. wake-up bell rang. I groggily forced myself to my feet. I stowed my mattress and used the toilet. Then I assumed the dreaded seiza position. While waiting for the roll call to commence, I gently probed my face with my fingertips. My bottom lip was split and my left cheek swollen and sore, both injuries courtesy of Jaws, who'd slapped me during the late-night/early-morning interrogation.

"Do not lie! The more you lie, the heavier the punishment. Tell the truth! Do penance for your crimes!"

"I have done nothing!"

"Admit your guilt, 232, and this will be over!"

"Have you ever heard of innocent until proven guilty?"

"You are guilty! You will go to hell so long as you continue to lie!"

"No, monsieur, *you will go to hell for being a corrupt oyster dick —"*

Slap!

In the distance I heard inmates shouting their prisoner numbers. Since I was now in a cell isolated from the others, I waited until a guard banged on my door before reciting my number. He didn't enter to search me, presumably because I had not yet been allowed to leave the cell.

I gobbled down my breakfast (served again alongside a toothbrush and a small tube of toothpaste), brushed my teeth (doing my best not to aggravate my split lip), and waited anxiously to discover what my work duty would be.

About thirty minutes later a guard carrying a large basket

entered my cell.

"Sit," he told me.

I sat on the mattress.

He set the basket in front of me, crouched, and withdrew a pair of disposable bamboo chopsticks and a paper sleeve. He slid the chopsticks into the sleeve and set the completed product on the ground.

I peeked into the basket and saw a whole lot of chopsticks and several stacks of paper wrappers.

Let the fun begin.

ΔΔΔ

At first I counted each pair of chopsticks I slid into their paper home, but by the time I was in the hundreds I could no longer keep the numbers straight.

While my hands worked on autopilot, I thought of my son Damien, missing him more than I'd ever believed possible. I thought of Blessica, the pleasant memories of her. I thought of my mother and brothers, the enjoyable occasions we'd spent together over the years. I thought of friends I had not kept in touch with, and those I had. I thought of vacations I had been on, parties I had attended, books I had read, anything to serve as a diversion to the mind-numbing boredom—and the dark specter of the very big elephant in the very tiny cell.

I was not a scientist; I was a pragmatist. Consequently, the possibility that parallel universes and alternate realities existed did not fill me with awe; it frightened me viscerally. Because whenever my mind inevitably fixated on this quandary, I couldn't help but wonder what happened to my family and friends living in Taured. If the country didn't exist in this dimension, did that mean they didn't exist here also? Or were they well and fine, living life as usual, only in a country called Andorra?

And what of me?

Did two of me exist simultaneously in this dimension? Or

had we swapped spots? Was there a doppelganger back in my universe, locked up in prison just as I was locked up here? Or had he evaded such an inimical fate? Was he instead settling into my life? Living in my house? Assuming my job? Tucking Damien in at night—?

Crack.

I looked at my hands. I'd snapped the pair of chopsticks I'd been holding in half. I cast an apprehensive glance at the door, saw no guard at the window, and tucked the broken sticks into the bottom of the basket.

I resumed working.

Sometime later.

I had no idea how much time had passed, but judging by the mountain of paper-cased chopsticks I'd amassed I guessed a lot.

For the past while I'd been having trouble keeping my eyelids open. They were slipping shut with more and more regularity. And then they simply didn't open again, and I sank like a rock into the murky waters of sleep...

ΔΔΔ

...something was tapping my head. I snapped open my eyes with a start. A string of drool dangled from my mouth. I wiped it away with the back of my hand.

"I am awake," I grunted, squinting up at the guard hovering over me. It was the one with the decent English who'd read me my punishments the day before.

"No sleeping," he said, still tapping my head with his foot.

"Fine," I said, flinching from his touch.

"No slouching."

I sat straighter.

"No stopping. Keep working."

I slipped a pair of chopsticks into a paper sleeve.

And then another.

And another.

And another...

ΔΔΔ

After I ate lunch, Foot Fetish and another guard took me from the cell. I was convinced they were taking me for an afternoon visit with Jaws. I was immeasurably relieved when I ended up not in an interrogation room but a concrete exercise yard enclosed in tall walls and wire-netting.

A few dozen prisoners—half wearing street clothes, the other half in green jumpsuits—were shuffling around, zombie-like, nobody speaking.

I joined them.

Before I'd completed a circuit around the yard, a guard with a bullhorn barked feedback-distorted orders I couldn't understand.

The inmates quickly organized themselves into three platoons. I slipped into the one closest to me, standing at attention like everybody else.

We began to march, military-style, in concert with the guard's repetitive shouting. When the front three columns of men reached the wall, the platoons spun around and marched to the opposite wall.

And so it went. Back and forth, back and forth. Everybody goose-stepping and swinging their arms to the height of their shoulders and chanting five mantras which I translated roughly as:

Always be honest.

Sincerely report.

Always be polite.

Keep a helpful attitude.

Be thankful.

I added my voice to the brainwashed folderol so I didn't stand out—though given the treatment I had received thus far in the Tokyo Detention House, the hypocrisy of the mantras were not lost on me.

ΔΔΔ

Ugo Ndukwe was sitting in the same spot in the communal room he'd been in the day before, his bald head shining like a lamp under the fluorescents. I slumped down next to him with a weary sigh.

"You look very tired, my friend," he said, a note of concern in his voice as he set his novel aside.

"Really?" I said cynically, leaning my head back and closing my eyes. "I feel wonderful."

"Hey!" he said, gripping my forearm. "What are you doing?"

I opened my eyes. "Huh? What?"

"You cannot sleep here. It is against the rules."

"I was not sleeping," I said. "I was merely resting my eyes."

"That is not allowed either. You will be punished."

"*Fuck* the rules." I glared at the guards. "*Fuck* them too."

Mini Vin Diesel stiffened, and I had the impression that he was contemplating moving away from me.

"I apologize, *monsieur*," I said, rubbing my forehead. "It has been a long day."

Mini Vinny hesitated, then nodded understandingly.

"I stink," I remarked, sniffing an armpit. "Are we not allowed to bathe here?"

"Three times a week—though don't expect a Turkish spa. The length of the shower is nine minutes in the summer, and twelve minutes in the winter. This includes undressing, drying off, and dressing again. The guards use an hourglass to measure this time exactly."

I wanted to laugh at the absurdity of the image of a guard watching inmates shower while holding an hourglass in his hand. But I had no laughter inside me right then.

"Here," Ugo Ndukwe said good-naturedly, producing a packaged cookie from his pocket.

"I cannot accept that," I said, though my stomach insisted otherwise.

"I have more, my friend. You can use something to lift your spirits."

I accepted the snack and tore open the package. My first instinct was to stuff the entirety of it in my mouth at once, but I knew that would be a waste. This was a delicacy. I needed to savor the flavor and texture of it for as long as I could.

I broke off a small corner of the cookie and placed it delicately on my tongue. The taste of melting chocolate was divine.

"Aaahh…" I moaned, smiling in borderline ecstasy. "Where did you get this?"

"There is a small store that sells food here."

"*Sells* food?" I swallowed what remained of the cookie and popped another morsel into my mouth. "Do we get paid for our work duty?"

Mini Vinny nodded. "We don't get wages, per se. Instead, we receive a gratuity each month of three thousand yen."

About a dollar a day, I thought, my stomach souring with guilt. "Thank you," I said, handing him back the uneaten half of the cookie. "It was delicious."

"No, my friend, finish it."

"Your generosity is too much, *monsieur*. It was delicious, but you purchased it with money well-earned. You should enjoy it. Please."

Mini Vinny hesitated, then plucked the half-eaten cookie from my palm. He rewrapped it quickly and deposited it back in his pocket.

I asked, "What is your assigned work duty?"

"I assemble parts in the factory for the automotive industry."

"Factory? I've been stuck alone in my cell wrapping chopsticks all day!"

"Do not get the wrong impression. The factory is hardly a social venue. You cannot speak, and you are not allowed to look at anything other than what you are working on. Even the slightest eye contact with a fellow prisoner is prohibited."

Impulsively I blurted: "I cannot remain here!"

"Unfortunately, the only way to leave, my friend, is to admit your guilt, whether it is real or manufactured."

"Which would only get me convicted and sent back here."

"No, not here. This is merely an immigration detention facility. You will be sent to a real prison."

"Even better."

"At least you will have a *sentence* there. You will not be held indefinitely. You will have a future to look forward to."

For the briefest of moments I contemplated giving up my fight and telling Jaws everything he wanted to hear. But the thought came and went in the flap of a fly's wings. Because who knew what my sentence for passport fraud would be? Two years, three, five? Toshio received a year for stealing a sandwich.

What other choice do you have? a voice asked me from a dark corner of my mind. *If your idea is true, and you're at the center of some cosmic shell game, then you're a vagabond with no legitimate identification and no country to call home. So what choice do you—*

"Has anybody ever...?" I asked, leaving the unfinished question hanging. "You know..."

Ugo Ndukwe's already stern face drew tighter, and it took me a moment to realize the clenched expression was one of fear. "That is not something you want to contemplate, my friend."

"Has anybody...?" I pressed.

He held my eyes for a long moment. "I do not know," he said. "What I *do* know is that if you are caught, you will be sent to solitary confinement, where you will be handcuffed, gagged, and left in the dark without a bed or mattress for weeks or perhaps even months on end."

The barbaric description of solitary confinement rose a prickle of alarm inside me. Yet rather than deter my nascent thoughts of escape, it only galvanized my will.

I would not stay in this hellhole any longer.

I could not.

"Humor me, *monsieur*," I urged. "If someone were to try…?"

"It is impossible," he stated flatly. Seeing I was about to interject, he held up a hand and added, "From the prison itself." He shrugged. "But from the hospital? That would be a different matter."

"Go on," I said intently.

"There is a hospital in the prison that provides basic care," he explained, "mostly for the growing number of older inmates. For acute or specialized care, however, inmates are taken to a general public hospital—Horikiri Chuo Hospital—a few blocks from here. That was where I was taken when I was…mistreated."

"What happened?"

"I killed a cockroach."

"What!"

"*Hush!*"

We looked at the guards standing at their stations, but they seemed to be staring off into their own thoughts—and it struck me that they were almost certainly as bored as the prisoners they lorded over.

"It was nighttime," Ugo Ndukwe told me quietly. "I woke up to find the cockroach burrowing into my ear. You can imagine my horror. I pulled it free, threw it to the ground, and smacked it over and over with the sole of my slipper. Hearing the noise, a guard burst into my cell. I tried to explain, but he wouldn't listen. Then he called me a name."

"A name?" I said, not understanding.

"If you have not already observed, the guards here do not accept foreigners as their equals. It is why they treat us as poorly as they do. You, as a European, are viewed more favorably than someone from a country such as mine, someone who has skin the color of mine…but make no mistake, you are still an uncivilized foreigner to them."

"What name did they call you?"

"What does it matter? It was insulting enough that I struck the bastard in the face."

"And the guard beat you?"

"Very badly. When I came around, I was in a private room in Horikiri Chuo Hospital. A police officer was posted outside the room around the clock, and he accompanied me wherever I went for tests. But." He tapped his knobby index finger gently on the table. "He was the only police officer I saw. I was there for two days. *And he was the only police officer*. I remember thinking at the time that had I been able to get past him—I don't know how I would have accomplished this, but I remember at least thinking that had I been able to—I might have been able to stroll right out through the hospital's front door like any other outpatient."

As I contemplated this, a wicked bubble of excitement—I might even go so far as to call it something bordering on hope —inflated inside me. At the same time, however, I couldn't help but be skeptical. Escaping from prison shouldn't, *couldn't*, be so easy as slipping past one guard.

I mentioned this.

"You are forgetting what kind of prisoner I am, my friend," Mini Vinny said. "A rapist? A murderer? No, I am nothing more than a common asylum seeker. And this is not a maximum-security prison. It is a detention facility. The majority of prisoners being held here are no more threatening than I am. People seeking a better life. People who have overstayed their visa. Lonely old men who have no other place to go."

"Only one policeman..." I mused.

"Only one policeman," he agreed.

"But to get to the hospital..."

"To get to the hospital, my friend," Ugo Ndukwe said gravely, "you are going to have to get royally fucked up."

CHAPTER 18

The middle-of-the night interrogation devolved into a physical beat-down.

Part of the reason for the violence was Jaws' growing frustration that his intimidation tactics weren't working, and that I wasn't going to break any time soon. But the greater factor in the equation, I believed, was my blatant insubordination. I'd adopted a brazen air of insouciance and stubbornness, which clearly got beneath Jaws' thin skin—so much so he'd resorted to throwing me against the wall several times, pounding me in the gut, and kicking me while I lay helplessly on the ground.

As I was led bruised and bleeding back to my cell in the early hours of the morning, one thing became abundantly clear: I was going to have to attempt something much more daring and rebellious than acting like a recalcitrant ass if I wanted to get sent to the hospital that Ugo Ndukwe had told me about.

CHAPTER 19

The next day in the exercise yard I paced in anticipation and fear. This was the moment I had been planning for all morning.

When Big Daddy Drill Sergeant arrived, a pair of Ray-Bans perched on the bridge of his nose, the prisoners formed three platoons and, in step with his guttural commands, commenced marching.

I didn't chant the hypocritical mantras, and I only gave the goose-stepping and arm-swinging a half-assed effort.

Big Daddy noticed right away and stomped over to me, shouting into his bullhorn, "*Ichi-ni! Ichi-ni!*" One-two, one-two.

"Yeah, yeah," I said, without improving my form.

The drill sergeant yanked me free of the platoon with such force I stumbled to my hands and knees.

Bending over, he pressed the bullhorn right up against my face and began spitting all sorts of incomprehensible insults.

I clocked him.

Big Daddy staggered away from me, stunned and shocked. His Ray-Ban's had flown off his face and now lay a few feet from him on the ground. I leapt at the asshole, throwing a haymaker that grazed his left cheek. I seized the back hem of his jacket and yanked it up and over his head, "jerseying" him as players do in ice hockey fights. I landed two solid uppercuts to his gut before the other guards arrived. They came at me from all sides, punching and kicking like a bunch of pansies.

One of them got me from behind.

His right arm slipped around my neck, while his left arm pressed with suffocating force against the back of my skull. Suddenly I couldn't breathe. My vision turned white and spangly. I shuffled backward in the hopes of knocking the guard over and breaking the chokehold.

He remained on his feet and applied even more pressure. I clawed at his forearm pinching my throat. I couldn't pry it free. Everything began to go dark and the strength and fight left my arms and legs.

Sputtering, I sank to my butt, realizing with black doom that the guard was strangling me to death. My last coherent thought before my consciousness faded to nothingness was that this had not been one of my better plans.

CHAPTER 20

Smiley and I lay next to each other in the snow burrow we had dug, our breathing slow and frigid, our bodies stiff and unmoving. Earlier, while we'd been hiking through the evergreen forest, our blood had been pumping, keeping us relatively warm. Now our body temperatures had plummeted. My face felt encased in a mask of ice and my chest oddly hollowed. Both my gloved and ungloved hands, as well as my booted feet, itched and ached.

Thanks to countless weekends binge-watching YouTube documentaries, I'd learned a little bit about how humans have adapted to live in frozen environments. Inuit hunters in northern Canada can hunt in the dead of winter without gloves due to the web of surface capillaries in their hands opening every so often to release a fresh infusion of warm blood into their fingers. Aboriginal Australians, during near-freezing desert nights, can enter a light hypothermic state while they sleep to suppress their bodies from shivering until the sun rewarms them in the morning. And perhaps most impressive of all, Tibetan monks have been known to raise the temperature in their extremities through meditation alone.

Unfortunately for me, I was neither an Inuit hunter, an Aboriginal Australian, or a Tibetan monk. I was a bony kid who got the sniffles at the first whiff of winter and whose cheeks turned a rosy red after only a few minutes in sub-zero weather.

Now, as my body began to tremble violently and uncontrollably, which I knew to mean the onset of mild hypothermia, I decided it had been a mistake to hole up in the snow. I pushed up my frosted jacket sleeve and checked the glowing numbers of my wristwatch: 10:51 p.m.

"We need to g-go," I said through chattering teeth.

"Where?" Smiley replied, her voice sounding cold and brittle in the dark. "Nowhere to go."

"Bottom."

"Bottom?"

"Of the mountain. Roads there."

"Too far."

"Can ski..."

"Ski? Only one s-set."

"Go slow. I s-s-stand on b-back."

Smiley was quiet. After a long moment, she agreed. I rolled away from her, my Gore-Tex jacket crackling like wrapping paper, and crawled stiffly out of the burrow.

Above me, a glowing skein of stars filled the black expanse of sky. The gibbous moon hung low over the alpine forest, casting silver beams of light through the boughs of the white-mantled firs and pines. It might have been a beautiful night scene had it not been for the invisible and deadly cold.

I helped Smiley to her feet, then plucked her lime-green Rossignol skis from the snow, which she'd planted vertically like twin flagpoles. I set them in parallel lines in front of her. She toed her boots into the bindings and clamped down her heels, locking them in place. I stepped on the skis behind her and gripped her waist.

"Ready?" she asked hesitantly.

"Go slow."

She pushed off with her poles. When we gathered a little speed, she turned the tips of her skis together in a weak-kneed snowplow while keeping her arms scarecrow wide for balance. Although our switchback descent down the mountain wasn't very fast, it beat walking. Even so, the muscles in my legs had long ago cooled and contracted and cramped up, and after only a few minutes my thighs and calves were burning with the strain of remaining in a fixed position.

I tried not to think about this by turning my thoughts to Dom and Laurence, the surprise and relief that would animate their faces when Smiley and I burst through the front door of the little wood cabin. How we would all laugh as Smiley and I recollected our misfortune. Sitting before a roaring fire. Bathing in heat. Cupping a mug of piping hot coffee between my hands. In fact, I could almost smell the smoke of the fire and the dense aroma of the coffee...

Smiley and I crested a small knoll, the other side of which proved to be deceptively steep.

We picked up speed.

"Slow down!" I said.

"Trying!" Smiley said.

We continued to accelerate. The skis beneath my boots vibrated dangerously. I knew I was going to wipe out.

Over Smiley's shoulder, I glimpsed a snow-covered log.

"Stop!" I said.

"Can't!" she said, jabbing her poles into the snow in a last-ditch effort to brake.

I could have leapt from the skis, but that would be like jumping ship with the captain still aboard. I gripped Smiley's waist more tightly.

The tips of the skis struck the log. We both flew headfirst through the air. I landed hard on my shoulder and tumbled down the hill. I came to a rest on my back, dazed and frightened. The middle-of-the-night forest was eerily silent. All I could hear was my ragged breathing and the pounding of blood in my ears.

"Smiley?" I called up the slope. Scratchy snow had rushed down the throat of my jacket. The meltwater trickled down my sternum and spine in icy rivulets. "Smiley?" I repeated, feeling a flicker of disquiet at the lack of a reply.

Standing, I spotted her a dozen feet uphill from me, her powder-blue snowsuit blending like camouflage into the shadow-dappled snow.

I took a step—and cried out in pain as I sank to my knees. My right ankle felt as though it had been replaced with a bagful of crushed glass.

Keeping my weight off it, I limped through the snow until I slumped beside Smiley. She was lying facedown.

"Hey?" I said, my concern metastasizing into full-mounted panic. I tapped her on the shoulder. "Hey?"

She didn't reply or move.

I rolled her over. The snow was red where her face had been. A three-inch gash ran across her forehead, just below her hairline. Her eyes were closed, her rime-flecked lips parted. I pressed my cheek to her mouth—and almost wept with relief when I detected small, shallow puffs of warm, moist air.

I looked left, right, then down the slope—as though the answers to our exigency would be waiting for me if only I could spot them.

I found no answers. Only the still forest, which almost seemed like a sinister, sentient being watching me to see what I would do next.

We could no longer ski to the bottom of the mountain. Smiley was unconscious. I had strained or broken my ankle. We could not go anywhere.

Which meant I only had one option.

Dig another burrow.

Using my hands—my ungloved one so numb it was immune to the bite of the cold snow—I dug frantically into a drift. Sweat dripped from beneath my wool hat down my forehead, stinging my eyes. My shoulders and arms blazed from the exertion. I kept digging until I had created a trench about six feet in length and three feet deep. Keeping weight off my bad ankle the best I could, I hooked my hands beneath Smiley's armpits and dragged her into the trench. I folded her arms across her chest, laid down next to her, and pulled her tight against my body to keep her as warm as possible.

Lying there in the inhospitable black night, I had never before felt so alone or afraid. According to my watch, it was nearly midnight. Dawn was another five or six hours away. Would we survive that long? And if we did, would it bring salvation? Dom and Laurence would have alerted the ski patrol that we were missing. They would organize a search-and-rescue operation at first light. Yet they would be tasked with finding a needle in a haystack. It could take them hours to discover us, perhaps even days.

And by then it would be too late.

Despite my weariness and sluggish thinking, the epochal stupidity of the situation was not lost on me. I'd heard numerous stories of people getting lost in the wilderness and perishing from dehydration, injury, or the elements. I'd always wondered how they'd gotten themselves into such perilous positions in the first place. Now I knew from firsthand experience. It began with a single bad decision—such as deciding to ski off-piste in unknown terrain—and it escalated due to a combination of mistakes and more bad decisions.

Suddenly and with great conviction, a stray thought informed me that I was going to die this night. This embarrassed me as much as it terrified me. After all the daring activities I had embarked on in my life (such as climbing to the summit of Mount Blanc in France and white-water rafting in Austria), and after all the dangerous situations I'd escaped (such as being accosted by a maniac with a knife in a German hostel and getting the bends while scuba-diving in the Mediterranean Sea), it seemed both comical and anticlimactic that I would meet my demise on what was supposed to be a relaxing ski trip with friends in the Pyrenees Mountains.

I hugged Smiley a little tighter, hating myself for getting her into this mess. It had been my recklessness that had caused us to collide while skiing downhill, knocking us both off our skis. It had been my decision to allow her to stick with me instead of doing the smart thing and going for help. It had been my insistence to dig the first burrow, and later, to ski tandem down the mountain in the dark. Everything had been my fault.

"I am sorry," I mumbled through lips that I could barely move. I squeezed my eyes tight, although tears still managed to leak free...freezing instantaneously on my cheeks.

ΔΔΔ

When I felt myself losing any real urgency or desire to live, I summoned all my willpower to climb out of the trench.

ΔΔΔ

I crawled through the snow for what felt like hours, though I couldn't be sure as the numbers on my wristwatch no longer made sense. I couldn't feel my hands or feet, as whatever blood had once warmed them had retreated to my core to protect my vital organs.

At some point I spotted a light in the distance. A cabin? *Our* cabin? Yes, I heard the familiar jingle of the bell that hung above the front door. Someone had come outside. Did they see me? Did they know I was here? I wanted to shout Dom's name, but I couldn't find my voice. In fact, I could no longer move at all...

ΔΔΔ

I was curled in front of a woodstove, fighting a powerful urge to urinate. Had I crawled here? Or had someone carried me? It didn't matter. I was warm, so warm, exercised. No, not warm—*hot.* Why was I so hot? Was I too close to the stove? Oh God, I wasn't merely hot; I was *burning.* I was on fire!

Sitting upright, I yanked off my jacket and my sweater and the long-sleeved shirt beneath, throwing the garments away into the...

...night?

I blinked torpidly. What was I doing outside? I had just been inside. I had been—

In a flash of cruel clarity, I realized there was no cabin and no stove; there never had been.

I swiveled my frozen—and nude—torso to look behind me. There was the trench I had dug, only a few feet away. I hadn't crawled anywhere.

Moving with glacial slowness, my blood as sludgy as crankcase oil in a cold engine, I dragged myself back into the trench-turned-grave and collapsed on top of Smiley so we could die together.

CHAPTER 21

I woke to the aseptic smell of disinfectants and bleach and the beep-beep sound of a vital signs monitor confirming I was alive. For a moment I thought I was in the hospital where I'd been taken after the search-and-rescue team had found me, barely alive, on the mountainside. But then the fog cleared from my head, and I realized that was impossible.

Propping myself up on my elbows, I discovered sensors attached to my chest and an intravenous drip feeding fluid and perhaps medication into my left arm. Muzzy, I looked around the institutional room. The walls were cream, the floor gray. A TV hung from a ceiling mount. Beneath it were two plastic chairs, bright green, the color of springtime and hope.

The confusion of why I'd been hospitalized lasted for only a moment before the memories came flooding back—the drill sergeant in my face, the prison guards rushing me, one of them choking me—and I thought with a bright species of amazement: *It worked! I'm out of the prison!* And almost immediately following this revelation: *But at what cost?*

I rubbed my throat, relieved to find no discomfort or bruising. I swallowed experimentally—and sharp pain exploded in my left ear. It felt as though someone had suddenly and gleefully shoved an icepick into my eardrum. I touched my ear gingerly, winced, and decided to leave it alone.

A little more exploring with my fingers revealed that the tissue around my right eye was sore and tender.

I didn't remember any of the prison guards striking me in the head, which led me to believe the trauma had been caused after

I'd already passed out.

I glanced at the door. There was a little window in it—not unlike the one that had been in my cell door—through which I glimpsed hospital staff and visitors.

Removing the sensors from my chest and the IV catheter from my vein, I swung my legs to the floor. When I attempted to stand, a wave of dizziness dropped me back to the bed. I waited, hoping the nausea in my gut would pass. It didn't. I shuffled to the bathroom, where I knelt in front of the toilet for a full minute before finally emptying my stomach into the porcelain bowl. Afterward, I still felt somehow...fuzzy...but at least not so squishy inside. I checked my reflection in the mirror above the sink. The skin around my right eye was swollen and red.

Back in the room, I went to the window, which appeared to open only from the top. Looking out, I discovered I was on the hospital's fifth or sixth floor. Uninspired concrete buildings, traditional Japanese houses with tiled roofs, and grid-like roads alive with traffic stretched to the hazy horizon.

I heard the door open behind me. I turned quickly and saw a female nurse dressed in a pink top and beige pants. She was in her mid-fifties and kind-looking with a stethoscope and identity card on a red lanyard dangling around her neck.

"You are awake," she said in English.

"Yes," I said.

"Are you feeling better?"

"So-so," I said.

"I will get the doctor."

She left. I went to the door and peeked out the little window. I couldn't see the police officer who would be guarding the room. I suspected he was sitting either to the left or the right of the door, out of my field of vision.

I returned to the bed and waited for the doctor to arrive.

A few minutes later a man roughly my age in navy scrubs entered the room. He wore thick black-rimmed eyeglasses and one of those ubiquitous surgical masks. The tips of a half dozen pens poked out of his left breast pocket.

He tugged down the mask. "Gaston Green," he said, reading my name from a form attached to a clipboard he carried. "I am Doctor Shigeaki Kobayashi. Have you been awake for long?"

"Only a few minutes," I told him.

"How does your ear feel?" he said, stopping before me. I caught a whiff of the leathery smell of carbolic soap.

"It hurts. I can feel the pain all the way along my jaw."

"May I have a look?" He peered into my ear canal. "It hasn't recommenced bleeding, which is good. But you will most likely experience some drainage over the next few days, blood and maybe pus as well." He stepped back. "Unfortunately, you have a perforated eardrum. You'll need to remain on antibiotics for the next seven days to prevent an infection. I can prescribe a painkiller as well, if you wish."

"What about my eye?"

"The swelling and discoloration should decrease within a few days. It should be back to normal within a week or two."

"I am being held at the Tokyo Detention House," I told him. "Guards attacked me. One choked me. That is why I was unconscious. I do not remember them striking me in the head. Did anyone explain to you what happened?"

"From what I understand," he said, "you attacked a guard in the prison's exercise yard. The other guards restrained you. But I do not know the specific details, no."

"How long will I remain here for?"

"I will recommend you stay overnight for observation, but I'm afraid you will most likely be returned to the prison tomorrow morning."

I didn't let my alarm show. *Tomorrow morning. So soon!* "What time is it now?"

Dr. Kobayashi checked his silver wristwatch. "Two thirty. You were unconscious for a little over one hour. Please rest now. I will come back to check on you later this afternoon."

When I dared to poke my head into the hospital hallway, I discovered not one but two police officers sitting watch outside the room, one on either side of the door.

I closed the door and despaired.

Had there only been one cop on duty, as Ugo Ndukwe had said there had been during his hospital stay, my plan had been to lure him into the room and incapacitate him in some manner.

But *two* cops? That was a game-changer. I could not take them both out. Which meant escape would be impossible and everything had been for naught—

The face of one of the police officers appeared in the window in the door. Glowering—he'd likely seen my reconnaissance of the hallway—he wagged a finger reproachfully.

I returned to the bed.

ΔΔΔ

Half an hour later the kind-looking nurse returned with a lunch tray bearing a bento box that contained vegetables, meat, fish, and tempura. There were also two tablets.

"They are for your pain," she said, indicating the pills. "You can take them after you have finished eating."

"Thank you," I said, accepting the tray and setting it on the bedside table. "Dr. Kobayashi mentioned he would check on me later this afternoon, but I have been feeling very ill. Would it be possible to see him now?"

"What do you mean by ill?"

"Lightheaded, dizzy. Sometimes I feel like I am spinning, like I might simply fall over, or pass out."

Concern flickered in her eyes, even as she offered a reassuring smile. "I'll go see if I can find him."

ΔΔΔ

Waiting in the darkened bathroom, watching the hospital room through the narrow crack between the door and doorframe, my heart pounded painfully in my chest as I second-guessed what I was about to attempt. Was it reckless? Yes. Would it succeed? Maybe not. But I had no better option. If I didn't escape the hospital today, I would be installed back in the prison tomorrow morning. I'd likely be sent to solitary confinement for striking the drill sergeant. I'd waste away there until eventually, inevitably, Jaws indicted me on his bullshit charges. I would be tried, convicted, and sentenced to years behind bars in an official prison. This was all worst-case scenario, certainly, but nothing had gone my way since landing in Japan, and I saw no reason to suspect that would change any time soon.

Unless, that is, I took matters into my own hands.

The door to the hospital room opened and Dr. Kobayashi entered. Every muscle in my body received a boost of adrenaline. I barely dared to breathe.

The doctor crossed the room to the bed. "Mr. Green?" he said, speaking to the lumpy form beneath the sheets I'd arranged with a combination of pillows, folded towels, and my balled-up green jumpsuit.

This would not fool him for long. I pushed open the bathroom door and stole toward him. Mumbling something to himself, he tore the sheet back with a flourish. In almost the same instant, he turned to look behind him.

Snagging his shirt below the collar, I shoved him backward off balance and jerked him forward again in a whiplash motion, lowering my head, driving the crown of my skull into his nose.

Cartilage crunched. His eyes rolled up in their sockets, showing the whites. His clipboard hit the floor with a loud clatter.

I eased his sagging body to the gray tiles and dragged the doctor into the bathroom. I stripped him to his briefs and dressed in his blue scrubs and black loafers. I snapped his surgical mask over my mouth and slid on his black-framed eyeglasses. My reflection in the mirror was a blur due to the prescription lenses. I pushed the glasses down my nose and looked over them.

It was a pretty good disguise, I thought, as Dr. Kobayashi and I shared similar builds and skin tones. The problem was my hair. I had none, while the doctor did. Would the police officers notice?

I hoped not. I prayed not.

But there was only one way to find out.

I returned to the room proper and collected the clipboard from the floor. Taking a deep breath to steady my nerves, I pushed the eyeglasses up my nose and opened the door. Stepping into the hallway felt like stepping onto a stage in front of thousands of spectators with every set of eyes trained directly on me.

Staring fixedly at the clipboard, I went left, passing the seated police officer, keeping an unhurried pace. I was certain he would say something or leap to his feet and restrain me.

He did neither. Elation surged within me.

It was working!

Nevertheless, I knew I wasn't in the clear yet. A doctor could stop me, or a nurse. Suspicious of my Western eyes, or wanting to ask me an innocuous question. Either way, I would be busted. They'd see my fright. They'd know I was an impostor. They'd alert the cops...

The hallway ended at a T-junction. I glanced up from the clipboard for the first time. Both directions looked identical. I was wondering frantically where the damned elevators were located when I spotted a little green exit sign depicting a running man.

PART III

Shinjuku/Shibuya

CHAPTER 22

I flew down the concrete steps two at a time. At the first floor, I hesitated, then continued down one more flight, emerging in a well-lit subterranean parking lot. I hustled past rows of parked cars until I came to the ramp out. I followed the pedestrian walkway that hugged the ramp to the top. I ducked beneath the boom barrier and continued along an alleyway crammed with ranks of bicycles that led to a residential back street.

The houses were quaint yet cramped, many featuring tiny gardens. Eventually I came to a large commercial avenue. I ducked inside a 7-Eleven and asked the young female clerk for directions to the nearest train station. All smiles and bows, she told me to walk south for ten minutes.

When I reached the station—Horikirishōbuen, the blue-and-white sign read—it struck me that I had no money to purchase a ticket. No matter though. The ticket barriers were not mini fortresses to stymy fare evaders like their counterparts in Western countries. They merely sported waist-high paddles. I pushed brazenly through the barrier farthest from the clerk manning the ticket booth and stopped before an information board.

This station was on the Keisei Main Line and offered eastbound services to Narita Airport Terminal 1, and westbound services to central Tokyo.

I climbed the steps to the westbound platform.

ΔΔΔ

As the train sped along the elevated track, I stared out the window at the scenery whizzing by, playing over my escape in my mind while trying to work out my conflicting emotions. I had never gotten into a fight in my entire adult life. I wasn't a violent person. Having said this, I didn't feel remorse at punching the drill sergeant. He was a malfeasant who took gratification in the humiliation of others. However, I *did* feel bad—terrible really—at head-butting Dr. Kobayashi. He was a good man who had dedicated his life to helping others. He did not deserve what I did to him. Moreover, what if the head-butt caused him a more serious injury than a broken nose and concussion? What if he began to suffer migraines or vertigo or other long-term complications?

I told myself not to dwell on it. What was done was done and couldn't be changed. In all likelihood, Dr. Kobayashi would be fine. A killer headache for the next few days, tape over his nose for the next couple of weeks. But after that he'd be as good as new.

Unfortunately, I was finding it difficult to conjure an equally positive outlook for my own future. Because what was I going to do now? I was no longer locked in a cage like an animal, but I had no money, no bank cards, no passport, no clothing of my own, no shelter.

"*Out of the frying pan and into the fire,*" crossed my thoughts, and right then the phrase had never seemed so apt.

CHAPTER 23

More than three million commuters use Shinjuku station each day, making it the busiest railway station in the world—a statistic not lost on me as I moved through the bustling shoulder-to-shoulder mobs.

Given I often stayed in Shinjuku during my visits to Japan, I didn't have too much trouble navigating the arcades and hallways to the West Exit, which deposited me in Nishi-Shinjuku, the city's business district.

The afternoon was warm, the air illogically fresh. I went west along the area's famous electronic street, which was packed with retail stores selling phones and cameras and anything else you wanted. Ten minutes later shiny office buildings soared above me. Around the corner from the cathedral-like twin tower Tokyo Metropolitan Government Building was my destination, the Park Hyatt Tokyo.

An eager bellman showed me to a tranquil lobby on the second floor that featured dramatic sculptures and quirky wall art. The hotel occupied the top floors of a three-stepped skyscraper, and I took an elevator up to the forty-first floor, stepping out of the cab into a light-filled atrium called the Peak Bar and Lounge, where in the past I had enjoyed afternoon tea. I followed a confusing twist of hallways past a European restaurant and through a library to the elegantly decorated reception area.

A male attendant at one of the check-in tables beckoned me over.

"Good afternoon, sir," he said, bowing respectfully. With his neatly trimmed hair and beaming smile and well-knotted necktie, he was as polished as someone making a little over minimum wage could be. "Do you have a reservation with us?"

"Yes," I said, butterflies in my stomach. "Gaston Green."

As he typed my name into his computer, I waited with bated breath. When I spotted the slightest frown crease his face, I knew exactly what he was going to tell me. The faint hope I'd been clinging onto sank like an anchor.

"Green?" the attendant said. "Can you spell that for me?"

"G-r-e-e-n," I said tightly.

"Green, yes, that is what I entered. Unfortunately, I cannot find a reservation under that name. Could it be under a different name...?"

"Possibly," I said, forging a courteous smile. "I will check and come back."

ΔΔΔ

"Devastated" would be an understatement to describe how I felt as I made my way back toward Shinjuku station. Not because I should have been relaxing in a posh hotel room right then, ordering room service to my heart's content, but because the fact the reservation didn't exist confirmed the preposterous speculation that had been brewing beneath my thoughts these last few days. Because I *remembered making the booking online with perfect clarity*, damn it! Sure, mistakes can happen. A glitch with the hotel's software, a human error. Something along these lines would have been my natural conclusion had this occurred on any other sojourn to Japan, and I would have patiently worked with the attendant to arrive at a solution.

Nevertheless, this was *not* any other trip; it was a descent down the rabbit hole where nothing was as it should be and the only explanation for the Bizarro World I found myself in was that, yes, somehow, inexplicably, *I was in a timeline that was not my own.*

ΔΔΔ

Heading away from the hotel, I tucked these miserable thoughts away the best I could. Attempting to solve an unanswerable problem would not only be a presumptuous waste of time, it would exacerbate my turmoil and perhaps drive me crazy in the process. Besides, if I wanted to avoid being apprehended by a police officer and carted back to the Tokyo Detention House, I had to get out of Dr. Kobayashi's scrubs.

I had two options. Shoplift some new clothes, or pickpocket someone in the hopes they had money in their wallet, which seemed likely given Tokyo was a cash-dominant society due to its abundance of ATMs and low crime rate.

Back at Shinjuku station, I followed the yellow signs through the sprawling complex to reach the opposite side. Crossing a plaza, I entered Kabukicho, a shopping district jam-packed with neon-lit restaurants, izakayas, karaoke bars, pachinko parlors, and retail shops all stacked one on top of the other.

I found a spot near a row of ATMs and waited as inconspicuously as I could, which would have been much easier had I had a phone to fiddle with. Instead, I leaned against a wall with my hands folded behind my back, my eyes lowered for the most part.

Within minutes I spotted my target, a middle-aged man who had withdrawn money from one of the bank machines. I followed him for a block but could not work up the nerve to pluck his fat wallet free from the back pocket of his trousers. When he entered a movie theater, I gave up and returned to the ATMs.

I didn't have to wait long for a second target. Another man, younger than the first, with an equally fat wallet bulging from his back pocket. I remained directly behind him as he weaved through the crowd, and just as I was about to attempt the old bump-and-grab he entered a gaming arcade.

I followed him inside.

The first floor was filled with people, photo booths, and

brightly colored crane game machines. The man stopped before one of the latter and plunked some coins into it. *Now or never, Gaston*, I thought, and bumped gently into him from behind. Apologizing in Japanese, I patted him on the biceps with one hand and snatched his wallet with the other.

Glancing over his shoulder, he appeared discombobulated at the sight of a foreigner and swiftly returned his attention to winning a Pikachu stuffed animal.

ΔΔΔ

As I hurried away from the arcade, I looked inside the wallet and found identification, loyalty cards, credit cards, receipts—and twenty thousand yen, or about two hundred dollars. Folding the notes in half, I stuck the loot in my breast pocket and dumped the wallet into a mailbox I passed, hoping it would find its way back to the owner, albeit a little lighter.

ΔΔΔ

A six-floor, gaudily designed Don Quijote chain discount store dominated a nearby intersection. A sign with the store's iconic penguin mascot and the word *WELCOME!!* greeted me. Passing a pink pig humidifier spraying mist from its nostrils, I entered the labyrinth of cluttered aisles, where the idiom *pile them high and sell them cheap* was taken to the extreme, as the shelves were overflowing with everything and anything imaginable. Smartphone accessories, cosmetics, *matcha* snacks (including KitKat and Aero candy bars), high-end jewelry and accessories at slashed prices, electronics (from hot eyelash curlers to massage chairs), and home appliances (such as rice cookers and washing machines). There was even an aisle dedicated to toilet seats, most of which came with electronic bidets.

To add to the sensory overload, the store's cartoonish theme tune "Miracle Shopping" was playing over speakers in perpetuity.

After nearly fifteen disorienting minutes, I found the men's clothing section on one of the upper floors. I picked out socks, boxer briefs, a tee-shirt, black trousers, and a pair of oversized sunglasses. After trying on the shirt and trousers in a tiny change room, I returned to the first floor and paid for the purchases in cash.

A block away, in a McDonald's restroom, I changed into my new duds, tossing the prison underwear and scrubs in the bin. Checking myself out in the mirror, I looked pretty darn good for an escaped prisoner—despite my black eye, which was now the color of a rotten prune.

I slipped on the sunglasses.

At the fast-food restaurant's hectic front counter, I ordered a Big Mac combo with fries and a Coke, as well as two additional cheeseburgers. Gluttonous, but I was starving. I found a free window seat and ate the meal facing the street, people-watching as I thought about my next move, which involved gaining access to the internet. I was sure the McDonald's offered free Wi-Fi. The problem was without a phone or computer, I had no way of connecting to it.

When I finished eating, I went hunting for a *manga kissa*, or internet café, which I knew to be everywhere in Tokyo, especially around train stations. Despite nearly everyone owning a smartphone with an internet connection, the cafés proliferated because they doubled as manga libraries, oases of calm in a non-stop concrete jungle.

A short time later I spotted a sign for a *manga kissa* on a higher floor of a multi-story building. Stepping off the elevator, I presented myself at the front desk, where an equine-faced, thin-hipped woman greeted me with a bow. Her fake-lashed brown eyes feigned spontaneous fascination each time I spoke in Japanese. Mostly I was asking about the payment packages. Initially I'd planned on getting an hour or two of internet only. But according to the laminated price sheet she showed me, there were twelve-hour packages available—and combined with the option of a private room, I realized I had just found low-budget accommodation for the night. I was also delighted to discover free showers on offer (though shampoo and a towel incurred a small charge), and *samue*—traditional old-man clothes—to relax in.

All told, everything set me back a little over two thousand yen—a bargain since any hotel room would be about five times that price.

The woman handed me a basket containing my room key, shower amenities, rolled towel, and folded *samue*. She led me down a wood-paneled hallway. Her mass of amber-dyed hair swished past her shoulder blades with each pigeon-toed step she took. Her stovepipe jeans hung low enough below the smooth knobs of her hipbones to make a plumber proud.

I entered a changing area, hung my recently purchased clothes on hangers, and stepped into one of three available shower stalls. The steaming water not only cleansed my skin but relaxed my knotted muscles and troubled mind. I remained beneath the spray for a good fifteen minutes before reluctantly shutting off the faucets. Once dry, I changed into the old-man clothes and went looking for my private room, finding it at the end of a hall littered with slippers. I followed etiquette and left my slippers in front of the door to my budget abode, which featured a reclining chair, a wood desk with a burgundy leather blotter, a computer and monitor, and a Blu-Ray player. A lamp with a lozenge-shaped shade stood in one corner, a sink in another. A rattan fan wobbled and creaked overhead.

Setting the basket containing my belongings on the floor, I sat in the chair and powered on the computer. As I waited for the machine to boot up, I became antsy and stressed all over again. By the time I accessed the web browser, I was borderline nauseous.

This was due to a desperate kind of hope, which right then felt like the worst kind of hope, because a part of me knew it was really wishful thinking. And when my search for "Taured" didn't bring up the country in which I was born, but rather a character in the MMORPG *World of Warcraft*, I slammed my fist into the keyboard, causing it to *bleep* in alarm.

I performed several more searches for "Taured," combining the country name with different keywords. Yet as I'd feared and expected, I uncovered nothing relevant.

Taured did not exist.

Not in this world, at any rate.

ΔΔΔ

Andorra, however, *did* exist, I told myself determinedly, and I started researching everything I could about it.

ΔΔΔ

According to several websites, Neolithic humans had first settled the small landlocked region on the Iberian Peninsula that would become Andorra during the Ice Age. Over the centuries it came under the influence of the Romans, who spread their laws and culture to the scattering of inhabitants, and the Visigoths, who spread Christianity. When the Muslim Empire annexed much of the peninsula, ousting the ruling Visigoths, a man named Mark Almugaber led an army against them, fighting on the side of Charlemagne and the Franks. As a sign of his gratitude, Charlemagne proclaimed the region an independent nation, naming it for the first time "Andorra," in reference to the Biblical Canaanite valley of Andor. Two centuries later the marriage of the Spanish overlord of Andorra and a French count led to both Spain and France laying claim to the principality. Eventually the conflict was resolved by an agreement that stated Andorra's sovereignty would be apportioned by both countries—and this "co-prince" arrangement continued to this day.

Why was any of this significant?

Because the history I'd learned in school about Taured *also* began with Charlemagne, only the army who helped him keep the invading Moors at bay was led not by Mark Almugaber but Louis Taured—the man after whom Charlemagne not only named the region but also made its overlord. There was never any matter of royal marriages or bickering heirs or proprietary claims of competing foreign powers to muddy the waters of who was the legitimate ruler of the principality.

Taured, since its founding, was, and always had been, under France's control.

Slumping back in my chair, I thought about the so-called butterfly effect in which minor changes in a complex system are believed to have consequential effects. And I found myself believing this phenomenon to be real, for all it took was one man (Almugaber) instead of another (Taured), spearheading an important battle, to change the name and direction of a country—*my* country—forever.

I tried to be excited about this revelation. I *should have* been excited about this revelation, as it offered an explanation as to how and why two different countries occupied the same physical location, albeit in different dimensions, on the world map.

Much to my dismay, however, I found myself decidedly not excited but blackly depressed, because it didn't change the fact—rather, it only seemed to *confirm* the fact—that I was trapped in an alien universe with no way of getting home.

CHAPTER 24

My mother, Claire, is a silver-haired, shiny-eyed woman with a kind heart and a forgiving nature. Retired now, she'd spent most of her life as a truck-stop cashier. Setting gas pumps, weighing incoming rigs, and selling scratch-off tickets was not a glamorous job by any means, but she'd never complained. She woke up every morning at the crack of dawn, made my father and brothers and myself a warm breakfast, dressed in her uniform (which she took pride in keeping meticulously starched and laundered), and drove twenty kilometers to the truck stop at the base of the Pyrenees mountains. She'd worked there for more than twenty-five years, beginning when my younger brother, Arthur, started elementary school.

My father Victor was a large yet deceptively quick man with a pockmarked face and predatory eyes. He'd been everything my mother was not: introverted, foul-tempered, prone to violent outbursts, both verbally and physically. In other words, one unpleasant son of a bitch. In fact, he used to scare my brothers and myself senseless when he was in one of his Bad Moods, which often manifested on nights he missed dinner and came home smelling of the bar.

Victor Green never stumbled or slurred when inebriated. He was just more bellicose and violent than usual. These were the times he'd hit my brothers or me—if he could find us or catch us. Arthur and I would usually hide away in the room we shared until he passed out on the sofa with the TV playing. Our oldest brother, Paul, would foolishly confront Victor, especially if the bastard turned his ire on our mother. Over the years the rewards for his gallantry had included a broken collar bone, a shattered forearm, two dislocated shoulders from being thrown around like a ragdoll, and countless cuts and bruises he did his best to cover up the next day when he went to school.

Although Arthur and I didn't provoke our father, he'd smack us around too. One night we had been searching the garage for something or other when we'd accidentally knocked a can of white primer paint with a loose lid off of a shelf. It took us about an hour to clean all the paint off the floor, but there was nothing we could do about the huge white stain left behind. As soon as our father got home—late, for it had been one of the bar nights—he burst into our room, eyes blurry from too many pints, face red from all the yelling he was doing. He didn't ask what happened. Just slid off his belt and began whipping us. When my mother tried to intervene, he threw her aside…which was when he abandoned his sally, got in his car, and left.

Where he went, I had no idea. I suppose a cheap motel, or his partner's house, as they'd seemed to be pretty chummy. But he didn't come home for two days.

Victor Green, part-time father and full-time vile human being, was a police officer. On January 14, 2004, he pulled over a dated Tokyo sedan with a non-functioning brake light. Video from his patrol car's dash-cam showed him approaching the sedan, speaking with the driver, then returning to his car—and the driver bolting on foot. My father's police report described him catching the man in a parking lot. During the ensuing struggle, the man grabbed his Taser. Fearing for his life, my father withdrew his handgun and shot and killed the guy.

Surveillance footage from a video camera in the parking lot evinced a different version of events.

Specifically, my father shooting the man eight times in his back as he fled.

Two months after this prima facie evidence came to light, a grand jury indicted Victor on several charges, including murder. He was held without bail for six months before being released on bond and confined to house arrest.

A few days before his trial was to begin, he disappeared.

No note, no explanation, nothing. He simply left the house one day and never came back.

I was managing the Four Seasons restaurant and lobby bar then. I often had lunch with Paul, who had recently been promoted to assistant butcher at the Clove and Hoof down the street from the hotel. We spent much of our meals talking about our father. Neither of us were exactly surprised (shocked, yes, but not so much surprised) that he had murdered a man in cold blood. We were inured to his temper and violent side. What we were surprised about was that he had gone on the lam. We might never have gotten to know him well, but as his sons we knew enough *about* him, and despite all his ugliness, it had never crossed our minds that he was a coward.

My theory had been that our father had fled to either France or Spain, where he could become anonymous in a big city like Paris or Madrid. Paul was convinced he was in Portugal, living hand to mouth in some little-known coastal town.

It was Arthur, home from university over the summer break, who suggested bluntly that our father was dead.

This proved true just a week later. Nearly one month after Victor had walked out on our family without a word, a young Italian couple hiking in the Pyrenees mountains discovered his body hanging from a tree branch—or what was left of his body, as it had been badly decomposed and savaged by wild animals. A coroner confirmed he had died from pressure to his neck consistent with hanging. He pronounced Victor's death a suicide.

The news barely affected me. I was too angry at my father for taking the easy way out, for leaving a permanent, ghastly scar on our family name...while also breaking my mother's heart. Despite a marriage defined by my father's hard drinking and pathological abuse and single-minded selfishness, she'd never stopped loving him.

In the weeks and months after his funeral, Paul, Arthur, and I visited our mother regularly. She put on a strong face for us, but it was clear her health was deteriorating quickly. We urged her to move out of the house. The change, we thought, would be good for her. New place, new neighborhood, new friends.

She refused categorically. She was only fifty-four, yet the lively spark that had animated her had died with her husband, and she seemed suddenly *old*.

My first three years living overseas in Manila, I returned to Taured every December to spend Christmas with her and my brothers. The fourth year I was unable to make the trip due to an important function in Hong Kong. The following summer I came back for Arthur's wedding in July—yet that was my final trip home. I would Skype my mother on special occasions and major holidays, but of course this wasn't the same as being with her in person.

My excuse for my prolonged absence: I was too busy.

Too busy to see my widowed mother. Too busy to see my brothers or my two-year-old niece.

Too. Damned. Busy.

ΔΔΔ

Opening Skype now, which was already downloaded to the computer's desktop, I tried logging into my business account. My email address worked, yet my password didn't. I signed up for a new account, selected Andorra from the Country menu, and punched in my mother's telephone number.

And got the same message as when I'd dialed her number on Supa-san's smartphone.

I tried Paul's number next, then Arthur's, and went oh-for-three.

I gritted my teeth. *Why didn't their telephone numbers work?* Was the reason as simple as my mother and brothers in Taured having different phone numbers than their counterparts in Andorra? They entered the Andorra Nokia store on a Tuesday instead of a Wednesday, as they might have in Taured, and consequently were given different numbers? That seemed a reasonable explanation.

Nevertheless, there was another sinister one that I couldn't ignore.

The possibility they didn't exist in Andorra at all.

Perhaps in this dimension my mother's father, my grandfather, had never met my grandmother. Or perhaps my grandmother had suffered a miscarriage while pregnant with my mother. Or perhaps she'd never become pregnant in the first place.

Any one of these events, or a thousand other seemingly insignificant ones, could have prevented my mother from being born in this dimension, my brothers from being born.

Me from being born.

After contemplating these nihilistic thoughts for several long minutes, I navigated to Facebook. It was the world's rolodex. You didn't need passwords or telephone numbers to get in touch with other people. All you needed was a name and a country.

When my login credentials once again proved invalid, I created another new account. In the search bar I typed: *Gaston Green Taured.* I paused then, deleted *Taured,* and replaced it with *Andorra.*

I hit Enter.

A single profile for a Gaston Green from Andorra appeared.

And the man in the thumbnail photograph was me.

CHAPTER 25

When I clicked on the bite-sized photo of myself, Facebook informed me the profile was private, which prevented me from seeing any posts. Too excited by my progress to be disappointed by the setback, I typed my mother's name. A single profile for Claire Green Andorra appeared.

The silver-haired, shiny-eyed woman smiling back at me was most definitely my mother.

And her profile wasn't private.

As I scrolled down through all her recent posts, I marveled at how *Tauredian* they were. By that I meant nothing stood out as unusual. Everything was exactly as might be expected—photos, names, comments—had I been back home in Manila before any of this inter-dimensional madness began.

Given I could not call her as we were not "Friends," I clicked the Add Friend button, then the Message button, and typed with trembling fingers:

Hello Mother,

I've forgotten my Facebook password and can't log into my account, which is why I've created this new one so I can get in touch with you. I'm in Japan for business right now, though I've been having some trouble with immigration. I no longer have my phone either, so please get back to me via this app as soon as you can.

Love,
Gaston

PS: This is really me!

I read the message over a half-dozen times before adding the postscript, since what I'd written sounded like an internet scam targeting grandmothers.

Satisfied, I pressed Send.

Standing on matchstick legs, I ran my hands through my hair and paced in the small room, my thoughts racing. When I sat back down slightly more composed, I found a post that both my brothers had commented on, and I spent the next few minutes clicking through to their profiles and sending them messages similar to the one I had sent my mother.

I then conducted a search for my ex-wife, Blessica Villainz. Finding her profile proved more difficult than finding my mother's since Manila had something like twenty-million residents. Nevertheless, I eventually found the Blessica I was looking for buried on the seventh page of results. I wrote:

Hey Bless,

In Tokyo for business. Lost my phone, wallet, etc. Also, Facebook password's not working. Please get back to me with a time I can video call you. Really important.

Gaston

I sent the message and began the waiting game.

ΔΔΔ

I sat in the chair facing the computer screen for twenty minutes—refreshing the web page at least once every sixty seconds to make sure I hadn't missed a reply—before I got up to walk off my nerves. I ended up down the hallway in a communal kitchen where free soft drinks were on offer. There were also two vending machines, one selling hot and cold cans of coffee, the other, Asahi, Kirin, and Sapporo beer.

I poured myself a Styrofoam cup of Coke and returned to my room. While I was fiddling with the key in the lock, Facebook's bubbly ringtone announced an incoming call. I burst into the room and dropped into the chair in front of the computer.

I didn't recognize the number on the popup window but immediately clicked the green answer icon.

"*Hello?*" I said, realizing I sounded a little bit manic right then. "Hello?" I repeated more calmly. "Can you hear me?"

"Yes, Gaston," my mother said. "I can hear you fine. But I can't see you. Gaston? Oh—there you are!"

"I cannot see you," I said, swallowing hard. "You have to push the little video button."

"Did that work?"

Her face filled the previously black box on the screen. "Yes, it works!" I exclaimed.

"Are you at one of your events, Gaston? You sound excited."

My mother looked just as she should, down to her compassionate hazel eyes and choppy silver haircut. "I am in...a hotel room."

"What are you doing wearing sunglasses in a hotel room? Take them off. They look foolish."

"My eyes are sensitive to light right now." I shrugged. "Bad eye drops."

"Why are you using eye drops in the first place? You shouldn't be putting anything in your eyes. Is it because of all that traveling you do? Where are you right now? You said you were having immigration trouble?"

"I am in Japan."

Her lips puckered. "You know, I'm not happy about you traveling to all those foreign countries. They're dangerous. I worry about you, Gaston. What kind of trouble are you having?"

"Do not worry, please. I am working it out. Where are you?"

"Me?" She blinked in surprise. "Where does it look like I am? I'm at home. Don't you recognize your old home anymore?"

I didn't know if I recognized it or not, given I could only see her face and a little bit of the wall behind her head. I said, "How is the weather in Andorra?"

"Cold," she said, not batting an eyelid at the mention of

Andorra. "It's been raining all week. We've needed it. This summer's been so hot. But there's nothing to do but stay inside. Are you feeling okay, Gaston? You look like you've seen a ghost."

"I am fine, mother," I said, smiling to mask my despondence. If my mother didn't find objection to her country being called Andorra, then the nightmare I was experiencing was reality. I could no longer pretend, or wish, otherwise.

"Just a little tired," I added, still holding onto the smile. "How are *you*?"

"Oh, you know. I had to go back to the hospital last week because they didn't get rid of all the cancer—"

"*Cancer?*" I blurted. "What cancer?"

"Skin cancer," she stated. "The mole on my shoulder. I got it removed, as well as a second one on my leg. Why do you sound so surprised? We've talked about this several times."

"Skin cancer," I repeated, relieved.

"Are you okay, Gaston? I'm serious. You seem...I don't know. It's this immigration problem you mentioned, isn't it? Don't tell me it's not. I'm not senile yet."

"I told you, mother, everything is fine."

"Is it work then? Is that company of yours working you too hard? You need a vacation. You haven't been home in so long. We all miss you here very much. And Paul's birthday is coming up. Have you spoken to him?"

"No, not for a while," I said, feeling guilty as sin. Paul would be turning forty-four. When was the last birthday of his I'd attended?

Would I ever attend another?

Yes, I told myself decisively. Taured might not exist in this world, but Paul clearly did. Once I got out of Japan...

"Is he doing well?" I heard myself asking.

"He seems to be," my mother said. "Oh, have you heard the news? Bridgette is pregnant again!"

"How fantastic!" I blurted. Bridgette was Paul's wife. "How far along is she?"

"It's quite early. They only told me the other week. I think she must be in her third month now. Third or fourth."

"I will congratulate Paul when I speak with him. Do you have his number?"

"I don't know it offhand, Gaston. It's written down in the kitchen. Do you need it right now?"

"If you do not mind. It is in your phone, no?"

"I suppose it is. But I don't have my phone with me...oh, there's your father. Let me ask him."

My thoughts went bright and blank. When the shock subsided, I heard my mother speaking with someone who sounded uncannily familiar.

Then, to me: "Your father says Paul's number is...do you have a pen?"

A pen? Did I have a pen? *Fuck the pen*, because didn't I just hear my father speak? It sure sounded like it. I hadn't heard his voice in nearly twenty years because—

Because he's dead, he hanged himself, you were at his funeral, this isn't possible!

"Gaston?" my mother was saying. "Gaston? Oh, *zut alors*, I think I lost him."

My father saying something in the background.

"Gaston?" my mother repeated. "Are you there? Gaston? This stupid computer—"

Fumbling for the mouse, I ended the call.

ΔΔΔ

I was on my feet, my head spinning, the world canting. I placed my hand on the desk for balance, but then I was shuffling backward, one step, two, three, accelerating—falling.

The back of my skull walloped something. Rocketing pain. Then I was on the floor, fighting to keep my eyes open, struggling to sit up.

Darkness.

CHAPTER 26

I wasn't unconscious for long.

When I got unsteadily to my feet, and checked the clock on the computer monitor, it was 7:14 p.m.

My head throbbed where I'd struck it on the porcelain sink. It wasn't bleeding, but I could feel a bump already rising on the back of my skull.

Yet this concern was ancillary.

My father was alive!

This should be impossible, of course...only it wasn't. Impossibilities went out the window when I couldn't find Taured on a map of the world.

A multitude of questions blazed through my mind all at once. *Did my father never shoot that man in the Andorra timeline? Was he never charged with murder here? Or was he found innocent in court? Or guilty, but on a lesser charge than murder? Did he serve his time...?*

"This is too much," I mumbled to myself, even as a weird sort of euphoria blossomed inside me. Not because my father was alive—he meant little more to me than a complete stranger—but because the fact he *was* alive meant...well, I didn't really know. Something profound about life and death certainly. Perhaps life wasn't fleeting, and death wasn't absolute. Because if they were, how could a man be alive in one dimension and dead in another?

My head began to ache. These thoughts were much too big for me right then.

I decided I needed to *do* something. I'd been cooped up in the tiny room for hours. I counted what remained of the stolen money. Sixty thousand yen. It wasn't going to last me long. And then what? I'd have to pickpocket someone else. And when that money ran out? Pickpocket another person. And another, and another, and another. At some point my luck would eventually run out. I'd get caught, maybe arrested, and then it wouldn't be long before I was back in prison, only this time booked on a crime I couldn't deny.

Old Man Toshio got two years for stealing a two-dollar sandwich.

How long would I get as an illegal immigrant pickpocketer?

I needed help. It was good to have spoken to my mother, and I felt immeasurably better knowing I wasn't alone in this world. But my mother was too far away to help me. Same with my brothers.

I needed to talk to someone local. I immediately thought of Toru Matsuoka, the chef of the Michelin-star sushi restaurant. The woman I'd spoken to on the phone had said Matsuoka was in Osaka for a month. On business?

Sitting back down in front of the computer, I searched for the restaurant Matsuoka. As I'd suspected, there was indeed a branch in Osaka. Using the Facebook app, I dialed the corresponding telephone number. The line connected and was answered promptly.

"*Hai. Ginzu Kojyu de gozaimasu*," a woman said.

"*Gaston Green to mooshimasu ga*," I replied. "*Matsuoka-san wa irasshaimasu ka?*"

"I'm sorry," she continued in Japanese. "He's not available right now."

"I have an event scheduled with him at his Tokyo restaurant. It is important I speak with him."

"Hold on a second, please. What was your name again?"

"Gaston Green."

I was put on hold for several long minutes before Matsuoka came on the line.

"Yes? I am Matsuoka," he said.

"Matsuoka-san!" I said. "It is Gaston Green."

"Yes?"

"You know me?"

"No, I'm sorry, I don't. Who are you?"

My alacrity flat-lined. "Gaston Green," I repeated dully. "I am organizing a whisky dinner at your Tokyo restaurant on Thursday...?"

"I'm sorry, I'm not aware of this. I think you may have me confused for someone else. I'm sorry, I must return to work—"

I was no longer listening.

ΔΔΔ

Back in the communal kitchen, I tossed my empty Styrofoam cup into the trash. I purchased three full-strength Asahi beers from the vending machine. I chugged one on the spot and brought the other two to my room, where I spent the next half hour looking up erstwhile Japanese clients I had worked with and contacting them through their websites. Of the dozen or so I got in touch with, not a single one knew who I was.

By that point I had a decent buzz going and wanted to keep it going. In fact, I had no better ambitions than drinking until I passed out.

I locked my room, took the elevator to the first floor, and stopped in the Lawson's convenience store next door to purchase a can of beer. Outside, I popped the tab and took a sip. While drinking alcohol in public might be considered bad form, it wasn't illegal in Japan.

I started down the busy street. A shopping district by day, Kabukicho turned into a red-light district at night. As a single male foreigner, I was a prime target for the hustlers and bar girls standing outside their questionable establishments. I politely deferred the first few propositions I received before eventually ignoring them altogether.

I made my way through the seediness to a darkened corner of

Shinjuku called Golden Gai. The twentieth century wasn't kind to Tokyo's architectural heritage. Whatever buildings hadn't fallen down during the monster earthquake in 1923, or weren't bombed during wartime air raids, were bulldozed into oblivion during the second half of the century when the city was reimagined in steel and concrete.

Golden Gai had survived with its pre-war charm intact. Boxed in by high-rise developments, the area was composed of six intimate alleyways, each too narrow to drive a car down, and festooned with over two hundred mismatched bars and restaurants. Many of them were dirty and tumbledown with steep steps leading to second-story shops or flats. In some windows, signs boldly stated, "No foreigners" and "Regulars only."

I stopped halfway down one lantern-lit alleyway, looking up at a second-floor noodle restaurant. I'd gone there with a work associate during my last visit to Tokyo. We had ramen and beer, then spent the rest of the night getting drunk on plum tequila at a nearby Edwardian/Gothic bar decorated with gilded mirrors, chandeliers, stag heads, and the occasional disco ball.

And look at you now, Gaston, a pauper on the outside looking in, with barely enough money to your name to afford the seating charge —

I started as a thought struck me.

With a renewed purpose to my step, I went looking for a payphone. Unlike many European cities, Tokyo still had a good number around, backup communication, I suppose, in case of cell phone reception failure during the overdue sequel to the 1923 earthquake.

A couple of minutes later I stood before a lime-green phone in the back of a convenience store. A ten-yen coin got me one minute. I dug change from my pocket and dumped fifty yen into the slot and dialed Okubo's number, which I'd committed to memory on Flight JL077.

"*Moshimoshi?*" the flight attendant chirped.

"*Konbanwa, Okubo-san,*" I said. "*Gaston desu. Ogenki desu ka?*"

"Gaston! Good evening!" she said, switching to English. "I

thought you forgot about me."

I had, in fact, utterly, until only a few minutes ago. By way of apology, I said, "It has been a hectic few days."

"Yes, work, I understand. I've just come back from Manila again earlier today."

"You said you would be in Tokyo for...?"

"Until Friday. So I am still free for the dinner you mentioned on Thursday."

"Yes, that is right... But the reason I am calling... Would you like to join me for a drink tonight?"

"*Tonight?*" she said, sounding surprised.

"I know, you just returned from Manila, and it is last minute..."

"No, I...yes, I can meet you."

"Fantastic!" I said, grinning. "Where do you live?"

"Daikanyama. It's near Ebisu station. Do you know Ebisu?"

"Of course. Next to Shibuya on the Yamamoto line."

"Where are you?"

"Not far—Shinjuku. So how about we rendezvous in Shibuya. I could use the change of scenery."

"I will need a little time to get ready. Is ten o'clock too late?"

"It is perfect. Meet at Hachikō Statue?"

"Okay, Hachikō Statue at ten o'clock. Thank you for calling me, Gaston! I'll see you soon."

CHAPTER 27

Stepping out of Hachikō Exit, I emerged smack-dab in the beating heart of Shibuya, a Blade Runner-like scene pulsating with lights and sounds and prodigious TV screens, all wrapped up in a frenetic, youthful energy.

As I navigated the bustling crowd, the lights for Shibuya Crossing flashed green. A flood of humanity whooshed past me as thousands of pedestrians crossed the giant intersection all at once with a hive-like efficiency.

I picked my way through the swarm until I reached the small bronze statue cast in the likeness of the Akita dog after which it was named. According to the lore, Tokyo's most famous pooch, Hachikō, journeyed every afternoon to Shibuya station to meet his master, a university professor, upon his return from work. When the professor died in 1925 (he'd suffered a fatal cerebral hemorrhage in his classroom), Hachikō continued to visit this spot daily until his own death nearly ten years later.

Due to his loyalty and fidelity, Hachikō had become a national hero to the Japanese, and his statue had become a universal meeting spot.

Now a steady stream of fashion-obsessed Gen Ys and Zs were snapping selfies in front of it. I found a spot to wait for Okubo several meters away. Leaning against a tree, I watched the crowds cross the intersection every two minutes.

I saw Okubo before she saw me, and I delighted in the way she moved and looked. She wore a beige trench coat over a white skirt and cornflower blue sequined top. The combo of heels and sporty striped socks gave the outfit that sartorial quirkiness often present in Japanese fashion.

From her Gucci clutch, she withdrew her cell phone, perhaps to check if I had sent her a message.

Smiling, I approached. Her eyes lit up when she saw me.

"Hello!" she said, holding out her hand.

"Hello," I said, shaking. A kiss on the cheek seemed a little too intimate considering she had been nothing more than my flight attendant only a few days ago.

"You look great," I told her.

"Thank you!" she said. "So do you!"

"Don Quijote," I said, indicating my clothes. "The airline lost my suitcase."

"They never found it? They usually do."

"Not this time, unfortunately." I plucked off the sunglasses and indicated my black eye. "Hence the shades at night," I said.

"Oh, Gaston!" She made to touch my face before her hand shied away. "What happened?"

"How about I explain later?" I stuck the sunglasses back on and rested my hand on the small of her back. "I know a place not far away. Hopefully it is still where it is supposed to be."

She looked at me quizzically. "Still where it's supposed to be?"

"I mean—" I cleared my throat. "It has been a couple of months since I was last in Shibuya. I hope it is still open."

I led Okubo across the chaotic crossing and down busy streets ablaze with brand-name shops and eccentric boutiques before branching off into the lesser-known backstreets of Inokashira-dori. Most of the people we passed were young and decked out in the latest trends, which ran the gamut from clashing prints to oversized layering to pop culture references and rainbow-hued dos.

Located between a busy record store and a hole-in-the-wall coffee shop was a little bar I had previously frequented on numerous occasions, as it served up some of the country's best craft beer.

The door was huge, unadorned, and rather intimidating. I

held it open for Okubo and followed her down a tunnel-like set of stairs into a cavernous space lined with benches, which were mostly empty.

"Lucky for us," I said. "The place does not seem too busy."

We passed through a heavy purple curtain into the bar that belied its exterior appearance with clean lines and light wood furnishings. Behind the glossy black bar, eight beer taps protruded from a wall with a textured mud finish. A dozen tables filled the small space, half of them occupied.

A bowing hostess, who seemed undecided as to whether to speak English or Japanese, made a few pleasantries in both languages before leading us to a free table.

I browsed the beer menu while Okubo's roaming eyes paused on the jazz band in the back corner. "This place is great!" she said. "How did you know about it?"

"A client took me here...must have been more than five years ago now. I try to come back whenever I am in Japan. You know, I am surprised it is not busier with the Olympics being here and everything."

"The Olympics?" Okubo said, frowning.

"The summer Olympics," I said.

"Have you been living under a rock, Gaston? The Olympics are in Turkey this year. Tokyo was the runner up."

"What!"

"Don't you watch the news?"

A white-suited waiter with lacquered hair approached the table.

"Toro!" I said, recognizing his quick smile.

His smile faltered. "You know my name?"

Unsurprised by his reaction, I said, "You served me before. It, uh, was a long time ago," I added, so as not to embarrass him for forgetting a customer. "I am Gaston. This is my friend, Okubo. Do you still have that microbrew from Hokkaido on tap? I did not see it on the menu."

"A very good selection." To Okubo, "*Go-chuumon wa okimari desu ka?*"

"I'll have the same," she replied. When he left, she said to me, "They always do that."

"Do what?" I asked.

"Speak to my foreign friends in English and me in Japanese."

"You *are* Japanese," I pointed out.

"But you were speaking English. I'm with you. He should have continued speaking English to me."

"Maybe he is not comfortable using English?"

"He's comfortable," she assured me.

"How many foreign friends do you have?" I asked cheekily.

"Many. I'm a flight attendant, remember? I speak with foreigners all the time."

"On airplanes," I said. "Do you hook up with many of them after you land?" I realized how that could be interpreted and shook my head. "I mean, as friends."

She was smiling. "I've been on a date with you—wait, is this a date?"

"Seems like one to me."

"I've been on a date with you for all of twenty minutes, and you're already jealous?"

Toro returned with our beers.

"Please enjoy," he said, promptly taking his leave.

"Hey, only English," I said. "Maybe he overheard you criticizing his etiquette."

Okubo was staring at her beer. "It's blue!" she exclaimed.

"The brewery makes it with water from melted icebergs in the sea of Okhotsk," I told her. "They add a blue pigment to represent this. Gimmicky, but it does not affect the taste." I raised my frosted mug. "*Kampai!*"

"*Kampai!*" she said, lifting her mug with two hands, clinking, and sipping. "Mmmm," she said, fingering foam from her upper lip.

"Are you hungry?" I asked, aware I had to be careful not to go overboard with expenses so I could afford the bill. "They have authentic pulled pork."

"I have eaten, thank you. But you go ahead."

"I am fine," I said, despite the fact I was ravenous. All I'd eaten today was the McDonald's burgers and fries. I took another sip of beer.

"You look like Stevie Wonder," she said. "Can you take off those sunglasses, please?"

I hesitated a moment, then took them off, setting them on the table. "You do not mind looking at me like this?"

"You have very nice eyes. I like seeing them."

"I could say the same thing about you."

She smiled again. "I've been wondering, Gaston. Why would someone do that to your very nice eye? Or was it an accident?"

"I was with my colleagues in Kabuchiko last night. A drunk spilled his drink all over one of them. I told him to apologize. He punched me." I didn't like lying to Okubo, but I couldn't exactly tell her I'd elicited the black eye from overzealous guards in order to execute a brazen prison escape.

"You have to be careful in Kabuchiko at nighttime," she said. "There are some bad people there."

I wanted to move on from the topic and said, "So…Ebisu. Great location to live."

"It's convenient," she said. "I've only been there for a few months, but I like it."

"The last time I was in Ebisu I was with hard-drinking business associates plying me with whisky. I do not remember much, to be honest." I held up my hands. "Do not get the wrong idea. Self-regulation is a big part of my job description. I am good at it. If someone in my position sat around drinking all the time, they would not be employed for long."

"Gala dinners, pub crawls, first-class flights…" Okubo folded her delicate French-tipped fingers together on the table and leaned forward. "What exactly do you do, Gaston? You're a mystery to me."

"I am a whisky sommelier employed by a family-owned company. They send me around Southeast Asia to promote their brand."

"Ah, yes! I can see you doing that. It sounds like a lot of fun."

"I enjoy it."

"In the name of disclosure...I'm more of a vodka girl than a whisky girl."

"I assumed that much."

Her eyes flashed amusedly. "*What?* What does *that* mean?"

"Vodka drinkers wear sequins."

Okubo glanced down at her top. "And what do whisky drinkers wear?"

"Black."

"I wear black."

"There is nothing wrong with liking vodka, *chérie*."

"What's another vodka-drinker stereotype?"

"They turn into emotional messes after one too many."

"And whisky drinkers?"

"Keep our shit together."

"Whatever! What else?" she demanded.

"You guys are the life of the party."

"Of course. And whisky drinkers?"

"Keep to ourselves."

"All right, two can play at this game," she said, leaning forward, her perfume redolent of lemon cupcakes. "Vodka drinkers are...sweet."

"Whisky drinkers are bold."

"Vodka drinkers dance on tables."

"Whisky drinkers dance in the limelight."

"Touché. Vodka drinkers love to talk."

"Whisky drinkers love to think."

"Ooh...that one hurt. Vodka drinkers...take selfies."

"Whisky drinkers...take punches."

Okubo laughed. "Yes, you do indeed do that!" she said, referencing my black eye. "No argument there." She sipped her beer. "So...that's what you're doing at Matsuoka on Thursday—promoting your whisky?"

I nodded. "The head chef creates the dishes. I match them with whisky tastings. People usually enjoy themselves and learn something new about our brand at the same time. Which is important with all the misinformation about whisky out there."

"Misinformation?"

I nodded again. "It is especially bad in Japan. There are probably more fake whisky experts here than in any other country I have visited."

"Why would Japanese want to be fake whisky experts?"

"They are not Japanese. They are Westerners. When they noticed the spike in the popularity of whisky in Japan, they came here to do pretty much what I do, only they do not have any real experience. Because Japan has a more introverted population, and individuals do not voice their own opinions very loudly, these fake whisky experts get a lot of attention."

"How complicated is whisky really?"

"It can be very complicated with all the different brands and terminology. Most people think all rye is spicy, yes? Not true. It can be tamed to create a very nice mouthfeel by using port or sherry or other ingredients. A lot of people think all bourbon is sweet. Also not true. They think flavored whisky is just sugared swill, or anything labeled 'single' is better than anything labeled 'blended.' False and false. The list of misinformation goes on and on."

"So the fake whisky experts just...make stuff up?"

"They post photographs of expensive bottles of whisky on Instagram, get a few thousand followers, and suddenly they think they are a bona fide whisky expert—and, yes, they talk out of their asses. But you want to know their worst offence? They propagate the myth that Scotch is snotty. They think you must have all this knowledge about Scotch before you can enjoy it. On Facebook, whisky groups light up every day. A happy drinker might post a picture in one of a whisky on the rocks, only for an 'expert' to come along and criticize the whisky they used, or the glass, or the garnish. Instead of helping to create a fun and welcoming environment for new drinkers, they push newcomers away. Me, on the other hand, yes, I will tell you how I think you should taste your whisky. I will tell you how you can maximize the flavor, what you should look for. But ultimately I am happy for you to drink it the way you want to drink it and enjoy it the way you want to enjoy it. Because, *chérie*, the best way to enjoy Scotch is however you please."

"Wow, you really *are* passionate about whisky, Gaston! Do you remember your first glass?"

"Aside from my father's Black Bottle as a little boy? Yes—Rosebank 12 Flora & Fauna."

"What's the best whisky you've ever had? Objectively. The ones you promote don't count."

I thought about this. "I suppose a Silver Seal forty-two-year-old Bunnahabbain."

"Favorite place in the world to have a whisky?"

"Is this a game?"

"Don't stop."

"In a comfortable armchair, in front of a peat fire on an autumn night, with a good book."

"If you could have a whisky with anyone in the world, who would it be?"

I was about to nominate a hammy Scot before changing my mind. "I think," I said, "I would have a good time enjoying a dram with you."

Okubo's cheeks burned red. She surprised me by downing her entire beer in a series of impressive and declamatory gulps.

"You are thirsty!" I said, regaled.

She raised a hand and waved Toro over.

"What are you ordering?" I asked.

"Whisky."

CHAPTER 28

Okubo deferred the ordering to me, and I selected a glass of Tyrconnell for her and Glendalough for me.

"Do I swish it?" Okubo asked when Toro delivered the drinks.

"No, you smell it first," I said, lifting the snifter to my nose.

She did the same. "Whoa!" she said, leaning back.

"Do not sniff it like wine, *ma choupette*. It is much higher in alcohol and can make you woozy."

"*Ma choupette?* I know *chérie*. But what's *ma choupette*?"

"Well, *chou* means cabbage..."

"You're calling me a *cabbage*? What, do I have a big head or something?"

"No, I mean... The closest English translation, I suppose, would be pumpkin."

She thought this over. "Pumpkins are cute. Okay, I like it. You can call me *ma choupette*—as long as you don't call all the other women you know cabbages...?"

"Only you, *chérie*."

"Good." Okubo took a second, hesitant sniff at the top of the glass.

"Yes, better," I said. "Now you can swirl a little and take another sniff." I demonstrated. "See how it is taking a while to drip down the sides of the glass? That means the liquid is viscous."

"What about the color? It's pretty dark."

"Darker usually means it has been aged longer. Okay, now we drink."

I sipped the Glendalough. It was mellow with notes of cherry and spicy butterscotch. Okubo sipped the Tyrconnell and made a sour face.

"You do not like it?" I asked, surprised.

"It's good! Just strong!"

"Try mine."

We swapped glasses. The Tyrconnell was fruitier, with hints of vanilla.

"Wow!" Okubo said, smacking her lips. "They taste so different!" She started coughing.

"But good?"

She cleared her throat. "Great!"

I was pleased she approved. "Add in a tale about your twenty-first birthday," I said, "or your first trip overseas, and you have the perfect drink."

"I think maybe I'm already drunk, because I have no clue what you're saying."

"Everybody loves a good dram of whisky," I clarified, "but what they love most is a dram and a good story to go with it."

"Okay, Gaston," she said, "tell me a good story then."

How about a man landing in a foreign airport only to be told he is from a country that doesn't exist? What I said was, "I have been doing too much talking. I think *you* should tell *me* a story."

Okubo shook her head. "I don't have any stories."

"You must! All the passengers you meet? You must have many stories."

"All right, fine," she said. "Once I presented the standard breakfast meal to a first-class passenger. He was a large man dressed in ornate clothing, and he yelled at me in a thick accent: 'Bring me the mother!'"

"The mother?" I said, perplexed.

"When I asked him to explain what he meant, he kept pointing at his omelet and shouting: 'The mother! Bring me the mother!'"

"He was asking for chicken!"

Okubo nodded. "Was that a good story?"

"Short—but good." I sipped the whisky. "Do you like being a flight attendant?"

"It's demanding, that's for sure. Trust me, I've seen it all. Grumpy mothers with their screaming infants. Female honeymooners shooting every flight attendant dagger looks. Bratty kids. Sleazy drunks. But it is also very rewarding, especially given the scarce alternatives for Japanese women in the workforce."

"The gender discrimination?"

She nodded. "Japan is historically and culturally a patriarchal society. Women are often treated like second-class citizens. It's become internalized in all of us. Do you know what my grandfather wrote in his diary on the day my mother was born? *I beat my wife again because she gave birth to a girl.* He was angry he had two daughters and no son to continue his bloodline."

"Japan's made a lot of progress since then."

"*Economic* progress," she said. "Definitely. Maybe more than any other country. Unfortunately, this has not included equal opportunity for women. In most office jobs, female workers get paid much less than their male counterparts and are often expected to make tea for them and tidy up after them. They are told not to have children because their maternity absence will augment the workload burden on all the others. During the last recession it was common for big companies to simply announce they would not be hiring any women that year. And none of this is likely to change any time soon...which is why I became a flight attendant in the first place. I understood I would be in a subservient position. But at least I would receive greater prestige than, say, if I worked in an office building, where subservience would be expected of me anyway."

"And you get to travel," I pointed out.

"That used to be a big perk," she replied. "I used to love staying in hotels between long-haul flights and having all-night pool parties with the other staff."

"All-night pool parties?"

"Oh, you would love it, Gaston! All the beautiful young flight attendants…"

"Perhaps you could take me to such a party one day?"

"You wish!" She laughed. "Anyway, what was your question? Do I like being a flight attendant? Yes, it's been a lot of fun. Exploring different countries during layovers. Meeting interesting people. Once, the captain let me and another flight attendant into the cockpit to have a feel of steering a Boeing 777. Don't worry, I was highly supervised."

"Flying a 777!" I exclaimed. "And you said you had no stories!"

Okubo pressed her lips together impishly. "Actually, I was just thinking of another story. Do you want to hear it?"

"Would love to," I said.

"A few days ago I was on a long-haul flight back from Manila, in the galley, doing my makeup, when this passenger pushes in through the curtains."

"Ah," I said, swallowing whisky. "One of *those* passengers."

"Yes, one of *those* passengers," she agreed. "And a foreigner too. He began talking to me in Japanese—"

"Show off."

"He asked for a glass of whisky. I poured him one. But he kept talking to me."

"Insufferable."

"No, he was charming. And handsome."

I grinned. "Imagine your luck!"

"*Cocky* too," she said, grinning back at me. "And then he asked me for my number right then and there."

"Surely you did not give it to this scoundrel?"

"I did. I couldn't help myself. I didn't think he was going to call me—but then he did. He took me out for a drink."

"Did you have a good time?"

"As a matter of fact, I had a very good time."

I met her glittering gaze. "Dare I ask what happened after that?"

"I asked him back to my place."

"I cannot imagine he turned down an invitation such as

that?"

Okubo only held my eyes with hers.

I stood. "I will get the bill."

CHAPTER 29

We walked back to Shibuya station through the manic nightlife. The energy in the air was palpable, rivaled only by Shanghai, Seoul, London, and a select few other megacities. It was a world apart from the austere quiet I had experienced in the Tokyo Detention House, and I vowed I would never return to that depressing place.

The eastbound Yamanote Line train arrived precisely on time. Okubo and I squeezed into the packed car for the brief ride. From Ebisu it was a pleasant ten-minute trek to her place. She lived in a multiple-unit building differing little in style and design than all the others in the area. Although there was an elevator, we took the stairs to the third floor. Her apartment was at the end of the corridor.

"It's not very big," Okubo warned me before opening the door.

I followed her into a small vestibule, where we took off our shoes. She tucked the footwear into a cabinet and led me down a short hallway. On one side was a shower and laundry room, on the other, a bedroom, inside which I glimpsed a futon, dresser, mirrored closet, wicker floor lamp—and a huge Winnie the Pooh stuffed animal.

The end of the hallway opened to a living room with butternut walls and a compact kitchen.

"No tatami mats," I said, tapping my socked foot on the polished parquet flooring.

"Easier to clean," she said.

"But not as pleasant to sit on."

"I use chairs." From a cupboard above the kitchen counter she withdrew two wine glasses. "All I have chilled is champagne. Is that okay?"

"Good with me." I opened the gray space-saver refrigerator, saw a lot of leafy vegetables and leftover takeaway food, and grabbed the bottle of blanc de blancs on the bottom shelf.

"Do you want to sit outside?" she asked me, tugging back a curtain to reveal a sliding glass door and cramped balcony. Two chairs overlooked the darkened neighborhood.

We sat and poured the sparkling wine.

"This is quite pleasant," I said, stretching my legs. "Quiet."

"You should hear the crows in the morning." Okubo reached beneath the small metal table separating us and set a tin box on her lap. She opened it to reveal a baggie of marijuana and rolling paraphernalia and several pre-rolled joints.

"I did not think Japanese smoked pot," I said.

"We've used it since the pre-Neolithic period."

"*Modern* Japanese. Where did you get it?"

"Roppongi. I met a couple of off-duty American soldiers there a few weeks ago. One of them kept talking about how many people he'd killed before he was transferred to Okinawa. I think he was pretty messed up."

"Killing people will probably do that to you."

"He was really drunk too. He gave me the pot to roll a joint, and then he and his buddy went dancing. When my friend and I went looking for them, we couldn't find them anywhere." She shrugged.

"What if your neighbors complain about the smell? Drug laws are so strict in Japan. I do not want to end up...in prison." I almost said *back* in prison, which would have been a definite mood killer.

"Don't be a wimp, Gaston."

Okubo lit one of the joints and inhaled, wafts of skunky smoke floating away into the night sky. She passed the joint to me. I took a few quick tokes, passed it back.

"Good?" she asked.

I was holding smoke in my lungs and could only nod.

We passed the jay back and forth in silence until it was finished. As I watched Okubo crush the roach out in a ceramic ashtray, I realized I had a major buzz.

"Really good," I said.

Okubo giggled. Clearly she agreed.

"These American soldiers..." I said. "Strong lantern-jaw types?"

"You're cute when you're jealous."

"I am not jealous. I do not know why you keep saying that."

"So jealous!" Okubo adjusted her chair so we were facing one another. "I want to hear a story from you," she said. "I told you two of mine already. It's your turn."

"That one about the chicken hardly qualifies as a story. It was barely longer than a knock-knock joke."

"The second one was good," she insisted. "So come on. Your turn. Tell me a story. A *good* story."

And in my psychedelic state of mine, I thought, *Why not just tell her?* In fact, it seemed like a good idea right then. What did I have to lose? I could always cop out and say I was kidding if things got too weird.

"Once upon a time there was this businessman," I said, swapping first-person for third as she had done earlier. "He regularly travels to different countries for his job."

"Promoting whisky, by chance?" she asked slyly.

"The man's most recent trip was to Tokyo. He had been there many times before, but on this particular occasion, he was held up at immigration."

"Smuggling drugs!" Okubo said playfully.

"Passport fraud," I said sternly.

Okubo's eyes bugged. I could see her thoughts ticking as she determined whether I was alluding to a real event or not. "Passport fraud...?" she repeated.

"The immigration officers claimed the man's passport was from a country that did not exist. They questioned him in a little room all day long. The man insisted they were mistaken. His country existed. Only he could not find it on a map."

"What!" Okubo was on her feet. "I need a cigarette for this. Do you smoke?"

"No," I replied.

"Hold on."

She swayed with her first step, regained her equilibrium, and ducked inside, returning a moment later with a pack of Marlboro Lights and a canary-yellow Bic lighter. "Okay, keep going," she said, plopping back down in her chair and lighting a smoke.

"Eventually the immigration officers gave up their interrogation. The man was placed under arrest and taken to a detention center. It was like an army boot camp. After two days the man could not take it anymore and attempted an escape. While in the prison yard, he attacked a guard. The other guards beat him into unconsciousness."

Okubo glanced at my bruised eye. Her brow furrowed. The coltish curl of her lips turned downward into an uncertain frown.

"As the man had hoped," I continued, "he was transferred to a public hospital to receive treatment for his injuries. Supervision there was much laxer than in the detention center. He was able to slip past the police officers posted outside his room and escape."

Okubo was regarding me with an unreadable expression.

"Your cigarette, *ma choupette*," I said.

She'd forgotten about it. The desiccated tobacco leaves and paper had burned away almost to the filter, leaving behind a precarious tower of ash. She stubbed it out in the ashtray.

"Although now free, the man had nothing," I said. "No money, no credit cards, no way to support himself. He resorted to stealing someone's wallet—something he had never done before in his life. With the illicit money he bought street clothes from a Don Quijote, hired a room in a *manga kissa*—and took a beautiful woman out for drinks."

Okubo was still regarding me with that unreadable expression. I sensed she wanted to laugh but couldn't quite bring herself to do that.

"You're convincing, Gaston," she said, settling for a wide smile. "I almost believed you. Almost."

"Almost believed what?" I asked her.

"Everything you've just told me!"

"It is all true," I said simply.

"You were sent to a detention center?"

"Yes."

"The guards gave you that black eye?"

"Yes."

"And you escaped?"

"Yes."

You could have heard a bedbug sneeze in the dead air.

Then: "Holy *crap*, Gaston!" Okubo said. "You really *are* telling the truth, aren't you?"

"Have you ever heard of Taured?" I asked.

"Taured?" She shook her head. "No, what's that?"

I steeled myself for her reaction. I'd gone too far to back out now.

"It is the country where I am from," I said.

CHAPTER 30

"Taured," Okubo said.

"Yes," I said.

"That's the country where you're from?"

"Yes."

"I've never heard of it."

"Neither had the immigration officers," I reminded her. "Which was what started everything."

"Where is it?"

"In Europe. Have you heard of Andorra?"

"Sure."

"That is where it is."

"In Andorra? How can a country be within another country?"

"It is not *in* Andorra. It *is* Andorra."

"Taured is Andorra? That makes no sense, Gaston."

"In one..." I struggled for which word to use. In the moment, *dimension* seemed too far out there. "In one...reality," I continued, "in this reality, Andorra is Andorra. In another reality, in my reality, yes, Taured is Andorra."

Okubo slumped back in her chair, appearing both confused and bemused. She lit a fresh cigarette and said, "I don't understand. I think I'm too high for this." She glanced at my glass of wine, which was still full. "What are you doing tomorrow?" she asked glibly.

I blinked. "Tomorrow?"

"Work. Don't you have work to do to set up the whisky tasting on Thursday?"

She'd switched off, I realized.

"No, no work," I said, not knowing what else to say.

A bubble of silence ensued, though it was not of the comfortable sort we'd experienced earlier while smoking the joint. It was heavy and perhaps hostile and neither of us could reach past it.

Okubo, I noticed, was rapidly tapping her right foot.

"Thank you for the evening," I said, standing. "I should be going."

"Where?" she said, standing also.

"Where?"

"Where are you going? To the *manga kissa*?"

It was not an innocuous question; it was a challenge.

"Yes," I said simply.

"You took it too far, Gaston."

I nodded but didn't say anything. How had I expected her to react? How would I have reacted had our roles been reversed, and she'd dumped this madcap revelation on me?

"Goodnight," I said, the word wrapped in genuine sadness. I slid open the glass door.

"Don't go," she said quietly.

I looked at her. She didn't seem confused or bemused anymore. Not angry either, not exactly—more like...frightened.

"I want to hear more," she said.

ΔΔΔ

We retook our seats and I spent the next ten minutes explaining to her in detail everything I'd been through since boarding Flight JL077. She did not laugh or deride or argue. She listened quietly until I'd gotten it all out.

Finally she spoke her verdict:

"I believe you, Gaston."

ΔΔΔ

I wasn't sure I'd heard her right. I'd been so certain she would say the opposite I had to ask her to repeat herself.

"I believe you," she said.

"You do not have to say that for my benefit."

"I'm not saying it for your benefit."

"You believe I am from"—*oh hell just say it*—"another dimension?"

"You do not seem like you are joking."

"No, I am not."

"Why would you make all this up?"

"I would not."

"So I believe you."

"I might be crazy."

"That crossed my mind. But you don't seem crazy either. Nothing about you seems crazy."

"I might be a good actor."

"I said I believe you, Gaston!" she blurted. "Why are you trying to change my mind?"

"I am not. Of course I am not." I cupped my face with my hands and rubbed my eyes. "It is just that...it all *feels* so crazy. Sometimes I accept what I have told you, and sometimes I cannot accept any of it. I cannot get my head around it. And that makes me..."

"Feel crazy," she said.

"But I am not. I know I am not. I did not imagine being interrogated by the immigration officers. I did not imagine the detention center. This black eye, it is not made up. This conversation...I have never had a conversation that feels as real as the one we are having right now."

Okubo leaned forward and took my hands in hers. "I do not believe in ghosts," she said. "But if I saw one tonight with my own eyes, if I saw one and was convinced it was not an illusion or a hallucination, I think I would have no choice but to believe ghosts existed, despite how much a part of me would want to spin it otherwise. I guess what I mean is...sometimes there is no choice but to believe."

"Even in the impossible?"

"Even in the impossible."

She leaned a little closer and squeezed my hands. I squeezed hers back.

And then her lips were on mine.

We ended up in her bedroom, on her futon, right alongside the giant-sized Winnie the Pooh. There wasn't room for the three of us on the mattress, so I grabbed the bear by an ear and tossed him aside.

"Jealous?" Okubo teased.

"Immensely," I replied.

It wasn't long before our clothes were off and we were tangled up together beneath the sheets. Naked, Okubo seemed somehow smaller, more delicate than she had been previously. However, she was anything but submissive, and we were both slick with sweat by the time the curtains had drawn on our sexual acrobatics.

I showered first, given the stall could only accommodate one of us at a time. Afterward, lying on the futon in the bedroom, I heard the water clunk on and rattle through the building's old pipes as Okubo began her shower. The repetitive, gushing sound lulled me to sleep, and I barely registered Okubo slipping beneath the covers a short time later, snuggling tightly against my body.

CHAPTER 31

I woke at some unknown hour, my sleep murdered by a vague yet haunting dream filled with laughter and friendship, snow and death, regret and loss.

The bed was unfamiliar. I made out Okubo's silhouette next to me. I recalled what I'd told her earlier, and more importantly, her reaction.

She believed me.

Or she said she did. She could very well be humoring me. But if that was the case, she'd have to accept the alternative that I had some serious mental issues. Why would she want such a person around? She wouldn't.

Which meant she likely did believe me.

Or at least wanted to.

"Are you awake?" she asked me, her voice sharp in the darkness.

"I did not mean to wake you."

"You didn't."

My hand found her bare thigh beneath the covers. I stroked it gently.

"Are you seeing someone, Gaston?"

My hand froze. "No," I said.

"No one?"

"No."

"If you are, please tell me."

Where was this coming from?

I said, "And you keep teasing *me* about being jealous..."

"Who's Smiley?"

At the mention of Smiley's name, a fissure filled with nostalgic affection cracked inside my chest. The dream I had just awoken from flashed vividly in my mind. I pushed myself up to my elbows. In the faint moonlight seeping through the window, I could see Okubo's eyes were open. "Was I talking in my sleep? I was told I do that sometimes."

Okubo twisted onto her side to look at me. "Who told you that?"

"I have been with other women in the past, *chérie*."

"Are you married?"

I hesitated. "Technically, yes, but—"

"What!" She threw the covers off and leapt to her feet. "You're *married*?"

"Yes, but—"

Okubo flicked on the light switch and tugged a satin kimono gown over her body. "I think you should leave."

"Can I explain?"

"Explain? What's there to explain, Gaston? You're *married*."

"I do not live with my wife. We have not lived together for a year and a half."

Okubo frowned. "Are you swingers or something?"

"We live separate lives."

"Why haven't you divorced?"

"We cannot. My wife is a Filipina. Divorce is illegal in the Philippines. I have tried to get her to agree to divorce outside of the Philippines, but her family is strongly Catholic and holds much sway over her. They believe fervently in the sanctity of marriage, especially since we have a son together."

"You have a son...?"

I nodded. "His name is Damien. He is four years old. He lives with his mother. I see him every other weekend."

Okubo drew her fingers along her brow, then down her cheekbones. Her shoulders sagged. She shook her head, exhaling. "I'm sorry for getting so worked up, Gaston. I—I know so little about you..."

"We have only just met," I agreed.

"One night together... For some reason, it feels as though I have known you much longer."

"I should have told you about my son. I probably would have last night had our conversation not gone off on such a tangent... What time is it?"

Okubo looked above and past me. I turned to discover a yellow Pooh-face clock on the wall. The hands read: 4:10.

"You and Winnie the Pooh," I added.

"He is *kawaii*," she said.

"Puppies are cute too. That does not mean I am going to go out and adopt a litter of them."

"Yes, but Pooh-san is not just cute. He holds an enviable worldview. He's comfortable doing nothing but eating honey. That sounds nice, doesn't it? Sometimes all I want to do is relax and pamper myself and *be* myself."

"Words to live by," I said, sitting up and stretching. "I know it is early, but I do not think I am going to be able to get back to sleep."

"I'll make some tea."

"Do you have coffee?"

ΔΔΔ

Not wanting to dress in yesterday's unlaundered clothes, I tossed them into Okubo's washing machine and set the cycle. I would have been content wrapping a towel around my waist for the time being, but Okubo insisted I wear one of her satin kimono gowns. It looked ridiculous on me but was admittedly comfortable against my skin.

While Okubo brewed drip coffee and prepared something to eat, I tidied up the balcony, dumping the contents of the ashtray into the garbage and rinsing the wine glasses in the sink.

We sat at the round kitchen table, a plate of leftover steamed rice, pre-made pickles, preserved kelp, and fermented soybeans between us.

"Do you like natto?" she asked, picking up some gooey soybeans with her chopsticks and dabbing them in a wedge of yellow mustard. "It's really good for you."

"It smells like old socks."

"Hence the mustard. It's so hot it burns your nose and you can't smell anything."

I sipped the demitasse cup of coffee Okubo had made me. "Mmmm..."

"You don't like tea?" she asked.

"At this hour I need something more robust."

She plucked some more soybeans from the plate and attempted nonchalance: "So your wife's name is Smiley...?"

"No," I said. "Smiley was someone I knew when I was younger."

"How much younger?"

"Twenty-two."

Okubo's chopsticks paused halfway to her mouth. "How old are you now?"

"Forty-two."

"You still dream about someone you haven't seen for twenty years?"

"Usually they are not dreams. They are nightmares." I cleared my throat, wondering if I wanted to tell Okubo any more about Smiley. Then I realized that whatever I said would be tame in comparison to what I'd confided the night before. "The last time I saw my friend Smiley was on a weekend skiing trip," I continued. "I was with four friends. We went looking for an off-piste track. Two of my friends turned back, but Smiley and I pressed on, finding what we thought was the perfect ungroomed slope. Halfway down it I wiped out and set off an avalanche."

"Oh God!"

"I was buried under the snow for close to ten minutes until Smiley dug me out. She saved my life."

"Oh my God, Gaston!"

"Unfortunately, we could not find my skis. I told Smiley to go for help. She would not leave me. I should have..." I shook my head. "I should have insisted she go..."

"What happened?" Okubo asked quietly.

"I thought we could walk back the way we had come. That was Mistake Number One, because the walk was a lot more difficult than I had imagined. The deep snow, the trees, the cold. When it became dark, and we still did not know where we were, I suggested we make a burrow in the snow to wait out the night. Mistake Number Two. We began to freeze within the hour. I suggested skiing down the mountain in the dark, tandem, me standing on the back of Smiley's skis. Mistake Number Three. A little way down we hit a half-buried log. Smiley struck her head on something. I do not know what, but when I climbed back up the slope to reach her, she was unconscious. She had a bad cut here." I pointed to my forehead. "It was deep and bleeding. There was nothing I could do. I could not carry her. I could not leave her. So I dug another burrow in the snow. In the morning rescuers transferred us to a hospital. Apparently I was frozen stiff in a fetal position. It took the doctors and nurses over an hour to rewarm and straighten out my body."

Okubo was staring at me in horror.

"Perhaps I should not be telling you this right now," I said. "It is not a very pleasant way to begin the morning..."

"No, please..." she said. "I want to know."

I took a sip of the coffee. It was lukewarm and bitter. "The hospital did not have a cardiopulmonary bypass machine. That is something that pumps cold blood out of your body, rewarms it, oxygenates it, then pumps it back in. Instead the doctors cut me open here." I opened the gown to show her the scar on my abdomen. "They used a catheter to flush warm fluid over my organs, heating up the blood in them, which my heart then pumped around my body." I smiled weakly. "Sort of like how a car radiator works but in reverse. All told, I should not have survived."

"Your friend Smiley...?"

"When I woke up in the hospital, I had amnesia. A doctor told me I had been buried beneath an avalanche. He told me I was wearing a neck brace because I had suffered a C7 transverse process fracture in my back and several torn ligaments that caused two of my vertebrae to slide around. He told me he had never heard of anybody suffering hypothermia with a core temperature as low as mine had been." I held up my right hand. "Almost lost all of these fingers. The frostbite blisters lasted for weeks. I kept waiting for my fingers to turn black and die, but the tissue miraculously revived. I still cannot move them very well..." I clenched my hand into a fist, opened it again. I took another sip of the lukewarm coffee.

"What about Smiley, Gaston?" Okubo asked softly.

"The doctor did not tell me anything about Smiley. Nobody did. They did not want to upset me in the frail condition I was in." I swallowed what felt like a roll of stuck-together pennies. "I did not find out she was dead until the day before her funeral."

ΔΔΔ

A sober silence followed. Outside a crow cawed.

Okubo said, "I don't know what to say, Gaston. I'm so sorry. I feel like such a terrible person for being so nosy—"

"You did not know," I said dismissively. "And it feels...good."

"What does?"

"Talking about what happened. I have only talked about that day to a handful of people, ever."

"Thank you for sharing it with me."

"You are...I do not know. You are easy to talk to. I feel...close to you."

"Maybe we are husband and wife in a different dimension?"

I chuckled. The release of tension was welcome.

I finished my coffee in one swallow and looked at the food remaining on the plate, though I had no appetite.

Okubo said, "So what happens now?"

I frowned. "What do you mean?"

"You don't have a job in this dimension, right?"

"Not that I know of..."

"No wallet, no identification?"

"No..."

"No passport?"

I shook my head.

"No way to get to your wife and son in the Philippines?"

"Not that I can think of."

Okubo grinned. "Looks like you're stuck here with me then."

"I appreciate your hospitality," I said, taking my mug to the sink. "But I do not wish to overstay my welcome."

"Nonsense!" Okubo said, joining me at the sink. "Stay. I'm off until Friday. I'd enjoy your company."

"Thank you, *ma choupette*, but I cannot. I would not feel comfortable imposing in such a way."

Okubo planted her fists on her hips. "Where do you plan to sleep, Gaston?"

I shrugged. "The internet café."

"How much money do you have?"

"Enough for another night."

"And then?"

"I guess I will have to pickpocket someone again—"

"Pickpocket someone!" Okubo exploded. "Listen to you! You are no common thief, Gaston, I know that much. And I am telling you that you can stay here with me. You don't need to go around pickpocketing people and sleeping in internet cafés!"

The offer was tempting, all right, yet... "I would feel like such a bum," I said despondently.

"Don't be silly. If I slipped through the cracks of space-time and landed in another dimension, I would want someone there to look after me until I got back on my feet."

A gleam in her eyes made me think she was trying to keep a straight face.

"You do not believe me, do you?" I said tightly. "Everything I have told you. You think I have made it all up—"

"No, Gaston, that's not true." She stepped close to me. "What you have told me seems fantastical. It seems impossible. But I believe you. I don't know *why* I believe you. But I do."

The admission meant the world to me right then. "Well, if you are happy to let me stay here for a bit..."

She ran her hands along my shoulders, then down my chest, to the sash holding the kimono gown closed.

"I'm happy," she said, tugging the bow undone and glancing down. "Very happy."

CHAPTER 32

After a second round of sexual acrobatics just as adventurous as the first, we showered and dressed, Okubo in a flowing black muumuu, me in my laundered clothes. At a little after eight Okubo went to the local supermarket to stock up on food, as she now had another mouth to feed. Being alone in her apartment felt strange, personal, and I felt gratitude at the trust she'd placed in me.

I sat down at the dining table with Okubo's Macbook. I logged into the Facebook account I'd created yesterday and saw three new messages. The first was from my mother, telling me the connection had dropped out and for me to call again when I had free time. The second was from Paul. He'd tried calling me but couldn't get through. I wondered again where the "me" was who owned the phone he'd tried calling. Back in my dimension? Or was he still in this one? In Manila? In Tokyo? If I got "my" number from Paul, and rang it, would I speak to *me*?

The concept was so daunting I didn't dwell on it for long.

Blessica had sent the third message. I'd expected her to react to the news I'd lost my phone and wallet with chiding indifference. However, she seemed uncharacteristically concerned, ending the message with "I'm around all day tomorrow. Call me!!!"

I tried video calling Paul first. I hung up after a dozen unanswered rings. Arthur hadn't accepted my friend request yet, which ruled out getting in touch with him. I wasn't prepared to speak with my mother again so soon, not with the potential of my Lazarus-like father lurking around in the background. So I rang Blessica next. She answered almost immediately, her face filling the thirteen-inch screen. She looked just like the Bless I knew, a young Gloria Vanderbilt with expressive brown eyes in milky skin, aristocratic lips curled upward at the corners, a broad smile, and strong white teeth. Her shiny black hair was styled long and straight.

"Gaston!" she exclaimed. "I've been waiting to hear from you! I tried calling but immediately got the message bank." She laughed. "Late night?"

"Huh?" I said, confused.

"The glasses."

"Ah, yes..." I said. "Bad headache. You are looking good," I added, to move on.

"Awww. You're so sweet."

Sweet? When was the last time she'd called me that?

"Thanks," I said a little uncomfortably. "How is everything? You seem...happy."

She laughed. "Thanks. I *am* happy. Swamped with work, but everything's going well. What about *you*? How did you lose your wallet *and* your phone? Were you robbed?"

"I might have forgotten them in a taxi."

"Damn. What are you doing for money? Do you need me to send you some?"

"I would love you to," I said. "But I do not have ID. I could not collect it."

"What? Nonsense. My parents sent me money when I was robbed in Thailand. I didn't have ID either. You just need to answer a question with a passphrase."

I sat straighter. "That is it?"

"Simple, right? How about my middle name?"

"Mariel?"

She laughed again. "You sound unsure!"

In fact, I hadn't been confident in my answer. If my father could be dead in one dimension and alive in another, Blessica's middle name most certainly could have been something else entirely. "Great!" I said. "The sooner you could send the money,

Bless, the better. I am still here for a while, and the hotel is not paid for, so I will need a fair bit..."

"Don't worry about it, Gaston. I've got you covered."

"Umm—can you tell me your phone number in case I have any problems and need to call you?"

"You don't know my phone number? I'm insulted! You are so good with numbers."

"It has always been in my phone. I have never needed to know it."

"Yes, I suppose that's true. You're forgiven." She told me her phone number, which I immediately memorized. "Anyway, another *week*," she added. "I already miss you so much!"

I blinked. *Miss me?*

I opened my mouth but was at a loss for words. Bless was still speaking.

"...we should do something when you get back. Like a trip. Somewhere fun. Maybe Bohol. We haven't been there for years. How adorable were the Tarsiers!"

And with abrupt conviction, I realized what was going on.

Bless and I are still together!

"What's wrong, Gaston?" she said, brow furrowing. "You look funny."

"I just remembered...something is on the stove."

"Where are you?"

"In my hotel room."

"Your hotel room has a stove?"

"It is a contained apartment."

"Aren't you at the Hyatt?"

"I—no... Ummm..." My mind was racing. How did you ask someone—your wife, no less!—if you were in a relationship. "Can I call you back?"

"Can you show me the apartment?"

"What? Why?"

She was getting that crafty look in her eyes I knew all too well. "I want to see it."

"I need to go. I will call you back."

"Why are you acting so weird, Gaston? Show me the apartment!"

"Say hi to Damien for me. Tell him I'll talk with him soon."

"*Who?*"

My heart stopped. "Damien," I repeated carefully.

"Who the hell's Damien, Gaston?"

"Damien!" I pleaded, dreading what I knew I was going to hear. "Our son!"

"Our son? *Our* son? What's wrong with you, Gaston? Did you hit your head? Do you need—"

I slapped the laptop closed.

ΔΔΔ

I rushed to the toilet and disgorged the watery contents of my stomach several times over.

CHAPTER 33

Damien.

Gone.

No, not gone.

Much worse than that.

He was never born.

He had never existed.

CHAPTER 34

No wonder Blessica had initially been so bubbly and happy during the call, and why it appeared our relationship was still intact and thriving.

It had been Damien's birth in the Tauredian timeline that had driven us apart.

Damien was not to blame, of course. Blessica and I were. We were compatible as husband and wife but not as mother and father. Having a baby to care for redefined our relationship and created a widening schism between us. We had to develop a new way of relating to each other, of running the house together, and it didn't work. Part of the problem, I believe, had been Blessica's naïve expectations of what parenting would entail. During the pregnancy she had been gushing nonstop about how much she was looking forward to becoming a mother. Her idealized version of this role included hanging out with all her other mom friends in the park, shopping with them for designer bodysuits, and posting cute photos on social media.

The reality that first year was diaper changing, around-the-clock feedings, and disagreements with me over how to handle raising a newborn.

When I came home from work, Bless would immediately list everything she'd done that day—from feedings, to tummy time, to cleaning spit-up from the floor—and say, "He's yours now." I enjoyed spending the time with Damien. What I didn't like was Bless keeping tabs on everything she did and everything I did and constantly claiming she was doing more. She was, granted. But she didn't have her events company then. She had many more free hours in her day than I did. It seemed she simply wanted a target, someone on whom she could dump all her frustrations. It got to a point where if I forgot to pick up orange juice on the way home from work, she would go nuclear. My business trips made everything worse. Bless got it into her head that I was making up the travel just to get away from the house, even though I was spending less time overseas than I had at any other point in my career.

On Blessica's thirty-fourth birthday, I took her to an Italian restaurant for dinner. Eating out had become a rare occurrence for us, despite the fact we had a live-in nanny to keep an eye on Damien in our absence. During the meal, it became painfully obvious we no longer knew what to say to each other. We were so accustomed to arguing we forgot how to be civil. We didn't speak in the car on the way home. I slept in the spare bedroom that night. In the morning, I slipped off to work without saying goodbye.

We both knew it was over.

I moved out a week later. Damien had been two and a half then. I missed him tremendously and made every effort to ensure my overseas business trips didn't fall on my visitation dates.

He seemed to grow so fast. Within months, he began to walk, talk, and develop a semblance of a personality. The first time he called me "Dadda" broke my heart.

Watching him develop over the following year and a half had made me not only incredibly proud but genuinely fulfilled in a way I had not previously believed possible.

And now he's gone, I thought with empty terror. *My boy. Never born. Never existed.*

I'm never going to see him again.

ΔΔΔ

By the time Okubo returned I'd composed myself for the most part. I was a dead emotional wasteland on the inside, but outwardly I was able to assume a sane face. It had crossed my mind to tell Okubo about the video call with Blessica, but I didn't think she would be thrilled to know that my wife still loved me in this dimension. More than that, I simply didn't think I'd be able to talk about Damien without cracking up.

Okubo set the groceries on the table and began listing off everything she withdrew from the plastic bag, as if to elicit my approval: soy sauce, miso paste, dashi stock powder, panko bread crumbs, soba noodles, shirataki noodles, umeboshi, yuzu juice, sencha green tea, bancha green tea...

"Eggs?" I asked, peeking over her shoulder into the nearly empty bag.

"There are already eggs in the refrigerator."

"Bacon?"

"Sorry."

While helping her put the food away, I said, "Thank you for letting me use your computer."

"Did you get through to your brothers?"

"Unfortunately, no."

"Your mother?

I shook my head. "I did not try her. We spoke yesterday."

Okubo turned to me, holding a jar of pickles in her hand. "She's living in Andorra, right? You told me your family is living in Andorra. So does that mean you're from Andorra too—in this world?"

"I believe so."

"Where's that version of you then? The one that was born in Andorra?"

"I have wondered about that," I told her. "My mother was not surprised when I explained to her I was in Japan, so perhaps the other me has the same job as I do, or a similar one. Perhaps he is here in Tokyo on business. Then again—who knows? He could be in...Alabama."

"Alabama? In the US?" Okubo looked amused. "Why Alabama?"

"It is far away. That was my point."

"Point taken." She pressed her lips together, thinking. "What if he's in *your* dimension? What if the two versions of you swapped places?"

"Cosmic foreign exchange students. Yes, maybe. Or maybe he poofed out of existence when I arrived."

Okubo's face dropped. "I hope not. That would be terrible."

"Why? You do not know him. You have never met him."

"But I know *you*," she said. "And you're *him*. Anyway, what was I getting at? Right. If the version of you in this world—"

"Can we give him a name? 'Version of you' is disturbing."

"How about Paul?"

I frowned. "Why Paul?"

"Paul McCartney."

"No, Paul is my brother's name. What about The Other?"

"That's a bit spooky, but your double, your call. So if The Other is from Andorra, then why not visit the Andorra embassy today? If you explained to them you lost all your identification, they would be able to reissue you a new passport"

"Trying to get rid of me already?"

"No! I'm just trying to help you. If you had a passport, you'd be one step closer to recreating your old identity."

"That would be nice, *chérie*," I said. "But remember I am in the country illegally. Even if the consular section issued me a new passport, they are not above the laws here. I could not remain under the aegis of their diplomatic powers. They would be compelled to hand me over to the police."

"So what are your long-term options, Gaston? Remain an illegal immigrant in Japan for the rest of your life?"

"No, I need to get back to Andorra."

"But that's impossible without a passport!"

"I am aware of the difficulty of the position I am in, *ma choupette*. I will think of something." Changing course on my earlier decision not to mention Blessica, I said, "I was able to contact my wife on your computer."

Surprise flashed in Okubo's eyes but all she said was, "Oh?"

"She is going to send me money today," I added. "I will not be a burden on you for much longer."

"You are not a *burden*, Gaston. I'm not trying to get rid of you. I promise. I like having you here."

"I appreciate that, though *I* feel like a burden."

"Did you leave anything behind at the *manga kissa*?"

"No, nothing. I do not have anything aside the clothes on my back." I shrugged. "I suppose I could stay one more night..."

"Don't sound so enthusiastic."

"I am sorry, *chérie*. I am confused. I feel like a pawn in a game far beyond my control. It is frightening and...yes...confusing. I am not myself."

Okubo chewed on that. "Where are you going to pick up the money?"

"A Western Union."

"What time?"

I shrugged. "After lunch?"

She put the jar of pickles away in the cupboard and returned to me for the plastic bottle of mayonnaise I was holding. She took it from my hand and said, "I think you should talk to someone, Gaston."

"A shrink?" Panic floored me. "You said you believed me—"

"I do believe you, Gaston! I don't mean a shrink. I mean someone who knows about space and interdimensional travel and all that stuff."

I relaxed. "Do you have someone in mind?" I asked her.

"As a matter of fact, I do. My brother."

"Your brother?" I repeated skeptically. "Is he a scientist?"

"No, but he is really, really smart."

Not only did Okubo's suggestion sound like a waste of time, I didn't know how comfortable I would be telling a complete stranger I was from another dimension. "I don't know..."

"What else are we going to do today, Gaston?"

"Western Union..."

"We'll go there this afternoon."

"Does your brother live nearby?"

"He lives in Tama Center about an hour from here."

"All right," I relented. "Give him a call."

"He doesn't have a phone."

I chuffed. "Who does not have a phone in 2020?"

"My brother. He's a little...different."

"What if we travel all the way there and he is not home?"

"He'll be home. Trust me."

"But how can you *know*?"

"Because he hasn't left his room in ten years."

CHAPTER 35

During the walk to Ebisu train station, and the quick three-stop ride to Shinjuku, Okubo explained that her brother was part of Japan's infamous world of the *hikikomori*, which she translated to mean "withdrawn." To qualify for such a dubious label, you had to have shuttered yourself away from society for at least a year. Most of these people were male, many lived at home with their parents, and there were up to a million of them hidden around the country.

After making our way through Shinjuku station, Okubo and I boarded the Keio New Line train. As we traveled west, we talked more about her brother's condition.

"Japan is a country of contradictions," Okubo explained. "It's both modern and traditional. The cities are bustling but also lonely. Restaurants and bars are always filled with customers, but if you look closely, most of them are eating by themselves. Customer service is impeccable, yet it's incredibly impersonal. A supermarket checkout cashier might perform her duties flawlessly, but she would never in a million years make small talk. We are fascinated by Western culture and Western people, but we are wary of them too. And in the streets, no matter the hour, you can find exhausted office employees who've worked themselves into the ground. The opposite, or balance, to this workaholic lifestyle..."

"Is the *hikikomori*," I said. "So these young men, instead of working, just sit around in their parents' house all day long doing nothing? Their parents should kick the lazy bums out to the street!"

"You don't understand, Gaston. They are not lazy. They suffer from a mental illness. They have profound social anxieties. Do they want to go out in the world and meet friends and lovers? Of course they do. But they simply can't." She fiddled with the zipper on her handbag. "When my brother was a teenager, he was like everyone else his age. But then he had a falling out with my parents. My father is a salesman at Hitachi. He wanted Akira—that is my brother's name—to find a similar job. But the last thing Akira wanted to be was one of corporate Japan's army of 'salarymen.'"

"What did he want to be instead?"

"A games artist—for video games. He is very artistic. He always has been. So when my father demanded he apply for a job at a large firm, he retreated into his room in protest."

"Why not just go out and apply for a job as a games artist? To hell what your father thought."

"Because that is not the Japanese way," Okubo said stiffly. "We have a collective-minded way of thinking. We don't rebel. At least not vocally. Rebellion comes in muted forms...like the *hikikomori*."

"I can understand that," I said, knowing just how dominant group-thought was from the interaction I'd had with my Japanese colleagues and clients. "But your brother has not rebelled in his room for a week or a month. You said he has been there for ten years!"

"As you probably know, Gaston, outward appearances and reputations mean everything to Japanese. We call it *sekentei*—the pressure a person feels to impress others. The longer a *hikikomori* remains secluded from society, the more shame he feels at his social failure. He loses whatever self-esteem and confidence he once had. His room becomes his only safe place. The prospect of leaving it becomes ever more terrifying." She shrugged. "It's a kind of vicious loop, right? The withdrawal from society becomes the source of the trauma, and the trauma prevents a *hikikomori* from returning to society, which in turn makes the trauma worse."

"*Oh la vache!*" I blurted as an alarming thought smacked me in the face. "Are we going to your *parents'* house?"

Okubo smiled at me. "You do not think they would like you?"

"No, I mean...I...look what I am wearing," I stammered. "And I do not have anything to bring them. And we have only been on one date—"

"Relax, Gaston!" Okubo said, patting me on the thigh. "We are not going to my parents' house. When they accepted that Akira was not going to leave his room or change his behavior any time soon, they bought him his own apartment."

"His own apartment?" I said. "So he lives alone...?"

"Why do you look so skeptical?"

"Because he is a *hikikomori*! He does not leave his house. Who does his grocery shopping? Does he order Uber eats every day?"

"*Uber?*" She gave me a blank look.

Uber had operated in Japan since 2018. I'd used their services countless times before. The fact Okubo didn't know about the company meant this was yet another inconsistency between this world and mine.

"It is a food delivery service," I said simply.

"Ah," Okubo said. "Like Zoom."

"Yes," I said, whatever Zoom was, though I figured it was this world's Uber equivalent.

"I don't know if Akira uses delivery services. He gets his food and anything else he needs from a woman my parents hired. We call her a rental sister, though I don't know if that is the best translation. She leaves food at his door, as well as a note, asking how he's doing and all that. Sometimes he replies with a note of his own, or if he needs something."

I pictured this transactional relationship and marveled at the absurdness of it. "Did your parents ever object to you becoming a flight attendant?"

"They didn't care what I did. In their view, it is the husband who is the breadwinner. They assumed my husband would take care of me, as they assumed Akira would take care of his wife.

That is why, as their only son, they piled all their hopes and dreams of success onto him."

"It must have been tough on you as a teenager with all this going on at home."

"It was not fun. I tried to stay out of the house with my friends as much as I could."

"I think I now understand your affection for the laid-back bear of the Hundred Acre Wood."

"Comfortably imperfect," she said.

"Words to live by," I said.

ΔΔΔ

Tama Center station was decorated top to bottom with Saniro characters. As Okubo and I exited we passed beneath a huge mural of Hello Kitty and Keroppi dressed as Keio Line station masters.

"Am I missing something?" I asked, perplexed.

"Yes—Sanrio Puroland is a short walk from here."

"Hello Kitty country," I grumbled, glad she didn't suggest detouring to the theme park.

Tama Center, I discovered, was home to large and blocky commercial and municipal buildings, though it was also a suburban area and a world apart from the hustle and bustle of downtown Tokyo. You still had shopping arcades and convenience stores and restaurants galore, but there was an abundance of greenery too, and everything just felt a lot more peaceful.

Okubo and I walked up a large set of stairs and through a heavily wooded park that would have been pleasant to picnic in under other circumstances. A few minutes later we came to an incongruous brown-brick apartment building. Okubo led me up the staircase to the second floor and knocked on a door with a Do Not Disturb sign in the style of a *noren* curtain hanging from the brass handle.

"Oniisan! Doa wo akete kudasai!" Okubo called, asking her brother to open the door.

I heard the sound of a deadbolt turning, a chain clattering free of its track. The door swung inward.

Given Okubo's brother had led a hermetically sealed life for the last ten years, I had imagined him as an anemic, Golem-like wretch. Yet the man who greeted us was clean cut with a healthy complexion. He was dressed in neat jeans and a fitted red turtleneck.

Seeing me, his almond-shaped eyes flashed wide with alarm.

He slammed the door shut.

Okubo knocked loudly, explaining that I was her friend and in trouble and needed his help.

"You have just alerted the whole building," I remarked.

"I keep forgetting how good your Japanese is," she said.

From the other side of the door: "*Shusshin wa doko desu ka?*"

Okubo said, "He's asking where—"

"Yes, I know." I raised my voice. "*Yōroppa desu.*"

"*Doko no kuni no hito?*"

Okubo said, "He wants to know which country in Europe—?"

I shook my head. I couldn't tell him Taured.

Okubo explained to her brother that my origin was a complicated matter, and it was why we had come to see him.

A few seconds passed before the door swung inward once more.

"Hello," Okubo's brother said, eyeing me curiously. "Come inside. Quickly."

CHAPTER 36

Akira closed the door behind us and engaged the deadbolt and chain. Looking around, I felt as though I had stepped into a self-storage unit rather than someone's living quarters. Floor-to-ceiling plastic containers holding who knew what towered everywhere, alongside endless stacks of cassettes, magazines, books, clothing, and more.

After a curt introduction, Akira led us down a narrow pathway through the clutter to a clearing in the center of the room that contained a glass desk and leather executive chair. On the desk stood three large flat-screen monitors, a custom-made computer chassis, two high-end laptops, as well as a scattering of electronic accessories: surround-sound speakers, a pair of noise-cancelling headphones, a mechanical keyboard, a mouse glowing with LED lights, an external hard drive bay, a USB hub, and some other stuff I didn't recognize.

In other words, a geek's paradise.

"Nice setup," I remarked.

"I spend most of my time here," Akira said in fluent English. "Did my sister tell you? I don't go outside much."

"*Ever*," Okubo amended.

There was no furniture to sit on, so the three of us remained standing around the desk.

"I panic when I interact with other people," Akira told me. "Not you, don't worry. I was surprised to see you on my doorstep, but that was all. You are fine."

"Why am I fine?" I asked.

"Because you're a foreigner," Okubo told me.

"Yes, foreigners I have little problems with," Akira said. "All my friends online are foreigners. American, Chinese, European, Australian—they do not judge me."

"That is why your English is so good," I said.

"Oh, thank you," he said, bowing. Then: "I haven't had a real guest in such a long time I have forgotten my manners! Just a moment."

Akira ducked into another room.

I eyed the random items piled high around me. "I feel like I am in a china shop. One wrong move..."

"And it all comes crashing down? I know how you feel."

Akira returned shortly carrying a tray with a Japanese teapot and three white mugs. He set the tray on the glass desk and filled the mugs with green tea.

"Thank you," I said, accepting a cup.

As we sipped without speaking, an awkward lull built, which Akira broke by saying, "May I ask what kind of trouble you are in, Gaston-san?"

I glanced at Okubo for guidance on how to broach the subject.

"Gaston is from an alternate dimension," she stated bluntly.

Akira's eyebrows shot upward.

I felt like slapping my forehead, but Akira did not laugh. He merely studied me with interest.

"Go on," Okubo said. "Tell him everything. That's why we're here."

I explained my story from beginning to end.

"Remarkable," Akira said simply when I'd finished.

"Do you doubt me?" I asked.

"Should I?"

"What I have said is true. Every word. I ask because I know how it sounds."

Akira sipped his tea thoughtfully. "Do you believe in the Big Bang theory, Gaston-san?"

I shrugged. "Sure."

"As do I. And if I can believe that all the matter in the cosmos

—trillions of stars and planets and so much else—was at one point an infinitesimal tiny singularity, then I can also believe in something as fantastic as interdimensional travel. Besides," he continued with a small shrug, "I have believed in the multiverse theory long before I met you. So although someone from a parallel universe showing up on my doorstep may be a surprise to me, the idea that other universes besides my own exist is not a surprise at all."

"See, I told you he'd believe you!" Okubo crowed triumphantly, punching me on the arm. "How many universes do you think are out there, *oniisan*?" she asked her brother.

Akira frowned in thought, and for the first time I noticed fine wrinkles at the corners of his eyes and lips. "A theory called inflation suggests that in the moment right after the Big Bang, space inflated rapidly before slowing down and creating the bubble in which the Earth, the Sun, the Milky Way galaxy, and billions of other galaxies reside today. If you accept this, there's no reason to think it was an isolated occurrence. Picture what happens when you pour Coca-Cola into a glass. Our universe may be just one of those bubbles in a cosmic fizz."

"So you're saying there could be *thousands* of other universes?" Okubo said.

"Thousands, millions, billions. Perhaps an infinite number. Another theory—one of the most popular today—comes from quantum physics. Proponents of it believe the universe splits in two each time there's a so-called quantum event. With such quantum events happening more or less continuously, the argument goes, the number of universes continues to increase ad infinitum."

"What's a quantum event?" Okubo asked.

"When something quantum happens," Akira answered.

"*Duh,*" she said.

"It's an event that is virtually impossible for the human mind to experience."

She rolled her eyes. "Can you try being less obtuse?"

"It's something that could not have happened according to

the laws of classical physics."

"For example?" I said.

"Classical physics describes the world in terms of definite outcomes. Think of Newton's laws of motion or gravity. Quantum mechanics, on the other hand, describes the world in terms of *probabilities*. Simply speaking, quantum mechanics argues that something can exist in many states at once. An electron, for example, can spin both upward and downward at the same time. However, when we observe the particle, we cause a quantum event to occur in which the particle adopts only one state at random. In the example I gave, it would be either spinning up or down, not both."

"Because it *knew* we were watching it?" Okubo said skeptically. "It's just a cute little electron!"

"I'm not saying it has a consciousness or awareness," Akira said. "We simply don't have the technology that would allow us to observe the state of the electron passively. The measuring equipment we use has an active physical effect on it."

I said, "So in any given situation, every possible outcome can occur at the same time?"

"Not can," Akira said. "Does. Each in its own separate universe."

"And this applies not only to subatomic particles but everything?"

"Everything."

"You mean like us too?" Okubo said. "So right now I can kiss Gaston. But if I don't, there's a universe in which I kissed him?"

Akira nodded. "The present universe gives rise to two daughter universes: one in which you kiss Gaston-san, and one in which you don't."

"And I'm stuck in the one in which I don't..." she said gloomily.

"Unless you *did* kiss me," I said. "Then you would be in the other one, the happier one."

She squeezed her eyes shut and shook her head. "This is too confusing! I want to be in the universe where I understand all this!"

Akira said, "Imagine your reality as a straight line and your alternate realities as branching lines that continue branching off of themselves."

She opened her eyes. "So you're saying right now there's another version of *me* out...there...somewhere?"

"No, Okubo, in these parallel universes, there could be *infinite* versions of you."

"The parallel universes would not all be identical to one another, would they?" I asked.

"Some would be," Akira replied. "Some would differ by a single particle's position. And some would be very different. In one universe, you might have gone to a bar with some friends and got so drunk you didn't remember how you got home, whereas in another you only had one drink, danced and mingled, and met your future wife."

Or you and your wife fall asleep one night in front of the TV instead of having sex, I thought abruptly and darkly, *and your son is never born...*

"So there's a universe right now in which I won the lottery?" Okubo asked hopefully.

"And one in which I'm not a *hikikomori*," Akira said gravely.

"One in which we're here having this exact conversation?" Okubo said.

"And one in which we are *not* here," Akira said, "because in it you never met Gaston-san."

"That would be *awful*!"

Blinking aside thoughts of Damien, I gave her a smile.

"As I mentioned," Akira said, "every possible outcome can and does occur at the same time. At every branch point, a new universe is created."

"Into infinity," I said, rejoining the conversation.

"If space-time is flat and continues forever, then, yes, into infinity. Hence the infinite universes and the infinite versions of you."

"Which means..." I said, trying to wrap my head around the

mind-bending science, "we have just had this conversation an infinite number of times."

CHAPTER 37

Akira refilled our mugs with tea.

"So is the name of your country—Taured—the only anomaly in this universe, Gaston?" Okubo asked me. "Or is there other stuff you've noticed?"

I hesitated a beat before saying, "When I was speaking with my mother yesterday, she spoke to my father in the background."

Okubo frowned. "So?"

"My father died when I was twenty-four."

"What! Oh, Gaston, I'm—I'm so sorry. I'm..." She lowered her eyes before raising them almost immediately. "But—well, that's exciting, isn't it? Because he's *alive* here!"

"Exciting?" I shook my head. "I would not use that word. I never got along with him. He was not a good person. I doubt he is any different in this world."

"I can relate to how you feel," Akira said sadly. "My father and I—"

"Today is not about you, *oniisan*," Okubo interrupted. To me, "Even if you never got along with your father, Gaston, I still think this is a great opportunity for you. *Your father is alive.* Maybe you can make up with him, or maybe you could—"

"I want nothing to do with him!" I snapped. Seeing the hurt on her face, I added more gently: "I do not want to speak with him, *chérie*. Not right now."

Okubo nodded. "I'm sorry. I understand."

Akira asked, "Are there other differences between your

world and this one, Gaston-san?"

"Some," I said without elaborating.

"Is John Lennon alive in your universe?" Okubo asked.

"No."

"Were atomic bombs dropped on Hiroshima and Nagasaki?" Akira asked.

"Yes."

"Did September 11—"

"We should stay on topic," I said brusquely. "For the most part, everything in this world seems the same as it is in my world." *Except your son was never born, Gaston. That's a biggie. That's one hell of a biggie.*

I asked Akira, "Have you ever heard of a case such as mine?"

"Someone phasing between universes?"

He nodded. "It happens all the time."

ΔΔΔ

Okubo and I reacted with exclamations of surprise and demands for him to elaborate.

"A simple Google search for 'multiverse portals' will bring up countless websites and blogs and forums documenting first-hand accounts from interdimensional travelers. It is a subject of great interest these days, especially to those into religion and mysticism. Because if infinite copies of this universe exist, then it's hard to make the argument that your life is singular and fleeting."

"Immortality," I stated.

"An alluring concept, certainly."

"Unless you hate your life," Okubo said.

"You are forgetting," I told her, "that there would be a universe in which you loved your life."

She squeezed her eyes shut again. "Brain freeze!"

"Regarding the international travelers," Akira said, "London has gained a reputation as the Grand Central Station—or the Clapham Junction, I should say—of interdimensional travel.

Portals are popping up all over town there. But they've popped up all over the world. Let me show you." He sat down in the leather chair. "I'm sorry, I don't have much furniture..."

Okubo and I moved behind him to see the monitors.

Akira clicked open a browser. His fingers flew over the keyboard. A few more clicks of the mouse and a page titled "Green Children of Woolpit" appeared. According to the story, in the twelfth century the villagers of Woolpit, in Suffolk, England, discovered two children, a brother and sister, in one of the many wolf pits that gave the village its name. Both had greenish-colored skin, spoke an unknown language, wore odd clothing, and initially refused to eat any food other than raw broad beans. The boy became sick and died, but the girl survived and integrated into the village. After learning to speak English, she explained that she and her brother were from a place where it was perpetually twilight. They had been herding their father's cattle when they heard a loud noise, and the next thing they knew they were in the wolf pit where they were found.

The webmaster went on to dismiss any historical explanations for the tale and argued that the children had come from a parallel dimension.

"You don't have green blood or anything do you?" Okubo asked me.

"Of course I do," I replied. "What color is yours?" To Akira, "That is an interesting story. But the twelfth century was a long time ago. Can you search for something more recent?"

Akira navigated to a different website. He scrolled through several articles, allowing us glimpses of haunting and otherworldly drawings, then returned to the first one. It concerned a woman named Carol Chase McElheney. While driving from San Bernardino to Perris, (both in California), she detoured to Riverside, her hometown, which she hadn't been back to in decades. Upon reaching the street she'd grown up on, she couldn't find her house, and all of the other homes were smaller and more rundown than she remembered. She drove to the street her grandmother used to live on. It too was different than she remembered. Frightened and confused, she went to the cemetery where her grandparents were buried—only it wasn't a cemetery but a fenced-off lot overgrown with weeds.

Years later, when Carol Chase McElheney's father died, he was to be buried in the same cemetery as her grandparents. When she arrived for the funeral, the empty lot she had expected to find was in fact a cemetery filled with graves dating back more than a century.

"That's creepy," Okubo said. "An ill-fated version of her hometown."

"What is the next article?" I asked, intrigued.

It concerned another woman, Lerina Garcia, who upon waking one morning noticed that her sheets were unfamiliar, and the pajamas she wore were not the ones she'd gone to bed in. Later that morning, when she arrived at her office building, she learned she worked in a different department under a boss she'd never met. And when she returned home that afternoon, her ex-boyfriend was in the living room—only he wasn't her ex but her current boyfriend. She was unable to reach the man she'd been dating for the last few months.

"*Mon Dieu*," I said.

"There are many more stories online," Akira said. "One website called *Mysterious Universe* is particularly good..." He began typing.

"No, it is okay," I said. "We do not need to read any more about these people. The important thing is that their stories exist. Can you explain the interdimensional portals you mentioned?"

Akira nodded. "Traditional thinking used to be that if there were parallel universes, they were vast distances apart, so vast we could never know of them let alone visit them."

"But...?" I said, expecting one coming.

"String theorists suggest something entirely different, namely that our—or *my*—universe might be located on a brane embedded in a higher-dimensional bulk."

"You're geek-talking again, *oniisan*," Okubo said.

"Their model of space," he explained, "has more than the usual four dimensions—three of space, one of time. It has extra dimensions. They are called the bulk."

"A kind of super-space," I suggested.

"Yes. Another name for it, in fact, is hyperspace. In any event, our visible universe is called a brane, short for membrane, because it's a kind of four-dimensional sheet. This brane is embedded in the extra dimensions of the bulk."

"I still don't get it..." Okubo complained.

"It might be easier to think of everything in two and three dimensions then," Akira said. "Imagine you are a two-dimensional being. You're flat, like a square. You live in a flat, two-dimensional universe."

"Like a piece of paper?"

Akira nodded. "This piece of paper is the brane. And it, along with many other branes, exist in three-dimensional space called the bulk."

"Why can't we detect the bulk?" I asked.

"Because physics as we know it is trapped on the two-dimensional brane. All the particles we know of—protons, neutrons, neutrinos, photons, electrons—are trapped on the brane. If light rays can only travel along the surface of the brane, they cannot illuminate any of the particles in the bulk—those off the surface of the piece of paper—and thus it is invisible to our eyes." Akira held up a finger. "Now here's where it gets interesting. It seems gravity, carried by gravitons, *can* escape into the bulk. This theory not only accounts for why gravity is so weak compared to other forces of nature like magnetism—its strength along the brane gets diluted by leaking away into the extra dimensions—but it also accounts for dark matter, that mysterious 'stuff' in our universe that nobody can seem to explain. String theorists suggest dark matter could be the gravitational shadow of matter in other branes like ours lying extremely close together in the bulk. Although we could never see the matter in these other branes, their gravitational pull would affect our visible matter, just as dark matter does."

"You're saying there are other universes right on top of ours?" Okubo said in disbelief.

Akira nodded again. "Stacked like pages in a book. Perhaps an infinite number."

"But we are not aware of them?" I said.

"Not stuck as we are in our three dimensions."

"How close are they to ours?" I asked.

"A distance vastly smaller than the size of an atomic nucleus."

"Impossible!" Okubo said.

"Not in a fifth dimension," Akira said. "Now this is my point with portals. Given how microscopic the distance is between branes, if our brane were to come into contact with another brane, an interdimensional portal could be a consequence of that interaction."

"Through which matter could be transferred," I said, understanding. "Matter like me..."

"Theoretically," Akira said, "it's a possibility."

"And how would one go about opening up another portal to get back to their brane?"

"They would most likely need to create a black hole—a very large black hole."

"Why not a small one?" Okubo asked.

"Because the intense gravity of a small black hole creates tidal forces at its event horizon that would squish you into something far finer than jelly. But if the black hole is large enough, and spinning quickly enough, you might barely notice passing through the event horizon."

"Got any super big black holes laying around?" I remarked.

"It is not very encouraging, I admit."

I sighed, which came out part groan. I had never expected Akira to have some magical *deus ex machina* to send me home, but the fact the only solution he could offer was a near impossibility was more than a little depressing.

Okubo rubbed my shoulder affectionately.

"Guess I will not be leaving anytime soon," I told her.

"I could think of worse things," she said, snuggling against me.

"Before you two start making out," Akira said, "let me tell you there remains one feasible option."

I perked up. "I am all ears," I said.

"You can wait," he said simply.

"Wait?" Okubo said.

Akira shrugged. "Nature has a way of righting her mistakes. And from what I've read, these people who find themselves trapped in a different reality often end up back in their own in due time."

"Like the woman with the rundown hometown," Okubo said. "At some point it returned back to normal. Or *she* returned back to where she was supposed to be."

"Yes, but how long was she in the other reality for?" I asked. "One hour? One year? Ten years? How long would I have to... wait?"

"I have no idea," Akira said. "But it seems most interdimensional travelers only make brief layovers in other realities rather than becoming permanent residents of them. Another example is a young American girl who vanished from her bedroom in 1960. Her parents thought she'd been kidnapped, but the police found no signs of forced entry or a struggle. A massive search party was organized but zero leads were found. Then hours later, in the middle of the night, the girl's parents discovered their daughter sleeping peacefully in her bed."

"Where did she say she had been?" I asked.

"She insisted she hadn't gone anywhere. Nobody took her. She'd been sleeping in her bed the entire time."

"Maybe she was lying," Okubo said. "Maybe she ran away?"

"And eluded the search party before slipping back into bed with no signs of being outside, no signs of exertion or distress?"

I said, "I guess I can only cross my fingers and hope I wake up in my own bed tomorrow morning."

Okubo folded her arms across her chest. "You wouldn't miss me at all?"

"Of course I would. But my life is not here, *ma choupette*. It is *there*."

"And if you don't wake up in your own bed tomorrow morning? If you end up stuck in this reality forever?"

"I am not ready to start contemplating that quite yet."

CHAPTER 38

Walking back to Tama Center Station, I said, "Your brother really knows his stuff."

"What else is there to do but read when you never leave your house?"

"An infinite number of universes..." I mused.

"An infinite number of Okubos..." she said.

"What do you think about that?"

"I guess it would improve my odds of meeting a nice guy for once." She missed a step. "Oh—I didn't mean it like *that*. You're great. I wasn't talking about *you*."

I smiled. "Do not worry, *ma choupette*. I understand. I have not made the best first impression. I should have kept the Mork from Ork story until at least the third date."

"You've made a first impression I will never forget." Her tone turned solemn. "And I do believe you, Gaston. Everything you've told me."

I kept the smile in place, but it had become forced, because once again I was questioning whether she did believe me. Maybe she had last night. But everything seems a little more possible when you're stoned. In the cold light of sobriety—that's another story. Because having to reassure someone you believe them is a little like insisting the weather's fine while in the eye of a hurricane.

"What has been the problem with the men you have dated?" I asked her.

"They've just been...bad. Take the last one, for example." She shuddered. "Total creep. He was a lot older than me. I don't usually date older men, but he was very charming—at first."

"Where did you meet him?"

"Manila. During a layover there. A flight attendant I work with heard about a new casino/resort that had just opened. A bunch of flight attendants went. We got into the VIP section. One thing led to another and we ended up at a penthouse party. That's where I met Shigeharu."

"He was Japanese?"

She nodded. "And apparently a big investor in the casino. Anyway, like I said, he was charming at first. And, you know... things happened..."

"You stayed the night?" I asked.

"I'm not a virgin, Gaston," she said.

"I know that from firsthand experience..."

"And I don't usually do...*that*...on first dates. You and Shigeharu were exceptions."

"So when did Prince Charming lose his luster?"

"After a couple of weeks. He was so mysterious, and not in a good way. He would never talk about himself, never open up. I actually think he might have been married."

"There is a winner."

"You're married."

"Not by choice."

"Anyway, I don't know whether he was married for certain, but he was always excusing himself to make phone calls. And he was living out of the Ritz-Carlton in Akasaka. He told me he lived outside Tokyo. When he was in the city for business he stayed at the hotel."

"Not unreasonable."

"Maybe no. But then after three or so weeks of dating he began to get *really* strange. Buying me clothes and jewelry and insisting I wear them when we went out. Instructing me how to do my hair and makeup. Calling me all the time while I was in a different country for work, asking who I was with and what I was doing."

"Sounds like *Single White Female* but in gender reverse."

"Yeah, he became totally obsessive."

"What did you do?"

"I ended it."

"I cannot imagine he took that well?"

"He never replied to my message. I guess I didn't really mean as much to him as I thought I did."

"You broke up with him via text message?"

"It's not like I knew him that well."

"And you never heard from him again?"

"No, thank God. But now you can see just what kind of guys I seem to attract."

"I can assure you, *chérie*," I said, "that although I might appear to have some issues right now, I am not a creep."

"I know you're not a creep, Gaston," she said affectionately, taking my hand in hers and kissing me on the cheek. "Which, by the way, is why I think I'm falling for you."

CHAPTER 39

From Shibuya station, we walked to a nearby Western Union. I wasn't sure whether Blessica would have sent the money after I'd hung up on her, but it turned out she did, and once I answered the security question with the passphrase, I received a whopping 500,000 yen. Having experienced the vulnerability and desperation that came with not having a penny to one's name, having cash in my pocket made me feel privileged and empowered and, most importantly, in control of my destiny once more.

Back in Okubo's apartment, she told me she was a member at a gym a few blocks away, was overdue for a workout, and asked if I wanted to accompany her. I declined, pointing out that I didn't have adequate attire.

"Why don't we go shopping then?" she suggested. "You have plenty of money now."

"I think I should save it for necessities, *chérie*," I replied. "Would you mind if I use your computer again while you are gone?"

"It's all yours."

While she disappeared into her room to change, I booted up her Macbook at the kitchen table. She returned in black tights, a fluorescent pink top, and white Nike runners. She filled a plastic drink bottle with water at the sink, then kissed me.

"Are you staying the night?" she asked.

"If you would like me to," I said.

"Maybe we could do something fun like order pizza and watch a movie?"

"No sci-fi multiverse stuff."

"What about a romantic comedy? Or are you too manly for that?"

"I am perfectly in touch with my feminine side."

"Think of a funny one then. I'll see you in a bit."

Once she left, I logged into my new Facebook account and discovered I had two new messages, one from Blessica, demanding to know why I'd hung up on her, and one from my older brother, Paul, who told me to call him.

I did just that.

"Gaston!" he said, answering the video call promptly. "Long time, *mon pote*. A moment."

I caught a glimpse of an intimidating knife, a hunk of meat, white walls. I heard the clank of a door, then saw bright light, which resolved into a nearly empty parking lot. The phone's camera refocused on my brother's bearded face. Thick eyebrows shaded steely gray eyes that belied his avuncular nature. He lit up a cigarette and blew smoke. "Beautiful morning."

"What time is it there?" I asked. "I did not mean to disturb you at the shop."

"Almost eight," he said. "Shit, look at that eye, *mon pote*! Don't bullshit me. You were in a fight, weren't you?"

"A minor one," I said.

"Remember that time I gave you a black eye? We were kids at the cabin. We were fighting and you got me on my back and I kicked you right in the eye. I've never heard someone howl so loud. Didn't sound human."

"It hurt."

"Whole thing swelled shut. I felt real bad." He took another drag. "Anyway, mom says you're in Japan?"

"Yes. How is...Andorra?"

Paul laughed. "You sound like you don't even remember what the place is called! You know about mom's cancer, right?"

"Skin cancer?"

"She had to go back to get it all out. They say she should be good now."

"And...dad?"

"Grumpy as ever. Still treating everyone like shit. But I think he's finally going to take mom around Europe. Think her cancer made him start thinking about their mortality. Mom's not going to be around forever, and he isn't either. It will be good for them, traveling."

I wanted to ask whether my father was still a police officer, whether he had ever shot a man, whether he had served time in prison or had been acquitted in court. But I couldn't ask any of these questions, I realized, not without sounding like a mental patient.

Besides, I suppose none of it mattered to me. Not right then anyway.

"When was the last time you were back?" Paul asked, taking another drag. "You should visit again."

"I would like to," I said. "You are well?"

"Well? Sure. Thinking about selling the business..."

"Selling it! But you have put so much work into it. I thought you liked—"

"Being a butcher? It's honest work, and it pays the bills. But, you know, being a butcher isn't like being a painter. You don't have a passion for it. At least, I hope you don't have a passion for chopping up animals all day long." Another drag. "I'm ready for something new, that's all."

"What are you going to do?"

"No idea. Take some time off first. Do some traveling. Might finally come to Manila to see you and Blessica. About time I meet her."

I frowned. Paul had been at our wedding in Boracay. He'd gotten that godawful rubber duck tattoo on his back! "You have never met her...?"

"You've never brought her home, *mon pote*."

"I know... But the wedding...?"

"What wedding?"

"My wedding!"

"*What*?" Paul blurted. "You *eloped*, you bastard! When?"

"I—" I was tongue-tied. *I'd never married Blessica here?* "I'm kidding," I added lamely.

"Kidding?" Paul chuffed. "You gotta work on your delivery. You think you're ever *going* to marry her?"

"Get back to work, Paul," I said, wanting to end the call.

He flicked away his smoke. "Back to dismembering Porky Pigs and Daffy Ducks. Will be nice to meet Blessica in person. Take it easy, *mon pote*. Take care of that eye."

ΔΔΔ

I'd never married Blessica.

Unlike Damien's non-birth, which remained a fatal wound to my heart—and which I was only dealing with by *not* dealing with it—this revelation barely fazed me.

I contemplated video calling Bless, but she would more than likely insist again that I show her Okubo's apartment, and a closetful of women's clothes would be hard to explain. Instead I sent her a quick message, thanking her for the money and promising to get in touch soon.

I was about to close the page but hesitated, nagged by a feeling there was someone else I should get in touch with...

ΔΔΔ

The possibility of contacting Miley "Smiley" Laffont—the possibility she might be *alive* in this world—sent such a shockwave through me so inclusive that for a moment I couldn't move or think.

Nevertheless, my reasoning was simple and valid:

If my father could be alive in this dimension, then so could Smiley.

I typed "Miley Laffont + Andorra" into Facebook's search bar and pressed Enter.

When I received no matches, it struck me that Smiley could be, and likely was, married. I dropped her surname and performed a second search.

No luck.

With my initial burst of hope fading quickly, I performed a final, broad search for the name "Miley Laffont" with no additional keywords.

I began scrolling through the results one by one.

I knew it was her without delay. She had the same blonde hair and sparkling blue eyes and namesake smile that I remembered so well—yet she was different too. There was a maturity to her features, a hardness forged by the natural process of battling life and growing old.

But it was definitely my Smiley, of this I was certain.

I sent her a message:

Hello Smiley,

I deleted the salutation, unsure whether she still went by the playful sobriquet, and started over:

Hello ma chérie,

Although this is a new Facebook account I am contacting you from, it is the same old me. Your profile says you are in Paris now? How exciting! In any event, I wanted to let you know of my new account in the event we could catch up. I'd love to hear how you are doing. Time passes too quickly.

Warmest regards,
Gaston

I read over the message several times before sending it. I didn't know whether the me in this reality already knew Smiley was in Paris or not, but I could not help that detail. If she replied, and questioned my memory, I would simply plead ignorance. What mattered was getting in touch.

I stood, feeling sharply buzzed, as though I had just drained a tot of good whisky.

Smiley was alive and well!

With a silly grin on my face, I capered across the room to the refrigerator. I withdrew the bottle of blanc de blancs from the previous night and poured myself a glass. Back at the computer I played some music on YouTube, sipped the bubbly, and refreshed Facebook constantly in the hope of receiving a reply from Smiley.

It wasn't until some fifteen minutes later, while I was singing along to A-ha's "Take On Me" and reading the penumbra of theory on brane cosmology, when a notification alerted me that I had received a new message.

I clicked it.

Gaston! I am so surprised to hear from you! Are you around right now? Can you talk?

I drained the little champagne left in my glass, turned off the music, and commenced a video call.

Smiley's face filled my screen, her brow drawn in concentration. I suspected she couldn't see me as I could her.

"Miley?" I said. "Can you hear me?"

Her eyes flashed to the camera, though there was no sign of recognition in them. "Gaston? I can hear you, but I can't see you."

For a moment I was lost in the green-blue depths of her eyes. I had seen them in my dreams for the last twenty years. They had always both warmed me with remembrance and chilled me with loss. Now seeing them for real was overwhelming.

"Gaston?"

"Yes, I am here. I can see you—"

"Oh! There you are!" Her brilliant smile lit up her face—then faltered. "Gaston, your eye!"

"Ah," I said, my hand automatically going to the still-tender bruise. "I am fine. Do not worry."

"It looks like it *hurts*."

"I am fine. You look wonderful."

Her smile returned. "So do *you*. Well, aside from the black eye."

We both laughed.

"*Mon Dieu*, Gaston," she said. "It is so nice to see you. This is so random! When was the last time we talked?"

"I cannot remember for sure," I said. "It must be..." I trailed off, hoping she'd finish.

"Ten years? It must be ten. At least." She shook her head. "Whatever happened with us?"

"Ten years..." I repeated, making sense of this. "That was about the time I moved to Manila..."

"I know. You were so excited. Everything must be going well there?"

"We should have stayed in touch."

"Yes, we should have. But marriage, a daughter..." She shrugged her delicate shoulders. "You can't stay young forever, unfortunately."

Marriage. I smiled, though no phonier smile had ever graced my lips. "You kept your maiden name?"

"No, but I took it back after the divorce. Oh—you wouldn't know, would you? My husband and I agreed to a divorce last year." She shrugged again. "People change, I guess."

"I am sorry," I said, doing my best to keep the smile from turning genuine.

Smiley was not only alive, but she was single!

"You are in Paris?" I said.

"My husband was from here. We moved four years ago. Esmée, my daughter, was born a year after that. I'd like to move back to Andorra, but joint custody...it makes for a logistical problem."

"Your daughter is three?" I asked.

"Yes, three. Where is she? Let me introduce you." Smiley looked away from the camera and called her daughter's name. "She's downstairs. I'm not sure if she heard me. What about you, Gaston? Are you married?"

"I—no, I am not," I replied, stymied by which reality to reference.

"I should have expected as much. You were always such a ladies' man! You could never stay with just one woman."

"Hardly!" I countered. "I dated Cecile all throughout university."

Smiley frowned. "Cecile? Who's Cecile? And if you dated her all throughout university, you kept her well-hidden!"

"I guess I did," I agreed in order not to tangle up realities. "In fact, we were somewhat on-and-off."

"That sounds more like the Gaston I knew!" She smiled wistfully. "Hey, do you remember the bet we made when we were younger? We said if we were both single when we were forty, we would marry each other."

"Yes, I do remember that! Forty seemed so far away then."

"I know! And now I'm forty-two…"

"Going on forty-three."

"Thanks."

"I am too."

"Two years overdue…"

"Move to the Philippines," I said lightly. "We can get married there and buy a little house on a beach."

"A beach on an island?"

"At the end of a private road. No neighbors or noise."

"Just the beach and the ocean. That sounds lovely, Gaston."

"But you would have to learn to drive a scooter."

"Would I?"

"Everybody on tropical islands drives scooters."

"I don't know," she said, biting her lip. "Those roads are so twisty-turny, aren't they? I think I'd be too afraid… Oh, look who's here!" Smiley left the camera's field of view, returning a moment later holding a little girl with bouncy gold curls and a smile to rival her mother's. "This is my precious Esmée!"

"Hello, Esmée!" I said, waving. "You are adorable!"

"Say hello, *ma puce*. This is my old friend, Gaston Green."

"I like green," Esmée said, hooking the corner of her mouth

with a finger. "My teddy bear is green."

"Where is Mr. Teddy from?" Smiley asked her daughter.

"The Lost Forest," the girl said. "Everything is green there."

"Sounds like a magical place," I said.

"Are you coming to visit us?" she asked me.

"Visit?" I said, caught off guard. "I would like to, but I am a very far way away right now."

"He's in Manila, *mon ange*. That's on the other side of the world."

I saw no point in correcting her that I was in Japan.

"You can take an airplane here, can't you?" Esmée said. "You can be our friend and I can show you the Lost Forest and you can make my mommy happy again."

"*Ma puce!*" Smiley said. Appearing flustered, she added, "What have I told you about keeping our private talks private?"

"I'm hungry, Mommy."

"I know, it's breakfast time, isn't it?" To me Smiley said, "And so the day begins... What time is it there now?"

"Afternoon," I said. "I should start thinking about supper myself."

"It's been good talking to you, Gaston. Thank you for getting in touch."

"It has been good talking to you...Smiley. Can I still call you that?"

"Of course you can!" She laughed. "I haven't heard it in years. But I like it. I miss it."

"Mommy..."

"Yes, I know. Can you say goodbye to Gaston?"

"Goodbye, Gaston," she said shyly.

"Goodbye, Esmée."

"Bye, Gaston, take care."

I raised a hand in farewell. Smiley clicked off, and the video window closed.

I sagged back in my chair, unsure if I wanted to laugh or cry.

CHAPTER 40

I remained sitting in that chair for a very long time. I thought of Smiley and the night she died on the mountain. I thought of the woman she was now, middle-aged, with a young daughter. I thought of the paradox that she could be both dead and alive at the same time, and what this meant about mortality, and life in general...and then when I felt my head begin to ache from sparring with the impossible, or what I'd always believed to be the impossible, I went to the fridge and poured myself the last of the blanc de blancs.

Goblet in hand, I ventured onto the small balcony. It was late afternoon, the city air warm and humid, the red sun swelling. A hornet half the size of my thumb lit on the armrest of one of the chairs before I swatted it away. I did not want to add anaphylactic shock to my list of grievances.

Elbows resting on the top of the concrete parapet, I noticed a man in a tight white suit on the sidewalk across from Okubo's building.

He seemed to be looking directly at me.

Sticking a cell phone to his ear, he began walking leisurely down the street.

I watched him until he reached the corner, where he turned around and wandered back the way he'd come, toward his original spot, still talking.

Deriding myself for being paranoid, I went back inside.

ΔΔΔ

Okubo returned from the gym thirty minutes later. By the time she had showered and changed back into her muumuu and slippers, it was a little past five p.m.

"I must confess I finished all the champagne," I said guiltily.

"Good thing I keep a secret stash then," she said, squatting before a cupboard beneath the counter. She transferred a bucket filled with cleaning supplies to the floor, along with another bucket overflowing with scrunched-up plastic bags, before saying "Ah-ha!" and fishing out two bottles of red wine. She set them on the counter and put away the buckets.

I studied the labels. An Australian shiraz and a French merlot.

"Preference?" I asked.

"None," she said.

I opened the shiraz and filled two glasses.

"*Kampai*," she said, holding hers high. "To movie night!"

I clinked. "*Kampai*. Did you think of a movie to watch?"

"No, *you* were supposed to do that."

"*Roxanne*?" I offered.

"Isn't that really old?"

"It is a classic."

"Is it on Netflix?"

"I have no idea."

"It has to be on Netflix."

"Maybe we should browse Netflix then?"

"You're a genius. But I want a cigarette first."

We went out to the balcony. I glanced over the parapet to the street—and was stunned to see the same man in the tight white suit down there.

"*Merde!*" I said. "Do you recognize that man?"

Okubo came next to me. "No," she said. "Is he looking at us?"

"He was down there earlier," I told her, "doing the exact same thing."

"*Chotto!*" she called loudly, getting his attention. "*Sokono kimi nani shiteruno?*" she added, asking him what he was doing.

The man continued to stare up at us.

"What a weirdo..." she mumbled.

I agreed with this sentiment, only I didn't think he was merely an innocuous weirdo; in fact, I was thinking uneasily about the characters Will Smith and Tommy Lee Jones played in *Men in Black*.

"You sure you do not know him?" I asked.

"One hundred percent never met him," she replied, lighting her cigarette.

Finally the man looked away from us and began using his phone once again.

"I do not like this," I said. "It is too coincidental."

"You think he's here for *you*? He doesn't look like a police officer."

"Have you seen *Men in Black*?"

Okubo laughed, although it was tentative rather than carefree. "You think he's a *secret government agent*? What's his mission? To round up intergalactic travelers who come to Japan illegally?"

The idea sounded absurd when spoken out loud, but it was nevertheless exactly what I was contemplating.

"I am going to go talk to him," I stated.

"*What?*" Okubo stabbed out her cigarette in the ashtray. "No way! What if he attacks you or something?"

"*What if he knows something about why I am here?*" I took a heavy breath. "I know that sounds crazy. But what else is he doing staring up at me?"

We both glanced over the parapet at the man again.

His back was to us now, his phone still pressed to his ear.

"Fine," Okubo relented. "Go down. But I'm coming too."

CHAPTER 41

The man in the tight white suit was right where he'd been, on the far sidewalk, on his phone.

I marched over to him. "Hey?" I said, not bothering with Japanese. "Hey?"

He swiveled on his heels to face me. Beneath a stylish shag dyed orange-blonde was an angled face defined by a svelte nose and prominent cheekbones. A comma-shaped scar to the left of his chin marred an otherwise smooth complexion. I could read nothing in his dark eyes.

"Do you know me?" I demanded.

The man said something quietly into his phone, then tucked it away in his inside blazer pocket. He looked me up and down with panache but didn't say anything.

Okubo repeated my question in Japanese.

The man remained mute.

I stepped up to him, my hands balling into fists at my sides. Although he appeared agile and fit, I was half a head taller and maybe twenty kilograms heavier. He lifted his chin, clearly posturing.

Okubo asked him why he wouldn't speak.

Ignoring her, he said to me, "What is your name?"

I blinked in surprise, partly because he had spoken, partly because the question was in English, but mostly because he didn't appear to know who I was after all.

"My name is Gaston Green," I told him. "What is your name?"

"That doesn't concern you."

"Why are you watching me?"

"That doesn't concern you."

"I think it *does* concern me."

The man tugged back the left sleeve of his blazer to read the time on a silver Bulgari.

"Some place to be?" I asked, annoyed at his nonchalance.

He looked down the street to the right of us. As if on cue, a blacked-out Toyota van rounded the corner and cruised toward us.

Okubo took my hand in hers. "Gaston," she said stiffly, "we need to *go*."

"You go!" I told her, tugging my hand free. "Get inside! Now!"

"Come with me! You don't know who these people are!"

"I need to find out!"

"Gaston!"

I brushed past the man in the tight white suit and marched in the direction of the approaching van. Okubo shouted after me. I ignored her. The vehicle lurched to a stop. The side door slid open and two men in gray suits jumped out.

Before I knew what was happening, they had me by the arms and were shoving me into the backseat of the van. They piled in after me and slammed the door shut.

Tighty-Whitey hopped in shotgun, and as the van squealed away from the curb, I glimpsed Okubo out the back window, waving her arms and running after us in vain.

PART IV

Yamanashi Prefecture

CHAPTER 42

We pulled onto an expressway and sped west along overpasses and through tunnels. The driver recklessly took the many sharp curves and multi-lane merges while aggressively weaving in and out of the traffic. All I could see of him was the back of his shaved head and a ruby earring. The two men in the middle row of seats appeared to be twins, both sporting goatees and long black hair tied into loose man-buns.

Eventually I broke the silence and said, "Where are you taking me?"

I didn't expect an answer and was surprised when Tighty-Whitey called back: "To see someone."

"Who?" I demanded.

"You will find out."

"Why not tell me?"

He didn't answer, and I was too unnerved to press him.

Gradually the large gray office buildings adorned with illuminated advertising boards dwindled and were replaced by low-rise apartment blocks and houses. As the sun dipped to the horizon, twilight crept out of hiding, spreading a darkness over the semi-rural landscape. The thought crossed my mind that I was being taken to a remote spot in the woods where I'd be forced to dig my own grave before being shot in the back of the head and buried. Yet I didn't really believe it, for I knew no reason why these men would want me dead...and even if they did, there were many less time-consuming and labor-intensive ways to kill someone.

Roughly an hour and a half after I'd been abducted, the Toyota van left the expressway, passing through a toll gate and turning right onto a smaller highway. According to road signs, we were in Yamanashi Prefecture, home to the iconic Mt. Fuji. We drove through a sprawling town, left the highway, and ended up parking before a small commercial complex with several buildings.

Everyone exited the vehicle. The night air was cool and fresh, carrying the sweet scent of pines. Stars never visible above Tokyo filled the black sky. The cars parked nearby were an eclectic mix of luxury European brands and American V-8s which, in the land of four-cylinder econoboxes, were a rare sight.

Tighty-Whitey asked me, "Do you know where you are?"

"Near Mt. Fuji," I replied. "Now will you tell me who you are and what you want with me?"

He seized me by the shoulder and shoved me forward. I stumbled but didn't fall. He opened the building's glass door and directed me inside.

The spartan reception lobby was devoid of typical furnishings. An elderly man behind a counter was arranging cherry blossoms in a red vase. Hanging on the wall behind him was an elaborate gold emblem depicting a Kanji character I didn't recognize. He paid obeisance with a bow. Tighty-Whitey bowed back. Then I was being herded up a staircase. Upon reaching the second floor, I was steered through a door into a large room. A dozen men engaged in jovial locker-room chatter stopped speaking midsentence at our arrival.

All of them straightened simultaneously and bowed to Tighty-Whitey, who dipped his head slightly in return.

Most of the men, I noted, were in their late twenties or early thirties and wore well-fitted suits like those of my escorts. One was dressed in a blood-red Champion tracksuit. The jumper was unzipped, revealing a heavily tattooed chest.

And two of his fingers were missing.

Grinning, he raised his hand and cracked a joke in Japanese, saying his fingers had flown away.

"*Yubi o tobasu!*" another man with russet hair shouted, and everyone broke into laughter.

Everyone except me.

I was frozen stiff with fear as I realized that I was standing in the heart of a yakuza lair.

ΔΔΔ

Tighty-Whitey once more shoved me forward. As I moved through the room I glimpsed more missing fingers, tattoos poking out from cuffs and collars, flashy cufflinks, ice-crusted wristwatches, groomed hands, perfect haircuts.

All the while I was failing spectacularly to grasp what was going on.

Why had the yakuza brought me here? What did they want with me?

I passed through a door into an office with bamboo lanterns and tatami mats. Behind a large desk were photographs of old men in wood-grain frames hanging on the wall, as well as an impressive man-sized wooden statue of a cobra poised to strike, a gold sake cup in its mouth.

Tighty-Whitey pushed me into a chair in front of the desk. The twins collected chairs from the margins of the room and seated themselves on either side of me.

"What is going on?" I demanded. "What have I—"

Tighty-Whitey slapped me across the cheek. "Quiet!" he barked.

I pressed my lips together and tasted blood.

Tighty-Whitey disappeared through a sliding shōji door, returning momentarily behind an older man dressed like a 1970s porn star, decked out in a batik shirt with a kaleidoscope design, checkered trousers, and crocodile-skin shoes. A gold medallion hung around his neck, matching his belt buckle.

Porn Star sat in the leather chair behind the desk, while Tighty-Whitey stood at his side, arms behind his back, legs spread, parade rest. The old man's face was uncomfortably lizard-like with flat features, small ears, and thin lips. From behind a pair of gold Cartier eyeglasses, his emotionless gaze seemed to penetrate through me.

"Say, '*Yoroshiku onegai shimasu*,'" Tighty-Whitey snapped.

"*Yoroshiku onegai shimasu*," I greeted.

"Bow!" Tighty-Whitey said.

I bowed.

Porn Star continued to stare through me, seeming to judge and dismiss me at the same time. He spoke in Japanese, his voice gravelly, unhurried.

Tighty-Whitey translated: "What is your—?"

"*Wakarimas*," I replied, telling him I understood.

Porn Star raised his eyebrows in surprise before bursting into croaky laughter. Tighty-Whitey and the twins dutifully joined him.

"My name is Gaston Green," I continued in Japanese.

Porn Star's laughter fizzled, as did that of his sycophants. He folded his hands on the desk.

"Why are you in my country?" he asked me.

"I came to Japan for business," I replied.

"What business?"

"I promote Glenfiddich for William Grant & Sons."

"The Scotch whisky distillery?"

"Yes."

"You are some sort of whisky expert?"

"Yes."

A smiled crept along Porn Star's thin lips. He leaned toward Tighty-Whitey and mumbled something into his ear. Tighty left the room. To me: "What do you think of Japanese whisky?"

"It is different than other single malt whiskys."

"You do not like it?"

"To the contrary, I find it very enjoyable."

This answer seemed to please the old man. "The water we use is very pure," he said. "It is mostly snowmelt from Mt. Fuji. Although Japanese whisky cannot claim centuries of history like its Scottish counterparts, it has come a long way in the last ninety years. It is no longer an exotic alternative."

"It has become extremely popular," I agreed.

Tighty-Whitey returned, carrying a filigreed silver tray with a bottle of whisky and two tumblers.

Porn Star indicated the bottle with a barely perceptible tilt of a hand. "A man named Shinjiro Torii opened the first whisky distillery in Japan in 1923. It was called Yamazaki. This"—another effeminate hand tilt, the gems on his Rolex glinting in the soft light—"is Yamazaki single malt. Have you tried it before?"

"Not for some time," I admitted.

Tighty-Whitey filled the tumblers and set one before me. "I would like to hear your expert opinion of it," he said.

Channeling my best whisky showman persona, I raised the tumbler to admire the liquid's amber color and gold highlights. I lowered my nose to the glass and sniffed. "Jasmine, cinnamon...peach," I said. "Plenty of nut oils and tropical fruits."

If Porn Star was intrigued, he didn't show it.

I sipped the whisky and swished the liquid over my palate. "Smooth, as expected," I said. "Full-bodied. Sweet with vanilla and citrus notes. There's an undercurrent of spice too." I swallowed and waited for the finish. "Woody...sweet...delicious." I smiled my approval. "A perfect introduction into the world of Japanese whisky."

"Do you know what I like most about whisky?" the old man asked me. "Each blend has its own distinct personality. It can be brooding or mercurial, spicy or sweet, mellow or intense. In that sense, whisky is much like women, would you agree?"

"And, in some cases, almost as expensive," I said.

Porn Star appeared oblivious to the joke. "In the West," he continued, "you have Scotch, which is very much like a Western woman: a wild clash of contradictions. Japanese whisky, on the other hand, is a crystalline spirit that knows what it is, knows what it should deliver."

"What should Japanese women deliver?" I asked, pursuing his metaphor.

"Obedience, subservience...fidelity."

Porn Star raised a hand and snapped his fingers. Tighty-Whitey withdrew his cell phone from his blazer pocket, tapped the screen a few times, and set the phone down on the middle of the desk.

"Look," the old man ordered me.

I retrieved the phone and looked at the screen. It showed a photograph of Okubo and I standing in front of Hachikō Statue at Shibuya Crossing.

I blinked in surprise.

"There are others," Porn Star said simply.

I swiped left. The next photo was of Okubo and I emerging from the craft beer bar. The next, Okubo and I walking hand in hand to her apartment. The next, us standing on her balcony, smoking the joint. The next, us kissing...

I set the phone on the desk and looked numbly at the old man.

"Do you like this woman?" he asked me.

"Yes," I told him, shaking my head in bafflement. "Is that a problem?"

"It is a very big problem," he said. "She is my girlfriend."

CHAPTER 43

My head spun as I tried to make sense of this revelation, then said, "Shigeharu-san...?"

"Ah!" Porn Star/Shigeharu said. "Okubo has spoken of me then? What did she say?"

"She told me..." My tongue felt thick, uncooperative. I heard a slowness in my voice. "She told me she met you at a casino in Manila, and you took her on several dates."

"What else?" he pressed.

"Nothing else," I lied, as almost everything she'd told me had painted an unflattering picture of him. "That is all. I—I only met her recently."

"Yet you have made a very strong impression on her, it seems. I am told you have not left her side in the last two days."

"No, well, yes." My mind raced. "My hotel is...not close. I didn't know she was still seeing someone..."

"Which is why you are not dead already," he stated flippantly. "Even so, ignorance is not an excuse. You have dishonored me. You must be punished."

I went momentarily woozy.

Punished?

Shigeharu slid open a drawer and withdrew a white cloth napkin that was rolled up like those in an expensive restaurant. He pushed it toward me.

"Open it," he instructed.

I unrolled the napkin and found a gleaming knife inside.

"The ritual of *yubitsume*," Shigeharu said in his unhurried way, "can be traced back to feudal Japan. If a Samurai committed an offense that caused him or his clan to lose face, he would cut off his little finger in atonement. His little finger's grip is his tightest on the hilt of his sword. Amputating it weakened him in battle, making him more dependent on the protection of his brothers. Under the yakuza code, *yubitsume* is also performed to atone for an offense, and to show apology to another."

"But I am not yakuza!" I blurted.

Shigeharu waved dismissively. "This is your punishment. There will be no discussion."

I stared at the short, small knife in horror. The blade featured a high point with a flat grind, almost like a sword. *I can't do it!* I thought. *I can't cut off my own finger!* Yet at the same time I knew I wasn't getting out of here if I didn't.

And losing your finger's better than losing your life.

Mustering all of my resolve, I forced my left hand palm-down on the napkin. I picked up the knife in my right hand. I hovered the blade between the top knuckle of my pinky finger and nail plate.

"No!" Tighty-Whitey said, rounding the desk to stand beside me. He pointed at the first knuckle in the center of the finger.

I reluctantly repositioned the blade.

"Now apologize," Tighty-Whitey ordered. "Say, 'All my mistakes and debt, I now repay to you by cutting off my finger. I hope you forgive me.'"

I repeated the instruction word for word. Before I could think about it, I rose slightly and leaned with my full weight onto the knife.

My severed nerves screamed all at once as an unbearable jolt of electricity shot through my finger and up my arm. In the amputation's immediate aftermath, the locust-like throbbing remained cold and hot and stinging all at the same time.

"Wrap it in the napkin," Tighty-Whitey told me.

I only stared in shock at the flat, offal-red top of my finger stump, and the ruined, discarded tip. My heartbeat pounded inside my head.

"Wrap it!" Tighty-Whitey shouted, slapping me on the back of the head.

This caused me to knock the stump against the table, firing off another jolt of electricity.

Unprepared this time for the pain, I cried out, a pitiful sound that tapered into a hiss. I folded the napkin around the dismembered fingertip and slid the package across the table.

Shigeharu didn't glance at the offering. Instead, he leaned forward and stared at me with his reptilian gaze and lipless sneer. "You must leave my country by tomorrow morning. That is your deadline. If you don't, I will know, and I will have you killed."

I stared at him in shock and dismay.

Leave Japan? How? I didn't have a passport!

I didn't dare mention this, for fear he would have me killed right then and there.

"Also," the abhorrent old man added, leaning back importantly in his chair, "you must never return to my country again. If you do, I will know, *and I will personally feed your balls to you.*" He flapped his fingers, as if brushing aside crumbs. "Get this foreigner out of my sight."

CHAPTER 44

After throwing me a fresh napkin for my bleeding finger, Tighty-Whitey gripped the neck of my shirt and dragged me through the building as though I were a dog on a leash.

"Tomorrow morning," he reminded me ominously as he pushed me through the front door with an added kick to my rear.

Grimacing, I turned around. "How will I get back to Tokyo?"

Laughing, he shut the door in my face.

ΔΔΔ

As I kept direct pressure on my finger stump with the reddening napkin, I crossed the parking lot and went north along a street studded with utility poles, which supported a messy network of electrical wires and cables. I entered the first drug store I came across and purchased medical supplies.

Two blocks farther on I found lodging. It wasn't a motel but rather a *ryokan*, or traditional Japanese-style inn. I stood in the stone-floored entryway with my bloodied hand tucked out of sight in my pocket and called out, "*Gomen kudasai!*" A pale woman wearing a kimono appeared from around the corner and invited me inside. I removed my shoes, stepped up to the main wood floor, and stuck my feet into the provided slippers. The woman led me to a reception area where she handed me a form to fill out.

While I was doing this, she asked, "May I have your passport?"

"My passport?" I said, recalling this was protocol in Japan when checking into any reputable lodging.

"It is required by law," she said. "I will give it back after I photocopy it."

"I do not have it with me," I replied. Thinking quickly, I added, "I live here. I am a resident."

She frowned. "You live in Japan?" She pointed to the address line on the form. "You wrote you are staying in the Park Hyatt Tokyo?"

"I live in Osaka," I lied smoothly. "I am staying in the Park Hyatt while I am in Tokyo."

"Then please write your permanent address there instead."

I scribbled away, hoping my rushed handwriting masked any glaring inconsistencies in the complex designations that made up a Japanese address.

Thankfully the milquetoast woman barely gave the false address a second glance before detailing the *ryokan's* available facilities. On the way to my room, she pointed out both the indoor and outdoor hot springs and their opening hours, as well as the dining room and the times of the meals (unfortunately, I had just missed dinner). In my room, she showed me where to find the *yukata*, air conditioning and heating control, and other amenities.

As soon as she left, I went to the bathroom, upended the paper bag of medical supplies I'd purchased onto the sink counter, and turned on the faucet. When the water was as cold as possible, I jabbed my pinky stump beneath it. The open wound stung with the ferocity of a thousand paper cuts. Gradually the gushing water worked its magic, numbing the pain while also cleaning away all the dried, brownish blood that had stained much of my hand. After five minutes, I shut off the tap and rinsed the stump with sterile saline before patting it dry with a towel. As delicately as possible, I applied antibiotic cream to the wound, covered it with a non-adherent gauze pad, and wrapped it with a stretchable adhesive.

Satisfied with the dressing, I left the *ryokan* and entered the first convenience store I spotted. I went directly to the refrigerated area and grabbed two cans of Asahi beer. After paying for them with my Western Union money, I stuffed one in my pocket and cracked open the other. The store didn't have any pay phones, so I continued down the street. My search lasted another fifteen minutes and took me all the way to Kawaguchiko train station, which was a hub of activity even at this late hour. The station was a brown-roofed structure, old but renovated, featuring timber and stucco and gables. Behind it rose the imposing silhouette of Mt. Fuji.

I squeezed between a pair of green tourist coaches and wandered through a gift shop and café before finding a bank of pay phones.

With the change from the convenience store, I called Okubo.

"Gaston!" she said even before I spoke. "Is that you?"

"It is me," I replied.

"Where are you? Are you okay?"

"I am okay," I told her.

"Thank God! I was so worried. Who *were* those men?"

"Yakuza," I said.

A pause. "Yakuza? *Yakuza?*"

She sounded genuinely confused, and I said, "You did not know your old friend Shigeharu was a yakuza boss?" I didn't want to come across as scornful or snide, but I couldn't help myself. I'd lost my finger and was being run out of the country because of a man she had dated.

"*Shigeharu?* A yakuza boss? What are you talking about, Gaston?"

"Shigeharu, from Manila, your ex. Those were his goons who threw me in the van. They brought me to some...headquarters, I suppose you would call it...where I had a lovely conversation with Shigeharu."

"*Shigeharu?* I—I can't believe this."

"Old guy who dresses like a porn star? Looks like a lizard? Wears a trashy gold medallion?"

"Oh my God! That's him! *A yakuza boss?* I had no idea, Gaston! He never told me what he did."

"Apparently he thinks you two are still dating."

A long silence. "He said that?"

"He said you were his girlfriend."

"That's absurd!" she exploded. "I broke up with him! Just like I told you."

"By text."

"Yes, by text."

"Maybe he never got it?"

"How do you not get a text message? It's right there on your phone. No, he got it. I am sure."

"When did you send it?"

"Last week."

I blinked. "Last week? *Merde!* I thought you broke up with him...I do not know when...but not last week!"

"It was the day before I flew to Manila. I was broken up with him when I met you on the return flight. I swear, Gaston."

I realized she was under the impression I might be jealous of Shigeharu. I almost told her the crazy bastard made me cut off my own finger and threatened to kill me if I didn't leave the country by tomorrow morning, that I wasn't jealous but *in fear of my life*. However, I decided this would only cause her unnecessary worry. Shigeharu wasn't her problem; he was mine.

"I believe you broke up with him when you said you did," I told her.

"I did! I sent him that message!"

"I believe you, *chérie*. Do you think it is possible he did not reply to your message because he wanted to see you in person? He seems like a guy who likes to take care of his business face-to-face."

"Knowing Shigeharu, yes, I think that's definitely possible." An epiphany lit her voice. "That's why his men came to my house today. They wanted to kidnap *me*, but when they saw you —"

"They have been watching us for the last two days."

"*What?* How do you know that?"

"They had photographs of us during our night out in Shibuya."

"So they've been spending the last two days trying to figure out who you are..."

"Or whether you and I are in a relationship..."

"Oh, God, Gaston," she said. "This is all my fault. Where are you? Where did they take you?"

"Kawaguchiko."

"Kawaguchiko?"

"In Yamanachi Prefecture."

"*Yamanachi Prefecture?* What are you doing there?"

"It is where Shigeharu's headquarters is."

"They drove you all the way *there*? But they let you go right? They're leaving you alone now?"

"Yes," I said simply.

I heard a sigh. "How are you going to get back to Tokyo?"

"I will take a bus in the morning."

"What time does it arrive? I'll meet you at Shinjuku station."

"I cannot see you anymore, Okubo," I said, the statement breaking my heart. Yet distancing myself from her was my only path forward. As a fugitive without a passport, I couldn't leave Japan in the morning as instructed, which meant I would have to go into hiding. Which meant I most definitely couldn't see Okubo again, for she would almost certainly be under watch by Shigeharu's thugs.

"You can't see me anymore...?" Okubo said slowly. "What are you talking about, Gaston?"

"Shigeharu told me I could not see you again."

"Shigeharu? He has no right! He can't decide who I can or cannot see! You can't let him intimidate you."

"He is a yakuza boss, Okubo! He runs a gang of violent criminals!"

"Did he threaten you?" she demanded.

"He made it clear I could not see you."

"We'll tell the police—"

"We cannot tell the police anything. As soon as I say who I am —"

"I doubt they have pictures of you taped up around the city —"

"Maybe not. But I will be in the computers. They will want to know who I am. They will ask for identification. When I cannot provide any..." I shook my head. "I am sorry, *mon amour*. I have far too many problems right now to add a vengeful mafia boss to the mix."

"We will think of something then, Gaston. I have a car. I will come and pick you up—"

"No!" I said firmly. "They will know—"

"How will they know?"

"They just will. They probably know I am talking to you right now." This thought unleashed a current of paranoia through me. "I have to go," I added. "When I get everything sorted out I will call you..."

"Gaston—"

"I have to go, *mon coeur.* I am sorry. I am so sorry."

I hung up on her.

CHAPTER 45

I stopped in a 7-Eleven across from the train station and bought two more beers for the walk to the ryokan. The streets were dark and largely deserted. While this might be a recipe for crime in most large towns or cities, it wasn't in law-abiding Japan. Yet I was very much on edge, my paranoia steadfast in its insistence the yakuza were keeping tabs on me even now. During the twenty-minute walk, I must have glanced over my shoulder a dozen times while scrutinizing every vehicle that drove past.

Once inside the relative safety of my room, I locked the door but could not relax. I definitely could not go to sleep. I thought about heading out again and getting something harder than beer, something I could drink until I blacked out. But it was already ten o'clock in the evening, and I couldn't risk sleeping in due to a drunken stupor. According to the schedule I'd picked up at Kawaguchiko station's information center, the first bus out of here was at eight o'clock in the morning, and I fully intended to be on it.

I punched on the TV and flipped between BBC World News and an American baseball game, the latter's broadcast no doubt due to the Japanese star pitcher on one of the teams.

Two innings later with my restlessness escalating, I decided to visit the hot springs. I stripped out of my clothes, dressed in the *yukata* hanging in the closet, and shoehorned my feet into a pair of too-small slippers. Towel in hand, I clopped to the outdoor hot spring I had been shown earlier. Affixed to the cedar wall at the gender-segregated entrances was a large sign that read NO! TATTOO. The small print explained that anyone found breaking this rule would be ejected from the premises without repayment or compensation.

Take that, yakuza, I thought happily as I pushed through the blue curtain for the men's bath.

I followed a string of white marble pavers set among smooth black river stones until I reached the geothermal spring, which was set amongst boulders in a grove of bamboo. I shed the yukata and my boxer briefs, showered, and waded into the rocky pool. Submerging myself to the neck with the exception of my injured left hand (which I rested on a warm boulder), I closed my eyes and sighed as the piping hot volcanic water leached the stress and tension and weariness from both my body and mind.

In this blissful state, I thought of Damien and Smiley and Okubo and even my father, I thought of multiple universes and parallel dimensions and mortality and immortality, I thought of my mother and brothers and the Taured I had not returned to in years and might never again see, I thought of all the intimidating challenges still lying in wait for me...and then I did my best not to think of anything at all.

CHAPTER 46

A noise awoke me.

I sat up on the futon, blind in the darkness, listening.

Another knock, stealthy.

I leapt to my feet, grateful the futon could not creak or groan like a Western bed. My eyes quickly adjusted so I could make out the general dimensions of the room. I pulled on my jeans and tee-shirt, which I'd left folded beside the mattress. Rounding the low table and legless pair of chairs in the center of the floor, I crept to the door, my footfalls silent on the soft woven straw of the tatami mats.

Another stealthy knock, as if the person on the other side of the door wanted to know if anybody was inside or not. My mouth went dry. My heart thundered. *Had Shigeharu learned of my phone call to Okubo? Had he reneged on his word to allow me until morning to leave Japan? Had he now sent one of his henchmen to murder me during the night?*

I needed a weapon, I decided. But what? A slipper? A teacup? A coat hanger? Those were the most lethal items available to me.

Run, I thought. *Get out of there.*

But how? There was only one door.

The window?

It was large enough to climb through, but I'd never slid back the shoji screen covering it, so I didn't know if it was a fixed window, or if it could be opened—

"*Gaston?*" someone said in a small, urgent hiss.

The voice sounded female.

I stepped cautiously toward the door.

"Gaston?"

"Okubo?" I said in bewildered relief. I flicked the lights on, unlocked and opened the door.

Okubo stood in the hallway with a wide grin on her face, dressed loudly in black-and-white striped pants, a zipper-infested leather biker jacket over a graphic yellow tee-shirt, and heels the same bold red as her lipstick.

"Hey!" she whispered.

I seized her by the elbow and pulled her into the room, closing and locking the door behind her.

"*What are you doing here?*" I demanded, my voice no louder than hers.

"I came to see you," she said cheerfully.

"Could you dress any more conspicuously?"

She frowned. "You don't like my outfit?"

"Yes, I do, you look beautiful, but—"

"Why are we whispering?"

"What time is it?" I asked, raising my voice only slightly. I folded my left hand into a fist to hide my bandaged pinky stump.

She glanced at her wristwatch. "Little past one."

"How did you find me?"

"Called about twenty hotels..."

I stiffened. "You have to go, *ma choupette*."

"Go? Sure, no problem. Grab your stuff."

I shook my head. "I cannot go with you."

She stomped a foot. "Stop this, Gaston! Stop—"

"Keep your voice down."

"Why? Who's listening? You think Shigeharu's listening? Is he God? Does he have magical powers?"

"You do not understand."

"Then explain what's going on to me!"

"Shigeharu..." I hesitated before thinking, *Just spill it.* "He told me I have to leave the country by tomorrow morning."

"That's ridiculous! You don't even have a passport."

"He told me if I did not, he would kill me."

Okubo flinched as if slapped. "Kill you...?"

"You can see why I am a little paranoid. And if he learns that you are here with me right now, I am sure he is not going to be happy about it."

"Kill you?" she repeated dumbly. "He can't *kill* you."

"He is a yakuza boss, *chérie*. I am confident he is very capable of doing just that. And if he is bluffing, that is not a risk I am willing to take."

I revealed my mutilated finger for the first time.

She stared at it, brow furrowed, mouth contorted.

"Oh, Gaston," she said. "What did they do to you...?"

"He will have his goons watching your place to make sure I am not still around," I said. "I have no doubt of this. Which is why I cannot see you. Which is why I have to disappear."

"But—but for how long?"

"I do not know," I told her, though the subtext was clear.

It would be a very long time.

Okubo finally understood, looking like a gambler at a roulette table watching the croupier rake away her life savings.

She turned her back to me. I wondered whether she might be crying. I took a single step toward her, but that was all. I wanted to touch her, comfort her, pull her into an embrace. Yet I couldn't. She had to leave. I had to disappear. There was no other way around this.

"Where will you go?" she asked quietly.

"I do not know," I said. "Somewhere in Tokyo. It is a big place. I will find an anonymous corner."

She turned to face me, her eyes watery. "Will I ever see you again, Gaston?"

"Yes."

"Do you promise me?"

"Yes."

Tears ran down her cheeks. "This isn't fair..."

"No, it is not—"

Okubo's gaze snapped past me.
I heard the noise too.
Someone was turning the door handle.

CHAPTER 47

I raised a finger to my lips.

The door handle turned again.

It wasn't hard to deduce who it was. *They must have been outside, perhaps parked across the street, keeping watch on the inn—*

The distinctive sound of a key sliding into the keyway of a lock.

The barely audible *click!* of the bolt disengaging the strike plate.

Startled, I leapt forward and locked the deadbolt again. I felt immediate torque on the twist knob as the person on the other side of the door tried turning the key a second time.

They have a key! How'd they get a key?

Most likely just flashed their tattoos at the reception and asked, came the immediately response.

Still gripping the knob, I whispered to Okubo, "*Get the table.*"

She stared at me, uncomprehending.

More torque on the twist knob.

"*The table!*" I pointed with my free hand.

Okubo hurried to the middle of the room, picked up the low table, and brought it to me. Bracing the door shut with my foot, I released the knob.

The bolt promptly disengaged. The door bulged inward, though my foot resisted the force. I took the table from Okubo and jammed one end under the doorknob and wedged the other end against the floor as close to the door as possible.

I removed my foot. The door bumped and shuddered. The

table held.

For the moment.

ΔΔΔ

At the window, I slid open the shoji screen. As I'd feared, the window was fixed in place. Waving Okubo back, I picked up one of the legless chairs and launched it at the window.

Glass shattered as the chair punched a hole straight through it.

Rapid chatter on the other side of the door—*there were at least two of them out there*—followed by loud thumping as they drove their weight into the door.

Grabbing the second legless chair, I swept the seat around the window frame, clearing the remaining jagged glass.

I stepped on the sill and leapt the five feet or so to the grassy ground. I held out my arms for Okubo. She hopped up onto the sill. I seized her beneath the armpits, wincing as pain flared in my left hand, and lowered her to the ground.

"Where is your car?" I whispered.

ΔΔΔ

She'd parked her car—a red Honda CRV—at the end of the block.

Just as we reached it, exclamations rose behind us.

Glancing back the way we'd come, I saw Tighty-Whitey and one of the twins skid to a stop on the sidewalk in front of the *ryokan*. Deciding we were too far to give chase on foot, they dashed across the street to a black SUV.

Okubo was already sliding behind the Honda's steering wheel. I ducked into the passenger seat, my door slamming shut seconds after hers.

She turned the key in the ignition, the engine roared to life, and we peeled away from the curb into the night.

ΔΔΔ

“Are they following us?” Okubo asked in an impressively calm voice.

I swiveled in my seat to peer through the rear window. “I cannot see—”

Before I could finish the sentence, a pair of bright headlights swerved around a corner fifty meters behind us and washed the back of the Honda in light.

“Yes—they are following us!” I said. “You need to lose them!”

“*How?*”

“Go faster.”

“We’re in the middle of a town! I might hit someone.”

“The streets are deserted. They are gaining!”

“I’m going as fast as I can, Gaston. I’m not a drag racer.”

I faced forward. “Find a police station.”

“You said you can’t go to the police!”

“Better than what these guys have planned for me!”

“I don’t know where one is.”

“Keep your eyes open,” I said. “We will be fine until we reach one. What are they going to do? Run us off the road?” I looked in the side mirror. “*Merde*, they are right behind us.”

We came to a four-way intersection as the lights turned red. Okubo blew through it.

As did the yakuza behind us.

I looked in the side mirror again. The SUV was nearly kissing our rear bumper. “*What are they doing?*”

“Trying to scare me.”

Okubo tapped the brakes. I whiplashed forward, the seatbelt pre-tensioners preventing me from slamming my face against the dash. The driver of the SUV blasted its horn.

“Get off my ass then!” Okubo yelled.

We came to another intersection and Okubo winged right, the Honda’s tires screeching in protest. The SUV remained glued to our tail.

"I can't lose them," Okubo stated.

"There must be a police station nearby—"

"There's a highway!" she said.

Before I could opine whether a high-speed chase would be prudent or not, Okubo juked right onto it. We passed beneath a pedestrian bridge and accelerated to over 100 kilometers an hour.

"They are still behind us," I said.

Now that Okubo was free of any hapless pedestrians, she continued to accelerate. We zipped passed a mini Kei trucks, then a white sedan.

The speedometer needle passed 130.

Nevertheless, the SUV—a late-model Lexus with a bigger engine than the Honda—had already caught up with us once more. It swung into the left lane and pulled abreast of us. The heavily tinted passenger window lowered to reveal Tighty-Whitey grinning sadistically at me, his styled hair whipped around by the wind. He raised his hand and pointed a finger gun at me.

"*Va te faire foutre!*" I shouted, flicking him the bird in return.

"Hold on," Okubo said—and jerked the steering wheel left. The Honda's flank broadsided the SUV. Metal popped and crunched, and I had the satisfaction of seeing Tighty-Whitey's gloating, vulpine smile dissolve into apoplectic rage.

The driver dropped his speed. The SUV fell behind us.

"*Mon Dieu!*" I cried, grinning wickedly at Okubo. "You are mad!"

"He deserved it!"

For the next several kilometers the Lexus SUV remained several meters behind us, the driver no doubt wary of Okubo pulling another stunt. The highway narrowed to two lanes separated by a solid yellow line, perhaps further enhancing the driver's caution.

The temporary reprieve from the all-out chase was welcomed, and I asked, "Where are we heading?"

"West," she replied.

"What's west?"

"The ocean."

"Great."

"It's a nice night for a coastal drive."

"You really are mad," I said.

In the distance, visible in the ample starlight, jagged hills rose against the night sky. I glanced at the fuel gauge: less than a quarter of a tank.

"We are running low on gas, *chérie*," I pointed out.

"I used most of it on the drive from Tokyo."

"Might be a problem."

"Want me to stop at the next service station?"

"I could use a toilet break."

"*Kuchi sabishii*," she said, which could be loosely translated to mean *Lonely mouth*.

"Are you hungry?" I asked.

"Fear works up an appetite."

I glanced in the side mirror. The Lexus's slanted headlights and bold spindle grille made it appear as though it were scowling at us.

I wondered how much gas *it* had remaining.

And was that the yakuza's strategy? To tail us until we ran out of fuel?

As I pondered this, the commercial buildings and houses and vegetable stands dotting the highway gradually disappeared until there was nothing on either side of us but dense forest.

"Are we in a national forest?" I asked.

"Aokigahara Jukai," she said.

"You mean—"

"Hold on!" she said, cutting me off. "They're coming!"

My eyes went to the side mirror. All I could see was a wall of light a moment before the Lexus rammed the back of the Honda, causing the smaller vehicle to lurch forward.

Okubo and I both cried out.

"Slow down!" I said.

"They'll hit us again!"

"They are going to hit us again regardless—"

Crunch.

The Honda jumped wildly.

Okubo braked, our speed dropping quickly to 100, then 80, lower.

"What should I do?" she asked, speaking in that oddly calm voice again.

"Pull over," I told her grimly.

"What? No!"

"There is no choice," I said. "If they run us off the road, then we will both be dead."

"I'm not going to let them—"

The SUV rammed us a third time. Although the impact wasn't as jarring as the previous two collisions, the driver didn't back off and indeed began *pushing* us.

"Help!" Okubo cried as the Honda's tires lost traction and the car's rear swayed left. Instead of turning into the skid, she made the mistake of turning in the opposite direction.

I grabbed the steering wheel to correct the move, but it was too late.

CHAPTER 48

If we'd been traveling faster, the Honda would have likely flipped and rolled, reducing it—and perhaps us—to a dismembered collection of individual parts. But because Okubo had already slowed our speed to fifty or sixty, the vehicle's wheels remained in contact with the asphalt as it performed a drunken slalom before slewing off the road and into the forest.

ΔΔΔ

Airbags are not soft fluffy pillows. They inflate fast and hard. The one that burst from the dashboard in front of me sounded and felt like a hot shotgun blast to my chest. For a moment I remained pinned to the seat, winded, a crisp, acrid stench in my nostrils. When the bag began to deflate, I sucked back a gulp of air and immediately started coughing, as I'd inhaled some of the talcum-like powder that clouded the air. I heard Okubo coughing too and looked over at her.

"Okay?" I rasped, still coughing. The car was making that *ding-ding-ding* noise when the keys are in the ignition and a door is open.

"Ugh..." she groaned softly.

Pushing aside the airbag, I released my seatbelt and shoved open the door. It struck a tree trunk with a flat crack, though there was enough room for me to extract myself. I rounded the car on jellied legs, keeping my shaking hands on the warm hood for balance. The front quarter panel of the Honda had merged into the thick trunk of a tall tree. I could smell leaking coolant.

When I reached Okubo's battered door, I ripped it open. She was slumped in her seat like a wilted flower and bleeding from the nose. Friction burns reddened her forearms. The band of her metal wristwatch had clipped open, and the watch was now lodged around her bicep.

Presumably she'd raised her arms to protect herself, and the rapid deployment of the airbag had smashed them into her face while driving the watch up her arm. Currently the airbag dangled limply over the steering wheel, wearing a smear of red lipstick and splatters of darker blood.

I unbuckled Okubo's seatbelt—noticing some of her teeth scattered on her lap—and asked, "Can you get out?"

She nodded but didn't move.

"They will be coming."

"Leave me here..." she said, the words reduced to fricatives as they squeezed between her barely parted lips.

I bent into the car, hooked my arms beneath her legs and back, and lifted her out. Her lithe body didn't weigh much, especially with adrenaline coursing through my veins.

My hearing seemed especially crystalline, and I made out conversation and footsteps coming from the road.

Holding Okubo tight to my chest, I picked my way deeper into the forest.

CHAPTER 49

Five minutes later I came to a red ribbon snaking into the sepulchral darkness, and I remembered where Okubo had said we were.

Aokigahara, also known as Aokigahara Jukai, as an aerial view of the dense, unbroken emerald forest gives the illusion of a "forest sea"—a *jukai*.

Those in the West call it the Sea of Trees.

Or Suicide Forest.

CHAPTER 50

I'd first learned about Suicide Forest fifteen or so years ago when a group of foreigners teaching English in Japan became lost in its depths. Some of them were attacked and murdered, and the story of their deaths made headlines around the world.

The forest is a sprawling thirty-square-kilometer tract of woodland. Due to the honorable (if not glorified) nature of suicide in Japan, as well as the stigma prohibiting the solicitation of psychiatric help, thousands of down-and-out Japanese have traveled to the hauntingly beautiful forest over the years on a one-way pilgrimage, believing it to be an ideal place to end their lives. During monthly sweeps, local police and firefighters and volunteers often recovered dozens of bodies in various stages of decomposition. They trailed behind them color-coded ribbons to indicate where they had searched and where they have found bodies or abandoned campsites. They also used the ribbons to mark the way they had come so they could find their way back out of the sylvan graveyard again.

I followed the red ribbon I'd come across through the fecund undergrowth, over mossy logs and volcanic rocks, between towering cypress and pines. Okubo's body quickly grew heavy in my arms, and I began resting against the trunks of trees to allow my strength to return. During these stationary moments, I listened. The forest was always perfectly and eerily silent, a chasm of emptiness. No leaves shivering in the wind. No animals rustling through leaf litter.

Only my rapid, ragged breathing, which sounded as loud as a

lion's roar in the stillness.

After about ten minutes of this stop-and-go travel, I came to a shadowed, root-strewn glade. Slumping again against another tree trunk, I decided I could go no further. I would hide here and —

My heart clogged my throat.

Someone was crouched in a small hollow at the base of a nearby tree, watching me. I could only make out a face and red shirt in the darkness, but it was definitely a person.

Breathless, I said, "Hello?"

The person didn't respond.

"Hello?" I repeated. "*Konbanwa?*"

No reply—and a ghastly realization struck me.

Gently, I lowered Okubo to the ground. I stepped toward the person. In the moonlight penetrating the canopy above me, I could see it was a man with a noose around his neck. He was not crouching but curled up into a tight ball like the carapace of a dead spider. Strands of black hair matted his nearly bald head. His pasty white face was wrinkled and sunken, his eyes stolen by scavengers, leaving behind wounded holes. His red shirt draped his wasted-away torso like a sail. Black pants did little to conceal knobby legs, while mummified ankles protruded from the hems. An open black briefcase lay next to him, as did water-bloated magazines, a defunct cell phone, crushed beer cans, and an empty bottle of booze.

I forced my gaze away from the gibbeted corpse and returned to Okubo, kneeling next to her.

"*Chérie*," I whispered in a skeletal voice, brushing her bangs away from her clammy face. "Can you hear me?"

Her eyes fluttered open, almost luminescent in the darkness, yet there was no recognition of me in them. They closed once again.

"What is wrong? Where do you hurt?"

When she didn't reply, my concern spiked. Up until this moment I'd assumed she'd been mildly concussed. Now I was wondering if it might be something more severe. A serious brain injury? Fractured bones and internal bleeding? Spinal trauma?

Delicately, I spread open her black leather jacket and slid her yellow tee-shirt up her chest.

A virulent bruise ran diagonally across her chest and horizontally across her abdomen, forming a Z with no top line—contusions made by the decelerating force of her body impacting the seatbelt.

I thought again of broken bones and internal bleeding and cursed. Had I known her condition was so dire, I would have left her in the car. Yes, the yakuza would have found her, but their vendetta wasn't with her; it was with me. They would have taken her to a hospital. She would have received medical attention.

What had I been thinking?

I looked around the glade with a breathless feeling of near panic. No help anywhere, of course. I was going to have to take her back to the highway, set her on the shoulder, get the yakuza goons' attention so they knew she was there. They might catch me before I could flee, but I couldn't keep her here without knowing the extent of her injuries.

When I returned my attention to her, I noticed something was...wrong. I couldn't immediately pinpoint what it was, yet the longer I studied her, the more I knew it was serious.

I pressed my ear to her lips.

She was no longer breathing.

I nearly scooped her into my arms and charged toward the highway. However, she needed immediate help. I placed the heel of one hand above her bruised sternum, placed the other hand on top of it, interlocked my fingers—and hesitated. What if she had broken ribs? What if the compressions pushed the bones through her lungs or heart or aorta?

Moot point, I decided. She'd only just stopped breathing. She wasn't clinically dead, and although CPR might cause collateral damage, it offered the possibility of reviving her. If I did nothing, she'd go from being *mostly dead* to *all dead* very quickly.

I started CPR.

CHAPTER 51

I performed two compressions per second for several exhausting minutes, stopping only to administer intermittent rescue breaths.

ΔΔΔ

At some point—five minutes later or twenty; time had lost all significance—I resigned myself to the fact she was dead, *all dead.*

ΔΔΔ

Out of shock I tried to stand but couldn't. Instead I pulled Okubo's lifeless body against mine and buried my nose in her hair. Even dead, she smelled of lemon cupcakes.

It's called Shalimar, I thought, making a vague decision to buy a bottle at some point. Then with more clarity: *She shouldn't be dead. It's my fault. Smiley died because of me, and now Okubo died because of me...*

An anguished sound escaped my lips and echoed through the shrouded forest in mournful, ghostly half notes.

CHAPTER 52

"You killed her," a voice said.

I surfaced from the abyss into which I'd sunken to see Tighty-Whitey, limned in moonlight, stepping into the glade. With his tailor-cut suit and expertly styled shag and ten-thousand-dollar wristwatch, he couldn't have been more out of place in the insidious, primeval forest.

"*You* killed her."

"Should have let us get her help."

Rage bloodied my vision, not only because of the apathetic manner in which he was speaking about Okubo's death, as though it held no more significance than the passing of a pet budgie, but also because he was right.

"How'd she die?" he asked. "Hit her head? Crushed her chest?"

Pushing myself to my feet, I glowered at Tighty-Whitey with a hatred more intense than I had ever felt before. If it weren't for him, I would be back in Tokyo with Okubo, in her bed, sleeping soundly. Not in this death-stained forest that had just claimed another body and soul as its own.

Someone called out in Japanese. He sounded far away.

I expected Tighty-Whitey to call back. When he did not, I believed he was going to honor a fair fight...until he pushed a button on a knife that had been concealed in his right hand, causing a blade to spring forth from the handle.

"*Coward,*" I hissed venomously.

"Any other last words?"

I spat on the ground.

He came at me holding the knife in a hammer grip, the blade above his thumb. He swung it like a swashbuckler, carving the air with fast attacks from multiple angles.

I escaped unscathed only by ducking backward. He kept coming, slicing and stabbing. Knowing it was inevitable I would get cut, I positioned myself sideways, offering my left arm as a target rather than my chest and vital organs.

Slashes crisscrossed the flesh of my biceps and forearm. I countered with a right hook, my knuckles shanking his chin.

Tighty-Whitey issued an "Ooph!" and jabbed the blade blindly, grazing my stomach. I attempted another right hook. He stepped out of the way.

Bleeding from the lip, he now appeared cagey rather than smug. He flipped the knife in his hand to an icepick grip.

Tighty lunged and tried to sink the blade into the side of my neck. I evaded the fatal attack with centimeters to spare. I threw up my forearms and batted his knife arm down and away. A third of a second later I smashed an elbow into the side of his skull.

He swung the knife, cutting me across the chest from shoulder to shoulder. I slapped my palm down on his face, shattering his nose. He noodled to his knees before keeling over as if he'd been poleaxed, his head dipping toward the ground.

With a grunt, I kicked him in the ribs, lifting him into the air and dropping him to his belly. I stepped on his right wrist and tried to pry the knife from his hand. His fingers were a vice on the handle.

I looked around for a broken tree branch or rock or some other blunt object to finish him off.

When I saw nothing suitable, I retrieved the red ribbon.

Crouching over Tighty-Whitey, I looped the ligature of satin around his neck and pulled it taut while pressing my knees into his back.

Tighty's body stiffened and lurched as he tried to buck me off him. His limbs flailed with uncoordinated convulsions. Quickly he lost consciousness, and then ceased moving and breathing altogether.

It took a couple of minutes longer before the oxygen supply in his bloodstream was exhausted and I was convinced he was dead.

CHAPTER 53

I didn't immediately move from Tighty-Whitey's corpse. His partner continued to call to him, sometimes sounding closer, sometimes farther away, but never nearby. Not that I cared whether he discovered me or not. My desire for revenge was spent.

So too was my desire to live.

Although a thousand thoughts battled inside my head, there was one louder and more insistent than all the others: *I can't go on.*

Okubo had been my single hope in this alien world. Now she was gone, and I was on my own again, with not only the Japanese police out to get me, but fate as well.

No Okubo. No Damien. No way out of Japan. No way home.

I was fortune's fool, God's little joke, a cosmic error, and it was all too much.

I glanced over at the old man in the red shirt. Judging by his state of dissolution, he had hanged himself months ago. I contemplated the bleak starkness of death, and while the mystery of it frightened me, it also calmed me. I would simply be going back to where I'd come from, wherever that was, and my problems would be over.

I pushed myself up and off Tighty-Whitey and went to the old man. I reversed the slipknot in the stiff and scratchy rope and lifted the noose over the man's head. His brittle body slumped farther onto its side.

He'd secured the anchor end of the rope to a branch only six feet off the ground. I gave the rope a tug. The branch seemed sturdy enough. I lowered the noose over my head and tightened the knot until the rope dug snugly into my throat.

Without thinking too much more about it, I leaned forward and let my weight do the work.

CHAPTER 54

I was seeing flashing lights and hearing ringing sounds and then a louder crack! Then I was falling through space and darkness.

ΔΔΔ

When I opened my eyes, the autumnal smell of peaty soil and decaying leaves filled my nostrils. It took me a moment to realize I was lying facedown on the ground on a bed of leaf litter, and a few more moments after that to remember I'd hanged myself.

Or, as it turned out, *attempted* to hang myself.

I rolled over onto my back. My mouth was cotton dry, making it nearly impossible to swallow.

Leafy branches weaved a web above me, blotting out the sky. The air was warm on my face, windless. I sat up with effort. The noose remained tight around my neck, but I couldn't be bothered removing it. A short hank of rope was attached to it. The rest dangled from the nearby tree branch, terminating in a frayed end where it had snapped under my weight.

I croaked a laugh—*your luck's so bad lately you can't even kill yourself, what do you think about that?*—and worked some saliva to lubricate my parched throat.

I lumbered to my feet, knowing there would be another suicide around somewhere, another rope to appropriate.

With heavy legs and flat-footed steps, I shuffled through the occluding forest. Even in the daytime it was shrouded in darkness, a contradiction of audaciously green vegetation and indistinct shapes. Because the trees had a tendency to grow tightly together, I was constantly swatting branches and hanging creepers out of my path. I also had to lurch through the obstacle course of fallen branches and rotten logs, often slipping on the feathery moss that covered it all. Several times I caught my toes on sharp, dried magma and stumbled. This same layer of magma prevented tree roots from burrowing deep, prompting them to slither across the rocky surface like tangles of woody varicose veins, adding more obstacles to navigate.

When I became trapped in a tangle of wild grape vines, I released my frustration with an angry bellow. This seared my throat and brought tears to my eyes. I barreled recklessly forward, banging my forearms and shins, until I burst free.

Breathing heavily, throbbing everywhere, I pressed resolutely on, shouldering past trees and splashing through murky puddles of water. Every so often I glimpsed evidence that others had been this way before: a discarded tent, a torn jacket, a single shoe, a bottle of bleach. I came across more ribbons too, some tied between trees, others meandering along the ground. Unfortunately, they were all made of flimsy plastic and wouldn't work as nooses.

After what might have been thirty minutes of this torturous trek, I was more than ready to give up the search for a suitable noose. Instead, I was thinking about crawling into one of the numerous hollows in the volcanic rock I had passed, curling up, closing my eyes, and simply allowing myself to waste away—

I noticed pavement beneath my feet.

Frowning, I looked up.

I was on the margin of a two-way road. For the first time since regaining consciousness I could see sky, blue with rafters of white clouds.

I looked back at the thicket of forest from which I had emerged, and then to where it continued just as thick across the road.

Too exhausted to deal with any more bushwhacking, I took the path of least resistance along the road, down the center of one of the lanes as there was no shoulder. When I heard a car approaching from behind me, I didn't yield. The car slowed as it overtook me. Then it was speeding up again and soon disappeared around a bend ahead of me.

Another car approached from behind. This one matched my speed and pulled up beside me. Someone was speaking, a woman. I ignored her.

She pulled ahead and stopped. By the time I reached the vehicle she had the passenger door open. She was speaking to me again.

English, I realized.

I stopped and looked at her. In her seventies, gray permed hair, round and wrinkled face. Worried brown eyes peered at me over the top of her bifocals.

"Will you come with me?" she asked. "I can offer you a place to rest."

She must have seen something in my eyes, because she boldly took my arm and guided me to the car.

I stood before the door for a long moment, undecided, before climbing inside.

CHAPTER 55

While she drove, she told me she was on her way back from Fujinomiya to the south. She'd gone there to visit her sister the day before. She described where they went for dinner and some of the lighthearted events of the evening. I listened but didn't say anything and eventually she stopped talking, aside from an occasional comment about the weather.

The woman, it turned out, lived in Kawaguchiko, in a beige two-story house that backed onto a parking lot. She parked in her driveway next to a garden filled with dainty blue hydrangeas and pinkish-purple lavender.

I opened the car door and stepped into the bright afternoon sunlight, thinking I should never have left the anonymous depths of Suicide Forest. Then the woman was at my side, taking my hand in hers, leading me inside her home. She sat me down in a chair in the kitchen and asked if she could remove the noose from around my neck. She interpreted my lack of a reply as affirmation and removed the rope, disposing of it in another room. When she returned to the kitchen, she boiled water in a kettle and placed a small plate of butter cookies on the table before me. The sight of them made me nauseous. When the water boiled, she set a mug of green tea next to the cookies and settled into a seat with her own mug of tea.

"Are you okay?" she asked me softly.

"No," I replied.

"Do you have family in Japan?"

"No."

"Is there anyone I can contact for you?"

I shook my head.

"Yamanashi Red Cross Hospital is nearby," she said. "I used to work there as a nurse. Would you like me to take you there now?"

"No."

"You have many injuries. May I look at them?"

"I should leave," I said, and started to stand.

The woman rested a wrinkled hand atop my forearm. "Please stay."

I hesitated, then sat back in the chair.

"You can stay as long as you wish," she told me. "It is only me here. My husband is no longer with me."

"Thank you," I said.

Smiling, the woman patted my forearm in a grandmotherly way. She rose and turned on the small television sitting on the kitchen counter.

"Drink the tea," she told me. "It will make you feel better. I will be outside in the garden if you need anything."

I watched the news for lack of anything better to do. A local marathon. Japanese volunteers helping to construct houses in Myanmar. World politics. I remained disassociated from it all, thinking only that I could not impose on the kind woman for any longer. I would tell her—

A graphic appeared showing the Olympic medal tally by country.

The tickertape read: TOKYO 2020

Tokyo? I thought, bewildered, and this was promptly followed by Okubo's chiding voice: *Have you been living under a rock, Gaston? The Olympics are in Turkey this year. Tokyo was the runner up—*

I jumped to my feet so quickly the chair crashed to the floor behind me.

ΔΔΔ

The old woman gaped at me when I burst through the front door of her house into her garden.

"I am okay, everything is okay," I told her giddily as I blew past her. "Thank you so much. Thank you."

At the sidewalk I skidded to a stop, ran back, and gave her a hug.

"*Uwa...?*" she said, laughing. "*Doshitano?*"

"Thank you," I repeated and took off running down the street.

ΔΔΔ

At Kawaguchiko station's ticket booth, I exchanged one Blessica's one-thousand-yen notes for one-hundred-yen coins. I dumped the coins into the same payphone I'd used to call Okubo the night before and dialed the Philippines.

My heart seemed to be stuttering almost loud enough to hear.

What if I'm wrong? What if I'm not really back?

These thoughts repeated until Blessica answered the call with a preoccupied, "Yes?"

"Bless," I said. "It is me, Gaston."

Her voice became accusatory: "Where the *hell* have you been, Gaston? You had Damien this weekend. Did you forget that?"

Damien.

My trembling legs gave out. I slid down the wall until I sat on the floor, the receiver still clasped to my ear.

"Gaston?" she said. "*Gaston?* Are you there?"

"I am here."

"Well? What's your excuse? I know you have one."

"There was a problem at work."

"A problem. Right. What was the problem, Gaston? What did you do?"

Her automatic assumption the make-believe problem was my fault would have previously boiled my blood, but right then nothing in the world—in the universe—could have dampened my mood.

I'm home again, I'm where I belong, and my boy is alive!

"I am sorry I am not there, Bless," I said. "I promise you I will make it up to Damien when I get back."

A pause. "What's going on, Gaston? You sound…strange."

"Is Damien there? Can I speak to him for a moment?"

"I'm upstairs," she said dismissively.

"Please, Bless, just for a moment."

"Seriously, Gaston, what's going on?"

"I want to get him a souvenir. I want to know if he likes… Hello Kitty."

"Hello Kitty? Isn't that for girls? Just get him something Star Wars related. He loves all that stuff."

"Bless…?"

A huff. "Damo!" she called. "Damo! Come up here! Your father's on the phone." At regular volume and directed at me: "What day are you getting back?"

"Soon," I said, though in truth I had no idea.

"Can you be any vaguer?"

"Tuesday."

"Morning or night?"

"Morning."

"Can you take Damien then? Make up for the weekend you missed? I could use the break."

"Yes, of course."

"He really wants to go to the new Lego store that's opened in the mall—here he is."

"Daddy?" Damien said a moment later in his small four-year-old voice.

I squeezed my eyes shut against a surge of dizziness. "How are you, *mon coeur*?"

"Okay."

"You were downstairs playing?"

"I was outside. I caught some ants. I put them in a jar with dirt. It's going to be their new home."

"How fantastic! An ant farm!"

"I want to show you it."

"I am far away in a different country right now. But you can show me as soon as I get home. I am going to bring you back something special. Do you know Godzilla?"

"The big monster?"

"That is right. What if I brought you a toy Godzilla? How does that sound?"

"Yes, please! Godzilla! Daddy...? I think Mommy wants her phone back."

"I will see you soon, *mon coeur*."

"Okay."

"Hey, Damo—I love you. I love you so much."

"Wuv you too."

I heard the phone change hands.

"Get your work problem sorted, Gaston," Blessica said to me. "We'll see you Tuesday morning."

CHAPTER 56

In the train station's souvenir shop I bought a tee-shirt with the image of Mt. Fuji emblazoned across the front from a saleswoman who did her best not to react to my pummeled appearance. A block away I stopped in a pharmacy and picked up all the first-aid supplies I'd purchased the day before, along with three additional rolls of crepe bandages. I checked into a cozy hotel with photographs of famous movie stars adorning the walls (using the tried I-live-in-Osaka lie to avoid producing a passport). The Western-style room had large windows offering an unobstructed view of Mt. Fuji. In the bathroom, I cringed at my reflection in the mirror. Although my black eye was no longer so black, it was still lumpy and swollen. My tee-shirt was a bloodied, shredded mess from the superficial knife wound across the top of my chest. My left arm stood out the most, as the incisions there were deeper and had bled freely, covering my forearm in flaky, brown blood.

After taking a hot shower and carefully patting myself dry, I spent the next half hour sterilizing and bandaging my wounds, including reapplying a fresh dressing to my pinky stump. I reluctantly put back on my dirty undershorts, jeans, and socks, though the clean Mt. Fuji shirt considerably improved my appearance. Certainly, I no longer looked as though I had just gone two rounds with a cranky grizzly bear. In fact, if you overlooked the pinky stump, I was just an ordinary guy with a slightly bruised eye and a bandaged forearm.

At the train station, I discovered the next coach didn't depart for Tokyo for another hour. Too antsy to sit around for that long, I negotiated a flat rate with the taxi driver for the hour-

and-a-half trip. While he didn't budge much on his price, I had plenty of money to cover the fare.

The ride passed in silence, and it wasn't long before Tokyo's skyline materialized, the buildings resembling ramparts of a distant fortress. Once we reached Chuo Dori, Ginza's main thoroughfare, I told the driver to pull over and stepped out into a world of frenetic activity and noise.

Like Shinjuku and Shibuya, Ginza was one of Tokyo's main shopping districts, only more upmarket than any other. Luxury boutiques and expensive restaurants lined the street. The majority of the cars parked along the curbs were Mercedes, Audis, BMWs, or other high-end makes, each scintillating with reflected neon light.

I joined the flow of well-dressed people moving hastily along the sidewalk for half a block until I came to a ritzy shopping center. I ascended through several glowing floors of cosmetics to the men's department, where I purchased an off-the-rack black wool suit, a blue broadcloth shirt, socks, boxer-briefs, a leather belt, and matching leather shoes. I changed in a restroom, tossing all the old clothes into the bin.

Looking at myself in the mirror, I shot my cuffs and buttoned my jacket closed. *Transmogrification complete,* I thought with satisfaction, feeling like my old self for the first time since I had landed in the Tokyo Detention House.

Outside on the sidewalk once more, I crossed the traffic-clogged street and walked two blocks to Matsuoka. The Michelin-star sushi restaurant was on the fourth floor of an anonymous building. A CLOSED sign hung in the window, but the door was unlocked. I entered. The elegant interior featured a minimalist dining area and several private dining rooms. Stopping before an eight-seat wooden counter, I called, "*Konichiwa?*"

A smartly dressed woman emerged from a door behind the counter. "I'm sorry, we are closed right now. If you'd like to come back—"

"My name is Gaston Green," I said. "I am here to see Toru Matsuoka."

"Mr. Green!" she said, her apologetic smile changing to one of uncertainty. "We've tried contacting you all week. Unfortunately, we had to cancel the event on Thursday..."

"That is why I would like to speak with Toru. Is he around?"

"He is in his office. Please wait here." She gestured to one of the counter seats. "Can I get you something to drink?"

"I am fine, thank you."

The woman disappeared and Toru Matsuoka emerged from the same door. He was as bald as a turtle with thick eyebrows and puffy lips that conspired to give his face a scrunched-up mien. He was fifty-two, though he could easily have passed as a man fifteen years younger.

"Gaston!" he said full of bonhomie as he rounded the counter. "Where the hell have you been? Ah—I bet it has something to do with that eye. What *happened* to you?"

I stood and embraced him, keeping my pinky-less hand in my pocket and patting him heartily on the back with the other. I'd held four previous events with him over the years, two here, and two at his nearby *kaiseki* restaurant.

"I must apologize, *mon ami*," I said with utmost sincerity. "I am so sorry for the lack of communication."

"Nobody knew where you were. Nobody could get a hold of you. We were worried. Did you have an accident? Sit, sit."

We both sat.

"I have spent the last week in prison," I told him, going with the story I'd worked out in the taxi.

"Prison!" His thick eyebrows slanted upward. "Whatever for?"

"Have you heard of the Tokyo Detention House?"

"In Katsushika City?" He nodded. "That's where they held one of the members responsible for the Tokyo sarin subway attacks. He was hanged two years ago."

"Hanged? In the Tokyo Detention House? *Merde!* I am glad I did not know the place housed an execution chamber! It had been horrible enough as it was."

"Whatever were you doing there?"

As with Okubo, I hated lying to someone I liked and respected, but I wasn't about to tell Toru I'd checked out to a different dimension for a week. "When I landed at Narita," I said, "I excited a sniffer dog. Immigration officers found marijuana in my luggage."

"Oh no, Gaston..."

"I had been at a party the night before in Manila," I continued. "Someone gave me some pot. I stuffed the baggie in my pocket and forgot all about it—and packed those same pants the next morning! In the detention center they did not let me speak to an attorney, did not let me call anyone. Your prison system here is a real bitch, I have to say."

The chef exhaled weightily. "You're lucky they didn't hold you for even longer. In 1980, Paul McCartney was arrested at Narita Airport for having marijuana in his suitcase. He spent nine days in jail. His tour was cancelled. I remember there being talk he could have received seven years for drug smuggling... Yes, you are very lucky." He indicated my black eye. "Did another prisoner give you that?"

I shook my head. "I got on the bad side of a guard."

"Now I know why you were so hard to get in touch with! Prison! Damn, Gaston. You're always saying a dram of whisky goes best with a good story. I suspect you'll be telling this story at your events for a long time to come!"

"It might be a little too personal to share with strangers, but who knows? Speaking of whisky, the woman I spoke to a short time ago..."

"My assistant, Haruna."

"She told me the event we'd organized was cancelled."

"We could not have a tasting without the whisky..."

"Of course. I mean...I feel terrible it was cancelled. The tickets we sold?"

"Refunded. Don't worry about it, Gaston. Everything has been taken care of. We'll do another event together in the future."

"Thank you for understanding, *mon ami*. It has been a very

distressing week."

"I only wish I could have somehow helped you during your incarceration."

"Actually...I *was* wondering if I could ask a favor of you?"

"Anything! What is it?"

"There was a woman I met on the flight over, a flight attendant. We made plans to see each other while I was here. For obvious reasons this was not possible. I fear she thinks I have stood her up. I would like to make it up to her, take her somewhere special tomorrow, somewhere out of Tokyo..."

"You need a car!"

I nodded. Toru Matsuoka owned a garage full of rare cars. He'd shown me his collection during one of our previous meetings, telling me if I ever wanted to take one for a spin I was more than welcome. "If your offer still stands...?"

"Of course it does!" he said. "Was there any car in particular you had in mind? I'll have someone drive it over right now."

CHAPTER 57

I parked across the street from Okubo's apartment in a 1973 Ford Mustang Mach 1. This muscle car had been the long arm of Japanese law from the mid-seventies to mid-eighties. At that time, Japanese vehicles were light years behind their American counterparts in terms of raw power. Consequently, few other cars in the country could outrun the American-made brute with its big-bore 429-cubic-inch Cobra Jet V-8. It was the apotheosis of attitude, Dirty Harry in the land of the Samurai, and it had more than likely put the fear of God into lawbreakers when they spotted it barreling down on them in their rearview mirror.

I didn't know how Toru Matsuoka had gotten his hands on one, or if he'd been responsible for its modification, but at some point after its retirement from service the police siren had been removed from the roof and its black-and-white livery had been painted a metallic silver.

I didn't borrow the Mach 1 to take Okubo on a romantic trip outside of Tokyo. The Okubo I was hoping to encounter today had never met me before. She was part of the Taured half of Flight JL077, the Hallie Smith half. And I didn't remember ever seeing Okubo during that portion of the flight, let alone speaking to her.

No, the reason I'd wanted the car was so I would not have to stand around on the sidewalk waiting for her to either return to, or emerge from, her building. I could recall clearly how sketchy Tighty-Whitey had looked while he'd been waiting on the sidewalk for me.

Sitting in a car, I figured, would be much less conspicuous.

ΔΔΔ

Two hours later and Okubo had yet to appear.

I knew it had been a long shot catching her coming or going. If she was out, she might not return until the evening. If she was in, she might be snuggled up in a pair of Pooh pajamas with no intention of stepping outdoors all day. Then there was the strong—and disheartening—possibility she was overseas for work. Worst case scenario, she might not even live in this building at all. I knew all too well how something in one dimension could be altered in another.

I'd toyed with the idea of simply knocking on her door, but since I would be a complete stranger to her, I feared she might simply slam it closed in my face. Catching her on the street, on the other hand, meant she'd at least have to listen to what I had to say.

Which was?

The truth.

She had believed me easily enough the night we'd gotten stoned. I was hoping lightning might strike twice. Of course, I had much more going for me that first night than I did now. We had spent the evening together. We'd told stories and laughed and gotten to know each other, gotten to trust each other. I was not some random character with a story about interdimensional travel...

The more I played over these thoughts, the more skeptical I became that I was doing the right thing, that Okubo was going to believe me. In fact, she might not even listen to me. She might tell me to leave her alone, or threaten to call the police, or kick me in the nuts and run...

You're going to blow any chance you might have with her in this world. She's going to think you're delusional, or creepy, or just insane —or likely all three—and you're going to lose her forever.

But what else could I do? I was going to be leaving Japan as soon as I got a new passport sorted. If I didn't approach her now

—

Approach away! But drop the cockamamie story and just do what you did before. Strike up an innocent conversation, make a joke, ask her out. You don't have to tell her you're from a different dimension, one in which she died at your hands, no less.

Okubo emerged from the front of the building.

I was so startled to see her I could only stare. The rush of adrenaline coursing through me at the sight of her turned to dread as she crossed the street.

I looked straight ahead, my thoughts racing.

She stopped at the window and peered in at me.

"Can I help you?" she asked.

"Sorry?" I said.

"Are you waiting for someone?"

"I—um..." *Busted!* And on top of this: *Too late for an innocent conversation. You've really screwed everything up now.* "I was... uh...I was just waiting..."

"You've been watching my apartment. Don't deny it. I've seen you from my kitchen window."

I glanced past her. Curtains were drawn in her kitchen window, but there was a crack where they met in the middle. With all the bright sunlight bouncing off the glass, she could have been looking out at me, and I wouldn't have been any the wiser.

"Who are you?" she demanded.

"My name is Gaston. Gaston Green." *Tell her. You've got no choice anymore.* "I—I know you." I cleared my throat. "I mean, we know each other."

"Do we?"

"Yes."

"How?"

"It is...complicated."

"What's complicated about knowing someone?"

"I will tell you. But I must warn you that what I have to say may sound very strange."

"I'm a strange girl."

I laughed at this, knowing just how true it was.

Okubo didn't laugh. Didn't even crack a smile. But something shifted in her eyes. The hard suspicion remained, yet there was uncertainty too, as though she were wondering if she did know me after all.

"Can we go for a walk?" I asked her. "Around the block? It is a rather long tale I have to tell."

She glanced up and down the street, as if searching for a trap I might have set. Then she stepped back from the car and folded her arms across her chest.

Waiting for me.

I shoved open the door and got out, my body stiff from sitting in the same position for so long, my injuries protesting at the effort it took to extract myself from the low-slung vehicle.

Okubo asked with a hint of concern, "Are you okay?"

"I have been better."

"Are the yakuza's numbers so low these days they've taken to recruiting foreigners?"

She was looking at my bandaged pinky stump. I looked too.

"It is part of what I have to tell you."

"I'm listening."

CHAPTER 58

As we walked down the heat-beaten sidewalk, I described to Okubo how we'd met on Flight JL077, the accusations that my passport was from a country that didn't exist, the maladroit interrogation and my time spent in the Tokyo Detention House, including how I'd gotten the black eye and how I'd escaped from the hospital. I described the night in Shibuya she and I had shared, the stories we'd exchanged at her apartment. I described the giant Pooh Bear in her bedroom and the Pooh clock on the wall, the champagne she'd had in the bottom of her fridge, the tin she kept her pot in. I told her that she took me to her brother's place, that he was a *hikikomori* and a veritable expert on anything and everything to do with science and science fiction. I explained his esoteric multiverse theory and the possibility there were billions of universes existing in a higher dimension, each separated from the others by distances smaller than that of an atomic neutron.

By this point we had already walked around her block twice. Okubo had listened to everything I'd said without interrupting.

A woman pushing a stroller was approaching us on the sidewalk. We stepped onto the road to let her pass.

When the mother and baby were out of earshot, I picked up where I had left off, explaining how the yakuza had been watching her apartment, how they'd kidnapped and taken me to their boss.

Given how extraordinary everything else I'd told her had been, and her reticence to ask even a single question, I was surprised when she broke her silence to say, "Shigeharu is a *yakuza* boss?"

"You sound surprised."

"I am."

"This surprises you more than me being from a different dimension?"

Okubo's lips tightened, and she said, "Continue."

I described Shigeharu's headquarters in detail, as well as the man himself. I described how he'd made me cut off my pinky finger because I'd dishonored him, his imperative that I leave the country in the morning, and his threat of what he would do to me if I ever returned. I described my phone call to Okubo, how she'd shown up at the ryokan in the middle of the night, and our harrowing escape through the window.

Then I described the car chase and how it ended in Suicide Forest.

"I died?" Okubo said, staring at me in shock, and it was only then, hearing the honest disbelief in her voice, that I realized she believed at least some of what I'd been telling her.

I nodded, finding it suddenly difficult to speak. "I tried to save you, I tried CPR. It did not work. I was distraught. One of the yakuza heard me and found me. We fought. He had a knife. I have many wounds. I can show you them. Afterward, I attempted to kill myself."

"Attempted?" Okubo said.

"I hung myself with the rope that had been around the neck of the man I had told you about, the suicide. But it broke. The next morning I found my way to a road rather by accident. An old woman picked me up and took me to her house. It was there that I learned I had somehow returned to my own dimension."

"How?"

I told her how I had learned of my return but that I did not know how or why it happened, only repeating her brother's aphorism that nature had a way of righting her wrongs.

We had completed two more loops around her block and were now back in front of her apartment building.

"That is about everything I have to say," I said, stopping. "If you have any questions, or want me to clear up anything...?"

Okubo began shaking her head, and I realized with a lurch of despair that I had read her wrong. She didn't believe me. She didn't believe anything I'd told her.

I held my breath and waited for her to confirm this.

"When I first saw you sitting in your car," she began, "looking up at my apartment, I was alarmed and frightened. I nearly called the police. But I didn't, I couldn't, because the longer you sat down there, and I watched you watch me, or at least my apartment...I felt I *knew* you, even though I was quite sure I had never met you before. So when you told me we *did* know each other...I don't know...it was a surreal moment, and I think...I think I might have believed anything you told me that would explain how I felt I knew you too."

"Yet you do not believe what I have told you...?"

"You know where Akira lives and that he is a *hikikomori*."

I nodded that I did.

"You know I have a Pooh clock on my bedroom wall."

I nodded again.

"You do understand, Gaston Green, that most people would likely conclude you're a world-class stalker." She paused before adding: "But me? I simply can't accept that any stalker worth his salt would ever stake out a woman's house in a car like *that*. You can see it from a mile away!"

"So you *do* believe me?"

"I don't know what I believe right now...but let's just say that I don't *not* believe you."

I sank back against the Ford Mustang. "That," I said with immeasurable relief, "I can work with."

EPILOGUE

TWO YEARS LATER

My mother's funeral was a solemn and sober occasion.

She was buried in my hometown's only cemetery. It was an intimate family-only graveside affair. The minister led the memorial service, my older brother Paul gave the eulogy, and my younger brother Arthur read a prayer. I offered a poem. Then my mother's casket was lowered into her burial spot next to my long-deceased father, as had been her request.

After an informal receiving line of aunts and uncles and other relatives filtered past my brothers and myself, people began meandering back to their cars. The plan was to rendezvous at Paul's house for food and drinks.

I walked with Okubo and Damien to the sedan we were renting during our two-week visit to Taured and said, "Please wait here for me. I will not be long."

Okubo rested her hands on her six-month baby bump and said, "Are you okay, Gaston?"

"Yes, but there is someone else I need to see while I am here."

"Who is it, Daddy?" Damien asked. He was six years old now, big for his age, and missing his two top front teeth.

"Just wait here with Okubo, *mon petit monstre*."

I kissed Okubo on the cheek, ruffled Damien's hair, and started away. Looking back over my shoulder, I saw the two of them playing pat-a-cake and smiled. These last two years had been the best of my life. Although the distance between Okubo and I, along with our busy schedules, had made it difficult to spend much time together, we'd always set aside one weekend a month to be together. Sometimes I would fly to Japan. Sometimes she would come to the Philippines. Other times we'd meet in Vietnam, Thailand, or Singapore, or somewhere equally exotic.

After I learned of my mother's passing ten days ago, we were making plans to meet in Taured for the funeral (it would be Okubo's first visit to my homeland) when she surprised me by suggesting she book a return ticket not to Tokyo but to Manila. Ever since learning of her pregnancy, we'd talked often of her taking a leave of absence from her airline and moving to the Philippines, but I'd never expected it to happen with such suddenness. Yet now here she was in Taured, having given up her life in Japan to spend the indefinite future with me in a foreign country. It was a terrific sacrifice to make, and I couldn't have loved her any more for making it. I knew she would be not only a wonderful mother to our soon-to-be born daughter, but also an equally wonderful stepmother to Damien.

Which was why I had proposed to her the night before.

We had been out for dinner with my brothers and their wives. After we returned to Paul's house where we were staying, and tucked Damien into bed, I asked Okubo to join me for a walk. I took her to a nearby park where, beneath the boughs of a gnarled oak I had climbed often as a child, I got down on one knee and asked her to be my wife.

With these joyful thoughts distracting me from the much starker ones of my mother's burial, I picked my way through the old cemetery and all the hallowed tombstones poking out of the green grass like so many crumbling teeth. Weathered crypts rose aboveground as well, some casket-styled, some family chapel-styled, a good number featuring large sculptures of angels or other symbolic figures.

Smiley's grave was located on the eastern side of the cemetery, where the burial monuments were flat grave markers instead of raised headstones. Hers was one of the flat markers. A bouquet of slightly withered flowers rested against the granite stone base. A bronze plaque read:

Miley Laffont
May 16 1979 / November 10 2001
Our Daughter

It was the first time I'd visited her grave in more than a decade, and I fought a rage of emotions at the sight of it. A tightness in my chest stole my breath, and I forced myself to exhale.

Kneeling on the grass before the grave, I lowered my head, remembering the halcyon memories of our youths. Then I said, "I became engaged last night, *ma bijou*. Yes, for the second time. But this one is for keeps. I wish you could meet her..." I cleared my throat. "I never know what to say when I come here... I am forever sorry for the night on the mountain. It should have been me, not you..." I ran a hand over my dry lips. "There is no changing what happened. But I want you to know that I spoke with you two years ago. Yes, in a different world, you are alive and well. You are a beautiful woman. You live in Paris. You have an adorable young daughter." I wiped an errant tear from my cheek. "This is all true. You are alive, not in a memory but in person." Another tear, another wipe. "Maybe life, as unfair as it seems sometimes, is balanced out in the end, in the big picture. That is what I would like to believe. No—that is what I *do* believe. Goodbye for now, *ma bijou*. I need to move on, but you will always be in my thoughts."

I stood and made my way back through the graveyard to the two people who meant the most to me in this world, and perhaps in many others as well.

AFTERWORD

Thank you for taking the time to read the book! If you enjoyed it, a brief review would be hugely appreciated. You can click straight to the review page here:

The Man From Taured - Amazon Review Page

Best,
Jeremy

BOOKS IN THIS SERIES

WORLD'S SCARIEST LEGENDS

Mosquito Man

After a woman bangs at the door in the middle of the night, and promptly dies from her injury, a couple's remote cabin getaway becomes a psychological night of terror as they are hunted by an unknown assailant. Now they must go far beyond what they thought themselves capable of if they hope to save their young children and survive until morning.

The Sleep Experiment

In 1954, at the start of the Cold War, the Soviet military offered four political prisoners their freedom if they participated in an experiment requiring them to remain awake for fourteen days while under the influence of a powerful stimulant gas. The prisoners ultimately reverted to murder, self-mutilation, and madness.

None survived.

In 2018, Dr. Roy Wallis, an esteemed psychology professor at UC Berkeley, is attempting to recreate the same experiment during the summer break in a soon-to-be demolished building on campus. He and two student assistants share an eight-hour rotational schedule to observe their young Australian test subjects around the clock.

What begins innocently enough, however, morphs into a nightmare beyond description that no one could have imagined—with, perhaps, the exception of Dr. Roy Wallis himself.

ABOUT THE AUTHOR

Jeremy Bates

USA TODAY and #1 AMAZON bestselling author Jeremy Bates has published more than twenty novels and novellas, which have been translated into several languages, optioned for film and TV, and downloaded more than one million times. Midwest Book Review compares his work to "Stephen King, Joe Lansdale, and other masters of the art." He has won both an Australian Shadows Award and a Canadian Arthur Ellis Award. He was also a finalist in the Goodreads Choice Awards, the only major book awards decided by readers. The novels in the "World's Scariest Places" series are set in real locations and include Suicide Forest in Japan, The Catacombs in Paris, Helltown in Ohio, Island of the Dolls in Mexico, and Mountain of the Dead in Russia. The novels in the "World's Scariest Legends" series are based on real legends and include Mosquito Man and The Sleep Experiment. You can check out any of these places or legends on the web. Also, visit JEREMYBATESBOOKS.COM to receive Black Canyon, WINNER of The Lou Allin Memorial Award.